Danse Macabre

Danse Macabre

by
Paul Lacroix

translated, annotated and introduced by
Brian Stableford

A Black Coat Press Book

ISBN 978-1-61227-205-4. First Printing. August 2013. Published by Black Coat Press, an imprint of Hollywood Comics.com, LLC, P.O. Box 17270, Encino, CA 91416. All rights reserved. Except for review purposes, no part of this book may be reproduced or transmitted in any form or by any means, electronic or mechanical, including photocopying, recording, or by any information storage and retrieval system, without permission in writing from the publisher. The stories and characters depicted in this novel are entirely fictional. Printed in the United States of America.

Introduction

La Danse macabre: histoire fantastique du XVème siè-cle, by-lined *P. L. Jacob, bibliophile, membre de toutes les académies*, here translated as *Danse Macabre*, was first published in Paris in 1832 by Eugène Renduel. According to Eugène de Mirecourt's brief biography of the author, it was originally intended to be issued by a publisher named Cosson, but five of that publisher's employees died on the same day, of a cholera epidemic, and sparked a rumor, encouraged by the novel's theme, that the book was cursed. No one would touch it for several months, until the peak of the epidemic had passed, and even then it required some courage on Renduel's part to take it on. If this is true, however, any supernatural contagion the work carried must have disappeared long ago, and no ill-effects ever seem to have been attributed merely to reading the text.

Paul Lacroix, who signed the great majority of his works in the same tongue-in-cheek fashion as *La Danse macabre*, was probably born on 27 April 1806, although Mirecourt gives the date as 23 February 1807. His literary vocation got off to an early start, when he began writing plays and critical commentaries at school, and he never made any attempt to cultivate any other career in his youth, even though he went through the usual initial tribulations of young writers endeavoring to break into print or get their work produced on the stage. He doubtless took some encouragement from the fact that his father had published a novel, and his brother Jules also cultivated literary ambitions with some degree of success. He combated his early difficulties with an extraordinary productivity, entering every competition offered for prose or dramatic works—unsuccessfully—and seemingly achieving his eventual breakthrough by means of the sheer volume of his output, which remained prodigious from the late 1920s until his eventual death in 1884.

Eventually, Lacroix gave up on plays and novels to concentrate entirely on non-fiction and his belatedly-developed career as a librarian—he obtained the position that Charles Nodier had once held at the Bibliothèque de l'Arsenal—and it was his obsessive and far-ranging historical and bibliographical research that ultimately won him his greatest celebrity and respect, but in the early years of his career he was a key member of the Parisian Romantic Movement, more renowned for his acid wit and his talent for comedy than the masterly scholarship that was then still in embryo. His first substantial employment came when he was taken on to the original staff of *Le Figaro* to produce humorous squibs, although the vehicle for his more earnest and substantial work was the *Revue de Paris*, the principal organ of the Romantic Movement after 1830.

The full extent of Lacroix's works remains somewhat uncertain, because "P. L. Jacob, bibliophile" was not the only pseudonym he employed, and some of the other pseudonymous works tentatively attributed to him might not be his. On the other hand, some works signed by other authors—notably Alexandre Dumas—are perhaps partly, or even mostly, his. His unambiguously-claimed works, however, include two dozen novels, as many plays, some of them in verse, hundreds of volumes of non-fiction and a number of "ambiguous" works, including fictitious memoirs of the kind that was later to be developed on an industrial scale of Étienne Lamothe-Langon; although he certainly did not invent nearly as much "history" as his Toulousian rival or the notoriously unreliable Jules Michelet, he was not above making things up, and it is probable that a number of his earnest historical studies contain fugitive elements of pure invention.

Lacroix's tendency to exaggeration and embellishment is amply displayed in the material he fed to Eugène de Mirecourt for the latter's biography, which includes one anecdote that is a variant of one of the most common "urban legends." Although it is not impossible that Lacroix's supposed experience is a true instance of the tale, its citation dies not give one confidence in the general reliability of the life-story reproduced by Mirecourt. The book also includes an anecdote in which Lacroix narrowly escaped being murdered by the famous criminal Lacenaire, and Lacroix does seem to have been the kind of story-teller who could not bear the thought that he might have narrowly escaped being murdered by any common-or-garden ruffian. The episode regarding Cosson, the cholera and the alleged curse might also have to be taken with a pinch of salt. The one thing that cannot be doubted, however, is Lacroix's deep respect for documentary sources, of which he was an obsessive researcher and cataloguer.

Had its publication not been delayed, *La Danse macabre* would have followed much more closely on the heels of Victor Hugo's *Notre-Dame de Paris—1482*, which was set a few decades later than Lacroix's novel. Between 1828 and 1931, while Hugo's novel was in progress, Lacroix was a regular visitor to Hugo's home, which had become the beating heart of the French Romantic Movement, whose original *cénacle* had been Charles Nodier's salon at the Bibliothèque de l'Arsenal. Hugo was also in regular attendance at Lacroix's salon, which was far less famous but nevertheless played a significant role in the evolution of Romanticism. Lacroix was a more prolific writer than Hugo, and wrote a great deal more rapidly, so there can be no doubt that his own novel of the fifteenth century was, to some extent, an emulatory exercise, but given Lacroix' legendary bibliophily, it is more than likely that the research for both volumes was to some extent collaborative, and that Lacroix made a substantial contrition to the meticulously-wrought background of Hugo's classic.

The influence in question did not, of course, end with Hugo and Lacroix. Jacob the bibliophile undoubtedly made some contribution to the work of other writers in the circle, including Alexandre Dumas. Indeed, at a much later date, when Dumas' regular provider of plot outlines, Auguste Macquet, quarreled with the great man over the credit and payments due to him, Lacroix became his temporary replacement, until he too became sick of being asked to bear an ever-increasing burden of the labor of composition while the flow of recompense became ever-more sluggish.[1] More immediately, Lacroix was also closely acquainted with Jules Janin, who obtained him employment with *Le Figaro*. Janin made his reputation and founded the school of *roman frénétique* [frantic fiction] with *L'Âne mort et la femme guillotinée* (1829; tr. as *The Dead Donkey and the Guillotined Woman*) and numerous short stories of the kind that subsequently became known as *contes cruels*. The influence of Janin on the world-view of *La Danse macabre* is very evident.

Lacroix was also acquainted with the younger writers whose own breakaway salon became known as the *petit cénacle*, including Petrus Borel, who was also influenced by Janin and who took *roman frénétique* to its furthest extreme. There is no doubt that Lacroix—and *La Danse macabre* in particular—also exercised a crucial influence on the groundbreaking stories collected in *Champavert* (1833, also published by Renduel), which the author signed "Petrus Borel le lycanthrope." Lacroix is one of the authors cited in the exemplary headquotes employed in the collection, and Borel became fetishistic in his pursuit of historical and philological research in much the same fashion as Lacroix; they undoubtedly shared the fruits of their research to some extent. Lacroix wrote a rave review of *Champavert* for the *Revue de Paris*.

Like Janin and Borel, Lacroix found that it was at least politic, and perhaps necessary, to moderate the tone and content of his work in order to continue to publish. Just as Janin never wrote anything else as horrible as *L'Âne mort et la*

---

[1] Mirecourt records, presumably on the basis of Lacroix's own allegations, that some of the work that Lacroix did for Dumas' compilation *Les mille et un fantômes* (1849), including the supernatural novella "Le Femme au collier de velours" (tr. as *The Woman with the Velvet Collar*), is almost entirely Lacroix's.

femme guillotinée and Borel never came close to matching *Champavert*, Lacroix never wrote anything else as callously cynical or as deliberately nasty-minded as *La Danse macabre*; for a brief interval, however, Janin, Lacroix and Borel achieved a horrific extreme that was not to be matched for more than a century, and perhaps remains unmatched, in the raw ferocity of its attitude, even to the present day. *L'Âne mort et la femme guillotinée, La Danse macabre* and *Champavert* remain the most prominent reminders of the fact that "Romanticism" did not necessarily imply a romanticized view of human nature, and that its Gothic attributes were sometimes combined with a corrosive skepticism that makes the most brutal aspects of Émile Zola's "Naturalism" seem a trifle tame.

The connection between *Notre-Dame de Paris—1482* and *La Danse macabre* is closer and more elaborate than the common ground trodden in the development of their backgrounds. There are similarities in their story trajectories and in their narrative method, and the difference between them is adequately symbolized by the deliberately contrasted edifices that they employ as their central symbols. *La Danse macabre* also features a Notre-Dame, but not the great cathedral; it plot is centered on the Tour de Notre-Dame-du-Bois, a primitive edifice consisting of little more than a spiral staircase and a lonely platform, which had stood in the center of the Cimetière des Saints-Innocents before its demolition in the 1780s, when it had been one of the oldest edifices in the city. In Lacroix's novel that monument is where the musician and actor resides who is credited by the novel with the invention of the *danse macabre*.

Whereas Hugo's novel deliberately attempts to reproduce in print the grandeur and profundity of the cathedral at the spiritual heart of the French capital, Lacroix's mimes the needle-sharp brutality of the lesser edifice. Although both novels are thoroughly Gothic, in every sense of the word, Hugo's aspires to and achieves a kind of sublime majesty, carefully sophisticated in its psychological analyses even though

9

its plot deals deliberately in flamboyant melodrama; Lacroix's on the other hand, is a frank and scathing horror story, which flatly refuses to dignify its account of everyday human psychology with any sophistication at all, accounting for it entirely in terms of avarice and crazed obsession.

In one of the mini-essays with which *Notre-Dame de Paris—1482* is spiced, Hugo points out that the date of the story corresponds roughly with the advent of the printed book, and that the period in question was pivotal in the gradual replacement of architectural "documents" as records of past endeavor and present aspiration with books. There is a sense in which *Notre-Dame de Paris* the novel is offered as a kind of equivalent of Notre-Dame de Paris the building, ostensibly taking over its task of summarizing and encapsulating the evolving soul of the capital. In the same way, *La Danse macabre* the novel is similarly offered as a kind of equivalent of the *danse macabre* as a symbolic performance; whether its hypothetical account of the origin of the motif can be trusted or not, the novel does reproduce in narrative, with a visceral potency, the callous implication of the symbolic dance. To call it a *memento mori* would be a drastic understatement; it is not a reminder but a cruel and strident assertion, a stark celebration of the irresistible and ever-present force that that death represented in the 15th century, and still represents today, in a subtler and more cunning fashion.

There is no surprise whatsoever in the fact that *La Danse macabre* was not translated into English when it first appeared; it would have been considered direly indecent in Victorian England, and equally so throughout the greater part of the 20th century. By the time its horrific detail and the relative frankness of its sexual references would have been considered acceptable for English-language publication, the novel would have come to seem extremely equivocal because its depiction of 15th century life assumes an actual foundation for the blood libel—the nastiest of all the vicious lies that were invented by Medieval Christians to license their cruel and relentless persecution of Jews.

Any such assumption is bound to seem direly anti-Semitic in today's world, and it certainly provides reason for hesitation as to the propriety of translating the novel, even though the text is now freely available in French, thanks to scanned copies made available on the internet. Two points, however, need to be made with respect to that hesitation. Firstly, the blood libel was invented, malevolently, because it was the most horrific notion the would-be persecutors could imagine, and it is for the same reason that "Jacob"—who did not choose that pseudonym at random—wanted to incorporate it into what he planned as the ultimate horror story; he did not include it in order to libel Jews. Secondly, although the result of its inclusion is to reflect badly on one (manifestly insane) Jewish character, the whole point of the narrative is that its clinical eye does not spare anyone at all from insult; if the story is anti-Semitic, it is also anti-"Bohemian," anti-Catholic and, indeed, anti-human. To take that inference from it, however, would be a naïve way to read it. The purpose of its relentless and uncompromising assault on human cruelty, hypocrisy, avarice and cowardice is to deplore those tendencies, and to plead in favor of kindness, honesty, generosity and courage, all the more eloquently in taking for granted and lamenting their extreme rarity.

If that argument seems a trifle paradoxical, it is because *La Danse macabre* sets out to be a calculatedly paradoxical text. The narrative deliberately shuns all the literary devices implicit in conventional "moral order" of fiction, by which authors are expected to reward their virtuous characters and punish the vicious ones by means of the contrivance of happenstance. Although there are differences of kind and degree in their viciousness, the characters in the novel are operating in a world almost entirely devoid of virtue, and although the distribution of character-roles follows a conventional pattern, the particular fictitious individuals selected to fill them are deliberately flawed. Thus, the role conventionally attributed to the "hero" of a novel—the handsome "leading man"—is here attributed to a reckless egotistical rapist. By means of this calculated perversity the story's subtext is able to reach beyond the superficial symbolism of the dance of death—which merely serves to remind the casual observer that death will eventually put a end to all human careers—to offer an elaborate account of a more profound haunting, in which a largely-unapprehended metaphorical mortality and decay is already hard at work within the living, corroding their souls, their flesh, their hopes, their ambitions and their pretentions.

La Danse macabre was published two years before the critic Désiré Nisard published a notorious attack on Victor Hugo—and, tacitly, the entire Romantic Movement—accusing him of "decadence" in his style and subject-matter. Hugo rejected the description as nonsensical, but some of the younger members of the movement, including Théophile Gautier and Charles Baudelaire, gleefully took it aboard and reconfigured it a compliment; Lacroix sided with Hugo, but the fact remains that *La Danse macabre* really is a decadent novel, not merely in the supposedly-insulting sense intended by Nisard and the supposedly-complimentary sense adopted by Gautier and Baudelaire, but in the perfectly literal sense that it tells a story replete with both physical and moral decay, to the extent of super-saturation. Nothing else matches it in that respect, even though it conscientiously stops short of pornography in its descriptions.

Lacroix would, of course, have known that the particular ultimate horror he describes, and of which he makes much, had been described before in French literature, in the pornographic works of the Marquis de Sade, where instances of the act are repeated on a much more lavish scale. In Sade, however, the very repetition reduces the impact of the horror by making it tedious, eventually effacing any real force from the image. In Sade, too, the people who commit such acts are exceptional, forming a kind of aristocracy of amorality removed from everyday existence. In Lacroix, the act remains nauseatingly extraordinary, but the people committing it remain stubbornly ordinary—a combination that re-emphasizes its horrific character and narrative impact twice over.

All of these factors ensure that *La Danse macabre* retains an edginess and a capacity to disturb even today, nearly two centuries after it was penned. It is a slightly difficult novel to read—and poses stern challenges to a translator—because Lacroix was concerned at least to appear to be reproducing the language of the 15th century, and peppered his text with mock-archaic terminology, at least some of which he invented rather than discovered in old books, especially the various colorful oaths that his characters employ. As the use of mock-15th century French is supposed to add specific local color to an account of Old Paris there would be no more propriety in the employment of mock-15th century English than modern English, so no translation could aspire to do more than imply something of the flavor of the original, and some of the key terms have to be left in the original for lack of any viable alternative. Once Lacroix had set up his stage, however, he began to relax into a more determined reader-friendliness in order to develop his plot, making the business of hopefully-apt translation a good deal easier in the frenetic narrative crescendo that forms the second half of the text.

In spite of the awkwardness induced by the archaisms, however, *La Danse macabre* is by no means an artifact of merely historical interest; it remains a powerfully affective narrative, possessed of an admirable intricacy and dramatic tension, as well as a horrific impact undiminished by the time elapsed since its first appearance.

This translation has mostly been made from the copy of the Renduel edition reproduced on the Bibliothèque Nationale's *gallica* website, but that text is flawed by a number of gaps caused by scanning errors, and recourse had to be made in those passages to the alternative electronic version accessible via the Open Library, which poses a challenge to the eyesight because is considerably darker, but is complete.

Brian Stableford

Death, who, sooner or later makes all humans dance,
Will beat time for us by playing the rebec,
To which it will be necessary for us to dance in step:
Young or old, rich or poor, there is only one rhythm:
Pantagruel is dead and Badabec is dead.[2]
Until my time comes, as yours will too,
From one day to the next within this world,
Let all my life belong to yours.
My eyes fixed on your eyes, and your hand in mine,
In order that my death will also belong to you!

---

[2] In Rabelais' epic, Badabec is Pantagruel's mother, who dies giving birth to him because of his enormous size, causing his father Gargantua to lament the cruelty, malevolence and una- voidability of Death.

To the Voyager Taylor[3]

Paris, 20 March 1832

I saw you last Sunday, my friend, meditating on the destiny of the Théâtre Français: you, the impassive president of the tragicomic republic, the vigilant custodian of the genius of Corneilles and Molières, of the art of Talmas and Marses. Now I am writing to you today, without worrying about whether my letter will find you on the banks of the Nile or in the mountains of Scotland.

For you are a voyager by temperament as well as an artist at heart; you parade from the Occident to the Orient your indefatigable activity of body and mind; you study places and people as an observer, a philosopher, a painter and an antiquary; the world is not vast enough for your taste; you go from Paris to Babylon in less time than I take to blacken two hundred square feet of paper with writing; you surpass the Duc de Nevers, who climbed into a carriage on leaving one of Louis XIV's parties and said to his coachman "To Rome or Madrid!"

To see is to have, the poet says. To see is to know, the moralist says. The love of travel, that passionate, audacious, irresistible love that laughs at perils and accepts all vicissi-

---

[3] The indefatigable traveler Baron Isidore Justin Taylor (1789-1879) arranged the transportation of the Luxor obelisk to Paris in 1829, which was set up in the Place de la Concorde. In his capacity as a royal commissioner of the Théâtre-Française he was influential in promoting the Romantic Movement, assisting in the staging of Victor Hugo's epoch-making *Hernani* in 1830 and several of Alexandre Dumas' early plays. He had earlier collaborated with Charles Nodier in editing a series of volumes of *Voyages pittoresques et romantiques dans l'ancienne France* (1818).

tudes in exchange for a glimpse or a memory, you possess by nature; it draws you by need; it pursues you in your repose; you have sacrificed health, fortune—everything—to it, with faith and enthusiasm. I understand the crusades of the Middle Ages and pilgrimages to the Holy Land; you have the religion and the fanaticism of art. Down with the infidels!

Your devotion is certainly more admirable in the presence of our home-loving egotism; you gaily confront a murderous climate, the plague, the desert and the Arabs in order to draw the stump of a broken column in ancient Istakhar, to rummage in a tomb in Thebes of the Hundred Gates, to hunt for the name of Zenobia in a defaced inscription in Palmyra, to collect seashells from the Red Sea or Jordan; then, when rumors of your death have thrown your friends, who are waiting for you in their slippers by the fireside, into despair, when your charterhouse in the Rue de Bondy has remained deserted for months, you come back, chagrined by not having run more dangers, visited more countries and collected more treasures; you have nearly been robbed and murdered twenty times over; you have suffered hunger and thirst; you have escaped contagion; you have covered eighteen hundred leagues; your memory and portfolio are full of precious materials that will belong to us! Are you not leaving again tomorrow?

Away with those splenetic travelers that one encounters in all the inns on the continent, laden with embonpoint and ennui, shut away in their berline or sniffing the odor of a fine supper! They are German princes and English lords, whose doctors have prescribed the movement of carriages, the skies of Italy, the valleys of Switzerland, the pitching of ships; those sybarites of the highways squander enough money on every stage of their journey to feed a caravan from Cairo to Mecca, or collect a series of Syracusean gold medals. They have eyes in order not to see; they come back as ignorant and bored as they set out; their itinerary is mapped out in their accounts of expenditure; their album encloses statistics of the most comfortable hotels. They are people who bring nothing back from the Cape of Storms but a quart of Constance wine, and from China nothing but an edible swifts' nest.

You, on the contrary, my friend, reserve the best part of your voyages for us; you only think of enriching us at your expense; hence your despair at not being able to bring back with you the obelisks that you obtained in Luxor, which you gave to France after ten years of negotiation and solicitation; but your baggage consists of mummies for out provincial museums, manuscripts for our libraries, pieces of sculpture, collections of natural history, strange weapons, medallions and curiosities. That is not all: you retrace poetically with pencil and pen the inconstant peregrinations that take you from the Alhambra to Saint Sophia, from the basaltic grotto of Staffa to the Holy Sepulcher in Jerusalem, from Cologne Cathedral to the giant temples of Karnak. The Duc de Choiseul and the Abbé de Saint-Non would run out of breath in vain trying to follow you in that rude course.

For what a king has not done with his authority and his royal treasury, you have attempted alone with our excellent Charles Nodier, in an epoch when questions of art seemed anachronistic; you have commenced your *exegi monumentum* in sixteen folio volumes of plates and text! Old France, delivered to the horrors of the *Bande noire*,[4] lost her most beautiful monuments one by one, her Gothic churches and her feudal towers; thanks to you, Nodier and de Cailleux, Normandy, the Franche-Comté and the Auvergne are sheltered from the devastation of time, and men who are even more destructive than the years. Meanwhile, you completed your *Voyage en Espagne*, in which the English engraving-tool is the interpreter

---

[4] The *Bande noire* [black band] was the term attributed by an 1823 poem by Victor Hugo to asset-stripping syndicates of speculators who bought up ancient estates, especially châteaux and abbeys, whose owners had been ruined or dispossessed by the Revolution, during the Restoration. The members of the Romantic Movement, and Lacroix in particular, loathed them as desecrators and destroyers of the past.

of your sketches and your picturesque style; now you only need three hundred drawings and three folio volumes for your recent voyage to the ruins of Palmyra, Babylon and Persepolis. In truth, my friend, are you counting on attaining the age of the Comte de Saint-Germain, who is living in retirement, it is said, in some corner of Germany? Are you seconded by some Lord Kingsborough, who has generously provided 500,000 francs for the printing of *Antiquities of Mexico* in London?[5]

Alas, many a time I have deplored with you the ingrate fate to which our century of advanced civilization has condemned arts and letters; many a time I have turned my head toward the past, to envy with you the privileged condition of those who consecrated their studies and their labors to the increase of society's intellectual enjoyments. Philippe-Auguste, François I and Louis XIV loved and protected in the instinct of art and artists; an obscure pope or an unknown Italian Duc often did more for art than a dynasty of kings; the Benedictines of Saint-Maur were worth more to the scholarly world than all the academies in the world. Today the adequate stipend of the arts is pout out to stud; that of letters is paid out to *Le Moniteur*; the Rue Louis-Philippe is to be pierced and Saint-Germain-l'Auxerrois demolished: we are, however, a little less barbaric than Toulouse, where the twelve Caesars have recently been decapitated for the instruction of tyrants to come.

Where are the arts in France? In our galleries of painting and sculpture, so meanly economical, in our libraries, so brutally dilapidated, in the hearts of a few individuals, rare and more impossible from day to day. They will not encounter a single Pompadour to caress one of our national glories. The tares of bankers have stifled the good grain of artists; people

---

[5] Lacroix did not know, when he wrote this, that Viscount Kingsborough's financing of the lavish publication of *Antiquities of Mexico* (1831) would ruin him and land him in debtor's prison, where he died of typhus in 1837, but he would have appreciated the dark irony.

no longer read in gilded salons now that people in thatched cottages know how to read. Diderot would not succeed in laying the foundations of a new Encyclopedia; the capital of a column of the Parthenon would be changed into a mortar; grocers have become booksellers, and vice versa; there is a plan to change the marvelous church at Brou into military stables; apple-trees will soon be planted in the Tuileries; vaudevilles will be sung in the ancient chapel of Saint-Bacche; the pavement of Philippe-Auguste and the Roman road of Julius Caesar have been discovered without the event being the object of a scientific dissertation; people no longer talk about prose and verse, even at the Café Procope; the death of the younger Champollion and his hieroglyphic system is almost forgotten; a volume of poetry by Victor Hugo or Sainte-Beuve, a drama by Alexandre Dumas, a feuilleton by Jules Janin, a tale of the sea by Eugène Sue, scarcely gives rise to public gossip; the existence of our finest theater is voted by sitting down and standing up; Ecousse commits suicide at twenty;[6] Nodier writes masterpieces in order to live; Chateaubriand writes pamphlets and Scribe ballets; literature and modern criticism have taken refuge in the sanctuary of the *Revue de Paris*; pensions are given to men who destroy historic monuments! How can one not despair of the arts? Console me by your example, Taylor.

I love to travel in your tales and in the wake of your imagination in your books; I do not run any dangerous risk, not even that of fatigue; I travel alone and without leaving my study, through the shelves of a bookcase, trodden back and forth a hundred times over, like the soil of a Roman camp; I interrogate the debris of the Middle Ages, the ruins of edifices, the vestiges of customs and the dust of human beings; I trav-

---

[6] The suicide of the playwright Victor Ecousse was attributed by some observers—the allegation was put into print by commentator in the English *Monthly Magazine*—to a bad review by Lacroix's friend Jules Janin, so there might be a slight hint of disingenuity here.

erse the centuries, as you have traversed the empires of the Pharaohs, the Mages and the Chaldeans; I frequent the courts of exceedingly Christian kings and the châteaux of suzerain seigneurs: but none has honored me with the gift of a golden saber, as the Viceroy of Egypt has done for you; I enter with impunity into leper colonies and the worst of places: but I have not seen, as you have, my traveling companions perish from the plague or cholera; I gladly frequent abbeys and convents, but I have nothing to fear, as you have of the hospitality of the bastardized crosses of Bethlehem; I am safer the in midst of the *Cour des miracles*[7] than you, surrounded by your guides, who deliberately show you the bloody location where one of your homonyms was massacred by them; I walk by night through the streets of Old Paris with more confidence than you, penetrating the gorges of the Galaath Mountains,[8] where only one or two voyagers have dare to go before you in search of Amman or Djerach.

When I undertook this chronicle founded on the *danse macabre*, I was obliged to seek information from you regarding the traces that fantastic symbol in question has left in the monuments and beliefs of the populations of Germany, where it was born under the religious influence of the fourteenth century. The scholar Monsieur Peignot, in a particular work,[9] and

---

[7] The *Cour des miracles* was an ironic term invented to refer to the Parisian equivalent of the English "rookeries" and "slums" inhabited by the underclass of casual workers, beggars and criminals. It figures prominently in Hugo's *Notre-Dame de Paris*, although its development was much more obvious, if only by contrast, during the reign of Louis XIV two centuries later.

[8] Given its coupling with Amman and Djerath, Lacroix must have obtained this esoteric geographical term from Felix Fabri's account of his journey to the Holy Land, published circa 1480.

[9] Gabriel Peignot, *Recherches sur la Danse des morts et sur l'origine des cartes à jouer* (1826).

the doyen of bibliophiles, Monsieur Van Praet, in his learned *Catalogue des livres imprimés sur vélin*,[10] have published curious articles on this subject in which bibliography usurps the place of criticism excessively; I have probably profited more from our conversations, which recalled your excursions in Switzerland and along the banks of the Rhine; you painted for me in somber and romantic colors those round-dances of death that still unfurl along the choir of the Abbaye de Chaise-Dieu in Auvergne, under the arcades of the bridge at Basle, on the walls of the cemetery of Lucerne and in the charnel-houses of Germanic churches. Your tales, which have inspired me, your observations, which have enlightened me, are found accurately summarized in one of the later volumes of *Auvergne*. There is little to add to this passage, as clear as it is precise, as profound as it is picturesque:

"One curious, and now rather rare, object is the series of paintings contained in the choir of the Chaise-Dieu, and which represent the *danse macabre*. It is the first time that we have been able to copy that bizarre poem, which became, between the fourteenth and sixteenth centuries, a fashionable subject of sorts, which enjoyed great celebrity in Northern Europe. Everyone knows that the *danse macabre*, or the dance of the dead, is a chain of individuals that Death, and the demons that serve as his satellites, are animating in that fantastic fête to the sound of the rebec or the psalterion. The representation of that subject, originally designed for the funereal decoration of cemeteries, was infinitely multiple for a long time in wood engravings, in oil-paintings or frescoes in royal palaces, covered bridges, flights of steps, churches and stained-glass windows, and then in miniature in the margins of Books of Hours and missals; in the sixteenth century it can even be found carved into the hilts of swords and the sheaths of daggers. The round sometimes divides into as many minuets or sarabands,

---

[10] Joseph Basile Bernard Van Praet; the catalogue in question (of books held in what was then the *Bibliothèque du roi*, later the *Bibliothèque Nationale*) was published in 1822.

in which Death dances one by one with people of every age and estate. At other times the round becomes general and a bizarre, noisy, packed crowd describes a circle or develops a long line in which the genii of death alternate in the ranks with the dancers, contrasted with young men and young women, with lords and ladies clad in rich vestments, or poor people dressed in the rags of misery: a grave and terrible allegory of the annihilation of human beings and the equality of death; an invention initially emerged from the melancholy mysticism of Germany, which became the type-specimen of frightful grotesques in the somber and satirical inspirations of Holbein and Albrecht Dürer. The thought of the first person to treat the subject was profound; that of the last was perhaps a cruel and despairing mockery...

"No one knows why the dance is called *macabre*. Some scholars wanted to give the word an Arabic origin when it was generally agreed that everything came from the Orient, including the ogival arch, which the Arabs have never had in their monuments. What is certain is that no known representation is older than the one in Minden, in Westphalia, executed in 1383. It is not known whether it is an original or a copy. As soon as 1424 Paris had a sculpted dance of the dead at the Cimetière des Innocents; and it was painted in 1502 in the principal courtyard of the Château de Blois, beneath the elegant arcades that Louis XII had decorated with so much grace by the artists of the Renaissance.

"The subject is no longer found in France except in the libraries of lovers of old books, where the caprices of the sublime jester are reproduced in an innumerable series of precious volumes between 1485 and 1790, passing through Theodor De Bry, Jacques Callot and Matthäus Merian to arrive at Wenceslaus Hollar. It has been destroyed in almost all monuments; the paintings of Chaise-Dieu might perhaps be the last surviving example, and probably will not take long to be effaced; half of the task has already been completed on the right exterior of the choir: a layer of distemper has caused the picturesque costumes of the fifteenth century to disappear, and, of that

24

curious vestige of times past, like many others, only feeble outlines still remain. The present curé, who was formerly a monk in the abbey, did not know that the painting existed."

The *danse macabre* has tried the patience of etymological trackers who have searched all languages and vocabularies, often to discover an impossible combination of syllables, a monstrous coupling of roots. It appears that *macabra* in Arabic means cemetery; in English the first part might signify "make" and the second part "break"; in Hebrew *maccahbi* is explained by the Latin *plaga ex me*—it is me who does evil— and in Old French *ma cabre* is equivalent to "my goat"; others have claimed that Macabre was the name of the inventor of the dance, and indeed, there might have been a troubadour named Macabrus who composed ballads about death and human fragility. Finally, does not the word macabre have a certain analogy with the magical formula abracadabra?[11]

I shall not oppose you for having advanced the contention that the *danse mcbare* existed in sculpture in the Cimetière des Saints-Innocents; but there is mention of it in the history of Charles VII for the years 1424 to 1429, as a spectacle that the English had introduced into France. That spectacle, the representation of which lasted for entire months,

---

[11] More recent etymologists have offered further rival interpretations, most of which are scholarly fantasies. Noah Webster's dictionary took the same view as Lacroix; although noting the thesis that Macabre was an adaptation of the Biblical Maccabee, Webster refuses to endorse the rather fanciful derivation of *danse macabre* from the Latin *Machabeiorum chorea* (Dance of the Maccabees). The earliest detectable use of the word *macabre* in French, which renders it Macabré, apparently as a proper noun, is in Jean le Févre's *Respit de la mort* (1376); Lacroix must have been familiar with Gaston Paris's interpretation of that reference as the name of the painter who first depicted the theme, although he preferred to develop the thesis that the reference was to an actor/musician rather than a painter

must have been a pantomime with music. As for the dance of individuals by Guyot Marchant, printed for the first time in 1486, and since reprinted with considerable variations, it resembles the rhymed explanation of a painter, and the dizains give the impression of having been engraved on the scrolls that were then put into the mouth of each person, in drawings as in sculpture.

I persist in distinguishing the *danse macabre* performed in 1420 from the one printed in 1486. The latter is only a devotional paraphrase of the Ash Wednesday prayer: *Memento homo, quia pulvis es et in pulverem reverteris*. The detailed subtitle expresses the author's intention: "The present book is intended as a salutary mirror for people of all estates, of great utility, and a recreation for numerous items of information it contains, as many in Latin as in French, thus composed for those who desire to earn their salvation and want to have it." It is understandable how that sepulchral phantasmagoria might have been conceived in the cell of a monk, in the presence of an open coffin, face to face of a corpse.

I do not think that a date ought to be attributed to that bizarre imagination anterior to the fourteenth century. The numerous manuscripts that I have consulted are of the fifteenth and the beginning of the sixteenth; the importance of miniatures in several, executed with particular care, respond to the meaning of the distinguished Latin distich that serves as an epigraph to the series of ingeniously colored figures:

> *Haec pictura decus, pompam luxumque relegat;*
> *Inque choris nostris ducere festa monet.*

The *danse macabre* was so generally widespread by the end of the 15th century that a large number of editions in various formats and of different texts were published everywhere in the early days of printing. The dance is found again in Hartmann Schedel's folio compilation *Liber chronicarum mundi*, Nuremberg, 1493; Michael Wolgemut, Albrecht Dürer's mentor, engraved in wood therein a round-dance of skeletons with Death playing the hautbois. The Latin centons explaining the allegory are a simply paraphrase of this ominous line:

Morte nihil melius, vita nil pejus iniqua

The word *danse*, which seems strange and out of place today in connection with such a lugubrious subject, was once employed in a more general, if not different sense; it did not imply the idea of a lesson or moral, as Monsieur Dulaure claims in authorizing the proverbial dictum "to lead someone a dance." Works entitled *Danse des femmes, Danse des folz, Danse des aveugles*, etc., advertise in their titles a series of actors who come on to the stage in turn like the dancers in a ballet, to demonstrate their eloquence in monologues or dialogues. Perhaps these "dances" were accompanied by jumps, steps and pantomimes to the sound of instruments. I have adopted that supposition for preference, all the more probable because I have seen several mysteries and farces in a manuscript in the king's library intermingled with those sorts of intermediaries, which are allegorical coryphées[12] such as Death, Reason, Truth, etc.

The *danse macabre* does not recall any belief of pagan antiquity, which, in spite of the dogma of the immortality of the soul, paints and disguises death. In Greece and Rome, the ashes of the funeral pyre only inspired respect, without horror; Egypt hid her mummies beneath bandages, aromatic substances and adornments, so that the body did not perish in its entirety. It was the materialistic Jews who were the first to give death its hideous character; Ezekiel, in his prophecies, evokes skeletons, and Jesus resuscitated Lazarus in his shroud. The Christian religion has supported itself since then on the moral

---

[12] A coryphée—the word is transferred into English directly from French—is a ballet dancer who functions as the leader of a small group; the term ultimately derives from Greek drama, where the equivalent terms refers to the leader of the chorus.

principle of equality before death, and bones display the revelations of the tomb to the eyes; churches became charnelhouses with the cult of relics; cemeteries became places of pleasure and of rendezvous; people became accustomed in infancy to the spectacle of destruction; they dreamed of another life, in spite of the reality of annihilation; every Christian had the idea of the *danse macabre* incessantly present, which exists in embryo in the fables of Aesop as in the Gospels. It was an inexhaustible text of sermons, often sublime, by the fathers of the Church, preachers and confessors.

Now, thank God, death is no longer anything but the settlement of an account, the conclusion of a piece of music; a candle going out; people live as if they were never going to die; they die as if they were going to live again; fields of rest are English gardens; and without obituaries, funeral processions and the livery of undertakers, that tribute to our humanity would be entirely forgotten: even physicians give the impression of not believing in death. And yet cholera knocks at our doors, war comes to demand the youngest of our blood, the Academy often has empty seats and the Panthéon will not open again.

Perhaps I shall be reproached for having written, under the inspiration of the *danse macabre*, a book that deserves to be devoured by grave-worms, a book for the use of gravediggers, meditated on a tomb and written in ebony black. I have nevertheless rejuvenated the language of the fifteenth century out of deference to ladies who like dancing too much not to read mine.

For you, my friend, who will soon be departing with an escort of friendly good wishes truer than those of Horace to Virgil's ship, remember this book sometimes when you visit the cadaver of Tyr, the great bone-heaps of Thebes and Persepolis, the ashes of Carthage and Sparta. You will see in the old Orient the *danse macabre* of cities and empires. May we not see them in our young Europe!

P. L. JACOB, bibliophile.

THE DANSE MACABRE

The *danse macabre* calls
Which for men and women to learn
Is quite natural for all
Everyone taking their turn.
The Danse Macabre

I. Saint-Jacques-de-la-Boucherie

On the sixth of April 1438, Palm Sunday—the last week of 1437 according to the old calendar, which fixed the commencement of the new year on Easter Day—the offices, processions, vespers and benediction had concluded at six o'clock in the evening at the church of Saint-Jacques-de-la-Boucherie, which was still hung with tapestries, perfumed with incense and illuminated by candles, although the priests and the faithful had gone to their homes for supper and silence reigned inside and out, before nightfall.

That church, of which nothing now remains but the blackened high tower with its symbolic animals, and whose site is occupied by the Cour du Commerce, was not in the fifteenth century as it was seen at the beginning of the Revolution, when the demolishers' hammers had not yet let air and light into the Rue des Arcis and the Rue des Écrivains. In the fifteenth century, the tower did not exist and the ancient chapel of Saint Jacques, known as *la Boucherie* because of the proximity of the great butchery that Philippe-Auguste's encircling wall had enclosed within the city, had grown by degrees to become a considerable parish, although dependent on the Abbaye Saint-Martin-des-Champs, and had given its curé the privileged title of *archi-prêtre* or *prêtre-cardinal*.

The original chapel, which was not dedicated, as some have believed, to St. Anne or Agnes in the tenth century, since that saint was unknown in Paris until the thirteenth, had long been imprisoned in the midst of houses and particular fiefs, of whose owners it gradually acquired the devotion. By virtue of these successive augmentations, it eventually extended all the way from the little Rue du Crucifix to the Rue des Arcis, surrounded by a ring of chapels and enriched by several merchants' associations. The devotion of the butchers of the Grand Châtelet, the Arrode family, Nicolas Boulard and especially the scrivener Nicolas Flamel, who was reputed to know how to make gold,[13] aggrandized and ornamented their parish in an epoch when the silver marc was worth seven livres, when plaster cost one sou per sack and a stone mason earned four sous six deniers per day. Throughout his life, Nicolas Flamel, who bequeathed a part of his wealth to the church council, directed building-work, sculptures and inscriptions, which he spread most generously at Saint-Jacques, edifying the portal in the Rue des Écrivains opposite his Maison de la Fleur-de-Lis, having the stained glass windows painted and preparing his sepulcher, with the narcissistic vanity of frequently repeating his own image, the portrait of his wife Pernelle and the writing-desk that he had taken for his coat-of-arms.

In 1438, Saint-Jacques, newly rebuilt from top to bottom, no longer had any part that was old, black and severe except for its arched square bell-tower facing the Rue Marivault and its somber porch in the Rue du Crucifix, which opened on to the cloister designed to serve the cemetery, permanently full of filth that three demolished houses had amassed in a larger area, even though the curé complained about the putrid odors that penetrated into the baptismal fonts. Scriveners' booths in

---

[13] Nicolas Flamel died in 1418, twenty years before Lacroix's story is set, but he did not acquire a reputation as an alchemist until two hundred years thereafter, so this reference and others in the text are a trifle anachronistic.

wood and masonry were attached to the walls of the church like a hideous leprosy, and had invaded the public highway, over which their signs and awnings loomed, to an extent or three or four feet. A few buildings decorated with the title of town houses stifled the southern and eastern sides of the basilica, in which the intermediate habitations conserved windows, so that the profane was narrowly allied with the sacred; one could hear mass in one's bed or one's kitchen.

A veiled woman entered precipitately through the Porte de la Pierre-au-lait in the Rue du Crucifix, thus named for a cross that did not make its surroundings respectable. A man who was following her went in after her and neglected to offer her holy water. She seemed reassured by the presence of the holy sacrament exposed on the altar above the reliquaries; she slowed her pace and looked more tranquilly at the man she feared less than the house of God; but the holiness of the place, which offered an inviolable sanctuary even to criminals had no power against the audacity of the man, who traverse the nave without bowing and caught up with the fugitive under the arches of the northern aisle, which she had reached during her initial alarm rather than go to the sacristy; She tried to make the sign of the cross in front of the chapel of Saint-Leu and Saint-Gilles, but her hand was stopped in the middle of the line she was describing between her forehead and her breast. She uttered an inarticulate moan, which the echoes of the vault sent back into the organ-pipes, and fell, discouraged, on to a bench with its back to the epitaphs.

"In the name of Our Lord," she said, in a tremulous voice, "in the name of Our Lady, go away from this pious retreat and leave me in peace, Messire."

"Good God, Madame!" replied the young man, who was in no hurry to obey that plea, several times reiterated. "Are you afraid of me today? Has the Devil dressed my face?"

"Yes, the Devil hides beneath genteel semblances to tempt poor sinners! So, I beg you, stop persecuting me so obstinately. Go away; for love of my person and my honor, go!"

"No; for the greater love that I have for you, I shall stay here, whether you like it or not, and I shall tame your rebellious humor, for my heart is consumed by hope and despair."

"Oh well! Hurry up and recite your impieties to me, wretch, and the sin shall be entirely imputed to you at the judgment of souls—but for the sake of my eternal salvation, make sure that no one sees you!"

The woman, vanquished by obstinacy and violence, which she pardoned in the depths of her soul, by reason of their cause, resigned herself with a sigh that was not solely an expression of anxiety, and brought her veil down over her tearful face. She put out a hand to maintain an appropriate distance between herself and the bold young man. Her white and timid hand encountered a sepulchral marble, and shivered at that cold contact. The unknown came to sit down beside her and silently enfolded her in his arms in spite of the mute resistance that she opposed to the strange familiarity.

She was a lady of high status, as was appreciable by the richness of the silks and furs making up her costume. She seemed young and beautiful, although she was veiled, and the admirable perfection of her figure was an undeceptive testimony to the perfection of her features, which she disguised more out of prudence than coquetry, but the grace of her bearing, her dainty feet and charming hands would have made her recognizable to anyone who had seen her before. She wore a green satin gown bordered with grey, with flared sleeves and a heart-shaped neckline; her gilded belt and necklace, especially, advertised her rank and wealth. She wore a rounded hairnet with auricles, not unlike the head-dresses of the time of Saint Louis, and her black velvet shippers were protected from the mire of the streets by a double overshoe equipped with wooden heels and toes, akin to clogs. A rosary of nacre and lemonwood, or cedar, hung from her belt, and under her arm she held a large missal bound in silk with silver clasps, although fashion dictated that the book in question ought to be confided to some ancient follower, a companion obligatory for walking and worship.

The young man was no less recommended by appearances; his handsome face and elegant costume seemed a sufficient guarantee of his distinguished birth and fine position in the nobility. He was of medium height, and remarkable for the harmonious proportion of his supple and vigorous limbs, which was not disguised by his tightly-knitted hose of amaranth wool and the silky cloth of his close-fitting jacket, tightened around his waist with a perfumed Cordovan leather belt. The blue jacket, darker in the chest and slit at the bottom of each side, floated above the knee and did not impede any movement, as a long and ample cloak, like those religiously maintained by old men and the notable of the bourgeoisie, would have done. His boots of blackened leather, laced over the foot, terminated in a flap. His fox-fur cap rose up in a cone with no other ornament than a gold medallion attached to the external rim and a cross of the same metal, which had been missing from the lady's rosary for an entire week.

He had a singular beauty that gave evidence of a foreign origin. The Jewish character imprinted on his physiognomy did not come from a depressed forehead, an oblique gaze or red-tinted hair; his hair was a striking blond color, undulating over his shoulders in natural curls; his large blue eyes blossomed beneath the shade of lashes; the incarnadine of his lips, always parted by an ironic smile, contrasted with the white of his teeth; even so, the indelible sign of the children of Moses was marked somehow in his eyes and smile. No one would have dared to make the observation, the Jews having been expelled from France by Charles VI in 1394, unable to return on penalty of the noose or the pyre. Nevertheless, the lady had noted with an involuntary pleasure the resemblance the unknown bore to Jesus.

"For God's sake, Messire," she said, affecting an angry one, "Are you a Jew or a Saracen, to behave so scandalously in the house of the celestial Savior you see crucified there?"

"Do you think, most excellent lady, that it is necessary to be a good Christian to become a good lover? I see no divinity to serve here but yours."

"Fie! Don't proffer such outrageous blasphemies, for fear of damnation. Go about your business, I implore you; my confessor will impose too harsh a penance on me."

"In that case, I promise to take half of it. Let me see those lovely eyes that shine more brightly than stars and carbuncles; comfort me with love, my beauty."

"Abstain from that language, Messire; you know that I'm married, and the wife of Monsieur Louis de la Vodrière; I owe him the fidelity that he owes me, and will therefore love him conjugally, as my legitimate and only friend."

"Truly, Madame, you talked in a better style last Sunday, at vespers, and I remember that you promised me a kiss—the first, but not the last."

"Alas! Kindly forget my imprudence, of which I'm ashamed; that sin as committed in the church of Sainte-Opportune; that's why I haven't been there since the mass in question."

"Curse the confessor who has inspired such stupid fantasies and displeasing remorse!"

"Oh, don't curse that venerable priest, who governs me in all things and guides me along the path of virtue; I don't reproach him for anything, except my deplorable marriage."

"In sum, you're no longer saying no to my lamentations; your marriage really is fatal and pernicious; your spouse is austere and ill-disposed—what a piteous life you lead!"

"Not at all, Messire; my little child would be a remedy for the worst ills; you do not understand the delights of a mother, you who have learned the doctrine of the court, who invest your glories in horses, dogs, arms and largesse. Oh, my sweet lord, is he not another father to my dear son!"

"I would have given up the king's court, the dalliance of the hunt, the honors of war, even the title of gentleman, as the price of your affection, my darling, and I desire no other paradise!"

"You have the election of that place; it will not be taken away from you, Benjamin; persevere in your love without requiring allegiance."

"Jehanne, tell me to make me content: may I not see you alone before next Sunday during mass? Will you let me come to your house, by day or by night?"

"Be more indulgent, my friend; do not come to Messire de la Vodrière's house, for the sake of your life and mine; on Sundays, do not prevent me from taking communion."

"What! Dear lady, do you think you can get rid of me? Can I not see you without danger of death? It does not matter to us whether it is Sunday or the Sabbath, or Easter, provided that we can talk about our love, larded with tender gazes and honest kisses. For that purpose I would risk the most dangerous peril. Tell me, where, when and how I can take you in my arms, call you mine, set you afire with my flame? Tell me that, tyrannical sovereign: soon, tomorrow, tonight, just now?"

"I have a great desire, but little power. No, not soon, a long time—never! Adieu, Benjamin, go away now; I can hear my confessor coming. Go, I beg you!"

The sound of a massive door closing had resounded in the nave, and the tumulary slabs that paved the church sounded under a slow footfall. Jehanne de la Vodrière, as if woken up with a start by that noise, which she recognized, detached herself from an embrace that had become tighter by the minute without her being aware of it, and got to her feet anxiously.

She went to kneel down, her head bowed and her bosom agitated, in the confessional of the chapel opposite, while the young man, disconcerted by that unexpected flight, hesitated to follow her; but the refuge she had chosen and the presence of a witness prevented him from giving way to an excitement that would have compromised them both. Clenching his fists, biting his lips and shaking his beard, he slipped from pillar to pillar and out of the church.

The chapel of Notre-Dame, where Jehanne had taken refuge, has been consecrated since under the invocation of Saint-Michel. Simon Dampmartin, the king's *valet de chambre*, changer and bourgeois of Paris, had founded it in 1394, to the right of the choir, opposite the main altar, under a vault known as the crooked piece, so dark that it required illumination to read there even in broad daylight.

The chapel, painted with frescoes in the brightest colors and ornamented with bronze statues of the founder and his wife, lying on their tomb, was perpetually lit by a *roe*, a kind of circular chandelier on a pivot, bristling with candles and maintained by the donations of parishioners, notably the widow Philiberte de Rosières, the mother of Guillaume Sanguin, the merchants' provost. Today, a finely-woven carpet had been added to the ordinary decoration of the chapel, representing scenes from the *Roman de la Rose* and the person known as the God of Amour and Old Age. The butchers' daughters had dressed the image of the Virgin, and coiffed her in a crown of roses; the tombs were strewn with bunches of boxwood branches and green grass.

Scarcely had Jehanne de la Vodrière knelt down in the confessional, a prodigious work of wooden sculpture in the Gothic mode, than an old priest entered his compartment, after having murmured a prayer on the altar steps. Age, in wrinkling his forehead and creasing his eyelids, had not curbed his tall stature; his bald head, surrounded by an aureole of white hair, and his silvery beard gave an air of solemn majesty to his immobile face, whose ivory complexion, piercing eyes and bushy eyebrows imposed respect and confidence. His costume was that of the Dominicans, known in France as Jacobins because their primary convent was situated in the Rue de Saint-Jacques. Père Thibault, who had been brought up in that order since childhood, wore a white woolen robe and a black serge cowl falling to a point over the stomach and as a mantle to the heels, the hood hanging down; his hands were bare and his feet shod. He leaned toward the grille separating him from his penitent, still veiled, and a suave breath caressed the icy face of the old man, who was not only attentive to the confession delivered to his religious ministry.

Jehanne trembled in enumerating the slight faults that aggravated her, as she passed them before the eyes of a judge, a rigid depository of divine authority; only her youth and sex were guilty of errors, which she declared sadly in a voice punctuated by sobs.

The confessor listened in silence, without interrupting the admissions that followed one another at hazard: naïve admissions that would not have made a virgin blush, and whose conclusion was a profound sigh that she would rather have repressed.

Afterwards, she waited with pretended gratitude for the priest to prescribe a penance, and as he was slow to speak to her, she selected from her alms-purse a gold coin bearing a crown, worth fifty sols, and presented it humbly to the Dominican, who made the sign of the cross instead of accepting the offering.

"My daughter," he said, shaking his head, "A confession is only taxed at six sols, and that indecent simony pays the rent due to Monsieur l'Archi-prêtre de Saint-Jacques. For myself, I don't traffic in that fashion with holy things, inasmuch as Jesus expelled the merchants from the Temple."

"Assuredly, my venerable Father, I know your exemplary charity, and I ask you to distribute this money to the needy poor, in order that they might pray for the redemption of my sins."

"Their prayers will not have the power for which you hope, my daughter, of being able to efface a sacrilege, a certain sin concealed from the confession."

"Thank you, Father. My confession is not perfect, since you have not absolved me. Do you want to interrogate me?"

"How is it that you did not say a word about the young seigneur who is pursuing you amorously? Have you sent him away, as is appropriate? Has he repented of his own malignity?"

"Oh, most excellent Father, my tongue dries up in anguish and begs pardon in response."

"Now, I summon you to omit nothing, Jehanne, lest the evil be impossible to heal; I have seen and heard your husband, who complains, who is indignant at your follies, of which I demand an account in the name of God."

"Don't believe him, Monseigneur; the jealousy that is pricking him is forging imaginary terrors and false melancholy, by which I am greatly inconvenienced."

"Speak frankly, my daughter; have you not seen that insulter of conjugal innocence, that love of human vanities and satanic pomps, again?"

"He is not as you paint him, Father, and I call my guardian angel as a witness that I have done my best to avoid encountering him..."

"You see him in secret, then? What has he said to you? Has he told you his name and his title, his wealth and his offices? What have you replied to his villainous propositions?"

"Indeed, I won't deny it, he has approached me in this very place, and I have proudly insisted that he leave right away—which he did without a murmur, the worthy gentleman."

"Do you swear by the holy sacrament that this conversation will not have more grievous consequences, my daughter?"

"I shall do my best to make sure of that, I swear—but the spirit is willing and the flesh weak. How I regret not having married such a gallant seigneur!"

"Incline your ear to my advice, Jehanne my daughter; I am the one who baptized you, confessed you and married you, all very honorably, so you cannot doubt the true amity that advises you as to your interests. Do not delay any longer in expelling and avoiding this young man, whoever he is. If not, you will go from bad to worse, for adultery opens the door to all of the seven deadly sins."

"I would gladly avoid him, if it were possible, but I always find him in my way, and if I stay in my room he walks past the window along the Rue des Bourdonnais. When I go to masses or sermons he sits close by, speaking to me with his gaze no less than his mouth; finally, I have quit Sainte-Opportune, only to find him at Saint-Jacques."

"God be praised that Messire de la Vodrière has not discovered this impetuous rival. I wash my hands of the blood that would be shed to settle that quarrel."

"May it please Heaven that there will be no blood or murder! Take back that prophecy, Messire!"

Jehanne dissolved into tears at the idea of a lugubrious presage attached to her destiny. She seemed to hear a sentence of fatality, and the punishment inflicted on her guilty passion took the most menacing forms in her mind. She begged for mercy, her arms raised and her body trembling; she abjured the love that possessed her entirely; she plunged into a ecstasy of devotion, so common in those times when people only lived half on earth.

Père Thibault blessed her, and did not impose any other penance on her than expressly forbidding her to see the unknown author of her sin again.

"Jehanne," he said to her, generously, "I shall delay granting you absolution again; act in such a way that, after this holy week, you can take communion virtuously."

She left the confessional so dejected that she had to support herself on the mausoleum of Simon Dampmartin, without having the strength to move forward. Nightfall redoubled the obscurity of the church, where the consumed candles were going out, with sudden surges of their vacillating light. A mephitic air rose from the ground, stuffed with cadavers; a glacial fluid descended from the damp vaults; and in that vague dusk, illuminated by the smoky lamps that were burning for the dead, the pillars, statues tombs and hangings stood out in black, the slightest sound taking on a formidable resonance among them. One might have thought them an assembly of phantoms if an odor of cabbage soup and roast goose had not brought the mind back to the realities of animal life; the curé and the canons were at table.

Jehanne, who feared being stopped on the way and incurring the jealous fury of her husband, begged Père Thibault to accompany her to her home, to excuse her return at that late hour. The Jacobin, who had seen her as an infant in her cradle, remembered having been her mother's confessor; he was no longer of an age to furnish a text on calumny, and did not hesitate to escort the young woman, whom he regarded almost as his daughter.

She hastened her steps, and he ran out of breath following her through the narrow, tortuous, dark and stinking Rues de la Heaumerie, de la Tabletterie, des Lavandiers and des Males-Paroles, whose names have not changed any more than their aspect.

The streets were deserted, the houses silent and the windows dark, their inhabitants asleep before the curfew. Jehanne, however, turned round anxiously at the sound of footsteps that matched her own, and the rattle of a leper clicking behind her.

II. The Tour de Notre-Dame-du-Bois[14]

Until the closure of the Cimetière des Saints-Innocents in 1780, an edifice of the greatest antiquity existed, the origin and usage of which have occupied the research of the scholarly historians of Paris in vain. It was an octagonal tower some forty feet high and only twelve in diameter, because the elevation of the ground had interred three fathoms of the monument in its greatest width and the first story had become, in consequence, a black and noxious cellar. That tower, solidly built with hard stones and Roman cement, only contained, above the cellar, a spiral staircase worn away by feet, ending at a narrow platform, with open aches on the eight sides, surmounted by a pyramid that terminated in a kind of flower. The sole door to the staircase must once have been a low window, and the architecture offered no other ornament than a jeweled string around the lantern; the pillory of Les Halles was constructed on a very similar model.

It appears that the Romans, when masters of Lutèce, then still enclosed in the Île de la Cité, had placed that watchtower in the depths of the woods and marshes that covered the northern part of the city, to serve as both a guard-post and a beacon. By day, a detachment of soldiers protected the area around of the bridge, the merchants coming from the North and the inhabitants who were going to visit the temples in the vicinity; by night, a beacon lit at the summit indicated the road to stray travelers. Later, when Christianity began to be established among the Gauls, the chapel of Notre-Dame-du-Bois, situated at the same location where the church of Sainte-Opportune has since been built, applied its name to the tower, doubtless inhabited by a hermit who sanctified his dwelling by erecting a

---

[14] Lacroix renders the name in this form, although most other references to the edifice in question give the name as Notre-Dame-des-Bois.

41

holy cross at its summit and placing an image of the Virgin in a niche. The foot of the building was buried under the debris and earth that was brought to dry out the marsh of Champeaux, which the proximity of a chapel soon turned into a burial-ground. Philippe-Auguste conserved the monument by building the walls of the cemetery around it; it was then in the middle of the enclosure, before the foundation of the charnel-houses brought it closer to the southern gallery. Night-watchmen were no longer lodged there, however, since a good wall protected the tombs from profanation; a guard being unnecessary in the shelter, often called the *petit guifs*,[15] it was rented to recluses, gravediggers or even some guests of death.

In 1424, the Tour de Notre-Dame-du-Bois had acquired a strange tenant who had come to Paris with the English, who took possession of the capital during the deplorable rein of Charles VI, as a result of civil wars and intestinal dissents. That mysterious individual, to whom popular superstition attributed a superhuman nature and an infernal power, only showed himself in public on the occasion of a frightful spectacle of which he was the inventor, and which Parisians had seen performed during several months in 1424 and 1429. That spectacle, which the authors of the fifteenth century have sought to reproduce in verse under the title of the *danse macabrée* or *danse macabre*—the name that the inventor had taken—was nothing but an interminable procession of men and women chosen from all ages and ranks, which Death caused to enter into a dance, according to the proverbial expression, which signified the exit from life.

Macabre, the principal actor in that monotonous allegory, did not pronounce a single word, but his resemblance to a skeleton, his pantomime, alternately jesting and horrible, his

---

[15] So far as I can tell, the use of the term "*guifs*" in Medieval French is simply a version of *juifs* [Jews], but that does not seem to be the meaning intended here, where the reference is to the subterranean space employed in the story as a residence by Macabre, so I have left it as it is in the original.

diabolical laughter, and especially the unusual chords of his rebec, provided matter for curiosity and fear. In sum, the theater set up in the cemetery added to the prestige of the representation, which had a greater effect on a credulous audience than the thunderous sermons of preachers. The first time, the *danse macabrée* had lasted from the month of August to the following Lent, and the second time, from the holy weeks until Toussaint. The clergy had thundered in vain from the pulpit against that moral farce; confessors had tried in vain to prevent their penitents from going to see it; the attractions of the novelty had been stronger than the religious prejudice; the churches had been deserted in order that crowds might flock to the forbidden pleasure. The English, somber by nature, took pleasure in that sort of recreation, which Macabre had initially imported to their nation from Bohemia,[16] and the vogue was so stirring that the Duke of Bedford[17] regaled the ladies of the

---

[16] Macabre is clearly a Roma or "gypsy," the latter term incorrectly implying an origin in Egypt, but French terminology often referred to the nomads in question, equally incorrectly, as "Bohemians," a term subsequently borrowed for application to litterateurs who imagined themselves, or were viewed by others, as outcasts from Parisian society. "Egyptians" play a considerable part in Victor Hugo's *Notre-Dame de Paris*, in which Esmeralda, having been stolen as a baby, is ultimately recognized by her mother by virtue of a trinket she still carries—a device that was to become a staple of Romantic melodrama. Lacroix's seeming assumption that "Bohemians" really did come from Bohemia is a literary device, and Macabre's nostalgic references to his homeland are symbolic rather than literal.

[17] The title of Duke of Bedford was initially created for John of Lancaster (1389-1435), the third surviving son of Henry IV of England, who appointed himself regent of France on behalf of his nephew Henry VI in 1431, shortly after arranging the execution of Joan of Arc, whose appearance put a stop to the sequence of his victories over French forces.

court for a day with that hideous masquerade. In spite of general poverty, those two performances must have raised considerable sums of money.

The extraordinary rumors that had spread regarding the foreigner obtained so much credit among the vulgar that the Cimetière des Innocents was reputed to be a accursed abode; the rich citizens of the surrounding parishes bought the favor of being buried in a church, the paupers feared dying in the dependencies of the cemetery, and the manufactories protested to the bishop against the theater and the actor; but the bishop, who was obtaining a levy from both, wrote off the complaint. Such was the dreadful prejudice attached to the existence of the man of the dead, however, that people avoided going through the cemetery even in broad daylight, and the grass grew long there in every part; everyone preferred to take an indirect route to the markets, and no one dared venture into the surrounding streets after sunset.

A few strong minds asserted that Macabre was merely a skillful showman and musician, who was taking advantage the monstrosity of his person and amassing considerable wealth before returning to England. Nevertheless, for nine years he had not repeated his performance, and although he was invisible, it was well known that he was still resident in the tower, following the retreat of his pretended compatriots, whom the taking of Paris by the king's men had driven back to the provinces. Some said that Macabre's rebec awoke the dead by moonlight; others told tales of the prodigies accomplished by that instrument, which one never heard without being threatened by imminent death. The tales grew as they were passed from mouth to mouth, and there was not a single death in the fourteen parishes that the cemetery devoured that was not attributed to the *danse macabre*.

The eight o'clock curfew had sounded from all the bell-towers; the entire quarter of Les Halles was asleep, buried like a cadaver in the silence and the darkness. The Tour de Notre-Dame-du-Bois, which loomed over the gables of the Rue Saint-Denis was not as tranquil at its bleak and black exterior

implied; two living beings were quarreling in that subterranean chamber that the centuries had buried in the midst of so
many generations turned to dust. The immobile light of an iron
lamp, stolen from a tomb, scarcely pierced the deleterious
vapors that filled the cellar in question, bizarrely colored by
damp and corruption. The walls were giving way under the
pressure of heaped-up corpses, cracking and bulging, ready to
collapse in putrescence; the putrid exhalations condensed in
drops of water that fell at intervals from the ceiling on to a
muddy stone floor.

Yellow skeletons hung from the moldy walls were not
the only inhabitants of that cavern; an iron pot, a pewter goblet
and a few household utensils in wood and metal announced
that the imperious needs of life had not yet been banished
from such a sepulcher; a frightful bed, enclosed in a large box
also testified that the sleep of the living was not as deep as the
sleep of the dead.

A frightful couple lodged therein.

The woman, charged with a deformed obesity, oily and
green-tinted skin, rotten teeth, extinct eyes and greasy hair,
deployed her gigantic stature and her disgusting nudity; she
had no other garment than a tattered shroud draped over her
shoulder. It is true that she was getting ready to go to bed, and
the rags she had just taken off had been hung up instead of
curtains, swaying over her Eumenidean head.

The man, if it was a man, did not seem to be in a hurry to
lie down with his companion; he was meditating, his chin in
his hand and his hand propped up on his knee, curled up in the
depths of the lair. He was dressed in a black woolen robe
made from a mortuary cloth, so long and ample that it had
almost not changed employment, for on seeing him unmoving,
one would have suspected that he had been dead for a long
time. His marvelous thinness had made him a skeleton, with a
hollow mouth, the teeth uncovered, the eyes sunken, the nose
absent, the skull polished, devoid of hair, the pale brown skin
stuck to jutting bones, and the body so fleshless that the veins,
the sinews and the muscles were, so to speak, ossified. Never-

theless, he had pupils in the holes of his eyes and breath in his lipless mouth. He could not move, however, without his carcass rendering a creaky sound, as if his bones were rubbing together. Finally, the cadaverous odor that he exhaled incessantly bore the evidence of the society that he habitually frequented.

"Gallows-bird," said the lady of the house, with an anger that only made her wrinkled throat tremble, "Egyptian crow, avaricious Bohemian, are you more churlish than a Jew, then, more bitter than a Lombard, more rapacious than an Englishman? How long will you be satisfied with your heap of stones? Until it comes unstuck and falls apart? Tell me."

"Wife," replied Macabre, in a hoarse and phlegmatic voice, "when the display of characters and my dance are complete, we'll leave France for German soil."

"Vile hoarder, have you not amassed enough, in the thirteen full years we've been in Paris, me reading palms and you playing your rebec?"

"It's not easy to make a poor living! Our companions, who arrived at the Chapelle-Saint-Denis three years after us, numbering sixty-five, telling fine stories to open purses, were sternly expelled and are traveling the highways, with neither shelter nor abode, living on alms and larceny."

"I remember the Sunday of mid-August 1427, when our chiefs appeared on horseback, dressed as comtes, and announced their false pilgrimages for the crime of apostasy!"[18]

---

[18] Lacroix obtained this datum from a document entitled *Journal d'un bourgeois de Paris*, ostensibly written between 1405 and 1449, fifteenth-century copies of which survived in the Vatican and in Oxford, and which became an important source of information about the period. It describes the arrival of twelve "penitents" at the gates of Paris on 17 August 1427, including an ostensible duc and a comte, who claimed to have abandoned their own faith (the Roma, recently arrived in Europe, were pagans) and made a pilgrimage to Rome.

"Do you still regret, Giborne, not accompanying those horoscope-readers, those sellers of quack medicines, those master vagabonds of Bohemia?"

"Fie, wretch! It ill behooves you to insult and vituperate against our ancient relatives! Possession is not worth as much as liberty, and contentment surpasses wealth! You often envy me my daily pittances, and I'm racked by hunger!"

"Money no sooner comes in than it goes out; that's why I shan't stay in this city during the plague and famine that I've prognosticated by studying the stars."

"Indeed, I've heard it said in the gravediggers' lodgings that mortality is increasing in the hospitals, and the price of cheese in the Madeleine market is as high as in the days of the English."

"So it's necessary, then, to make haste to put on our play before the contagion and the famine arrive. For that, you need to go to the Lombards tomorrow to hire costumes.

"Right! They won't lend me an old rag without a pledge and caution. Can you just give me a few unclipped gold pieces to get dresses and trinkets?"

"A little silver and small change, gladly; I don't know whether there's any gold in my savings. Am I a money-changer? Do I have a forge and a stall under the Pont-au-Change?"

"Don't mock me, you liar! Do you think you can deprive me of sight, sense and memory? I have a suspicion that old Nicolas Flamel, the alchemist, has no better income than yours, changer of death..."

"Shut up, traitress! What if someone were listening? I'm merely a miserable player of the rebec and farces, Giborne."

"The said farces, twice danced publicly, in significance of joy and merriment for the English victories, were worth two thousand écus each, in addition to Bedford's gifts..."

"Oh! Wretched spy, are you daring to lay siege to me, to pillage and slay in my fortress? Those are defamatory lies, patent lies and insensate words."

"Will you similarly deny twelve thousand shrouds and winding-sheets, stolen from the dead of the cemetery and sold by me to the clothworkers under the pillars of the market, at the risk of being buried alive?"

"Shut up, chatterbox, or I'll tear out your tongue! Rather confess freely that those sales of drapery have produced large sums that you've withheld from me. Give them back immediately!"

"Do we not need to add to that account the income from bodies and bones delivered to physicians, apothecaries, necromancers, wise women and others?"

"Truce, she-wolf, viper, malign beast! I'll make you fast in penance for your perfidy and go to bed without supper. Make provision nevertheless to procure us what we need to start the dance by Thursday."

With these words, pronounced with a particular grinding of the teeth, Macabre fixed his bloodshot gaze on the gipsy woman and bolted the door as he went out. His furious wife shook the rusted hinges and the rotten wood, but, seeing that her efforts would be futile against her imprisonment, she growled like an angry tiger, broke earthenware jars with her kicking feet, shook the sonorous bones of a skeleton, put out the lamp in order to drink the oil from it, gnawed some crusts of moldy bread, and then lay down in the coffin that took the place of a bed and went placidly to sleep.

Macabre went slowly up the sixty steps that led to the platform, and his bony limbs creaked at every step like a rusty weather-vane in the wind. He sat down on the bare stone in the cool air of a spring night, and, from the height of his belvedere, he contemplated the cemetery below, half-hidden in the darkness, with its black crosses, its whitened tombs and its new enclosure of charnel-houses. Then he paraded his gaze over the horizon limited by painted gables, tiled rooftops and slate-lined bell-towers, which seemed animated in the sparse rays of moonlight. The wind whistled as it was engulfed in the chimneys, the back-streets and passages.

Macabre looked at the eastern part of the sky and sighed.

At that moment, a night-crier, in accordance with the statutes of the brotherhood based in the parish of Saints-Innocents, appeared at the summit of that church, in the Rue Saint-Denis, and repeated the cry: "Wake up, good people who are asleep, and pray to God for the poor dead!"

Will it be necessary for me to render my soul too, Macabre thought, when the crier retired, *and let go of so much acquired wealth? Oh, should I not return to the land of my ancestors, to Bohemia, where I was born?*

He was sad and preoccupied, as he considered the funereal space where he had labored for thirteen years, but a kind of laughter murmured in his throat when he had pushed a catch hidden between two stones which, sliding apart with a seesaw action, uncovered a hiding-place excavated within the thickness of the wall. Macabre plunged both hands in to it, drunkenly, and dipped them into the gold that streamed between his fingers.

A shiver of delight ran through his entire body, and the sound of the metal, stirred with excitement, restored life to his heart. He lulled himself with that unsteady harmony, which mingled with the sounds of the atmosphere; his eyes bulged in their orbits; his jaws imitated the rasp of a file; his knees knocked together crisply and his ribs rattled like the scales of a serpent. Finally, possessed by the strangest sensations, his respiration interrupted and his limbs shriveled, he plunged his arms into his treasure all the way to the elbows, and collapsed, rigid.

He did not get up from that fit for an entire hour, and its spasms had been so violent that several pieces of gold had warped and folded in his hands. He hastened to restore everything to its usual state, and to bid a tender adieu to the object of his frenetic amour. To efface the last vestiges of that exhausting crisis, however, he suddenly passed on to a gentle and natural enjoyment. He took down a rebec suspended on the wall alongside an Aeolian harp.

The rebec, whose Celtic name proves its antiquity,[19] and which it is wrong to confuse with the Hebrew zither, was an oval violin with three strings, with a neck sculpted in a grotesque figure and a curved bow broadly furnished with horsehair. Macabre tightened the strings of his rebec, bizarrely ornamented with a death's-head, and began to draw slow, plaintive and moaning chords from it, which borrowed the accents of the human voice; it was an expressive and eloquent music, the modulations of sobs, tears and sighs; at times, a clear and melodious sound was exhaled, like a celestial prayer.

Macabre experienced dreamlike and fantastic sensations of another kind; he nodded and raised his head in cadence, marking time with the movement of his chin, and abandoned himself to ecstasy. The surrounding objects submitted to the charm of his music; the tower seemed to rotate, gently suspended in the void; the houses were uprooted without disorder and formed silent dances, intersecting, meeting up, coming apart and coming together. Here and there, massive belltowers swayed above the moving crowd. Then the musician's rebec burst forth in harsher and more mysterious sounds.

Down below, in that bewildering round-dance, the charnel-houses were dancing around the cemetery, whose terrain had been lifted up by the power of the instrument; and while the obelisks, crosses and monuments yielded to the general vertigo, an ever-increasing number of shades and specters revived, mingled and took flight with lightning rapidity. The moon, carried away amid the clouds, presided over the mute frolics, and Macabre allowed himself to be drawn in spirit into the fête he was giving for the dead. The vision of Ezekiel was realized.

---

[19] Some etymologists link the name of the instrument in question—the ancestor of the violin and similar stringed instruments—to the Arabic term for a similar instrument, but Webster agrees with Lacroix in deriving it from the French *bec* and hence to hence to the Celtic-derived *beak*.

Weariness forced him to stop before the strings were broken by the energy of his playing. The entire magical ball stopped at the same time, and Macabre, wiping away his involuntary tears, searched in vain for traces of the transformation he had briefly believed that he had wrought in the order of nature. He abandoned his rebec for a spade, pincers and a hammer; the artist became a workman again. He went down into the cemetery to rob the newly-buried.

III. The Boîte-aux-Lombards

The Jews of the Middle Ages were hated and persecuted in all countries and by all religions. It is necessary to attribute that universal horror less to Judaism itself, which shares much of the Christian dogma, than to the antisocial character of the Jewish nation. A people without a homeland, dispersed among other peoples, from whom it isolated itself obstinately by its customs, its costume, its worship and its prejudices, only receives a grudging and intolerable hospitality. It is true that the calumnies spread by Christian priests against a religion they scorned contributed to rendering contact with Jews odious, who established an eternal barrier between themselves and the worshippers of Christ. To that grave reason for division was added various personal and local reasons that were handed down from father to son. Their impropriety, their fanaticism, their avarice and their egotism were ineradicable flaws that they did not strive to hide; finally, their activity, industry and wealth served to aliment envy rather than emulation.

It was, therefore, to please the people and the clergy that the kings of France punished the Jews tyrannically, even though they contributed to the commercial prosperity of the kingdom. The most barbaric ordinances were devised for their ruination and shaming; between 1096 and 1394, there was no end to the insults, cruelties and injustices that they experienced. Before Saint Louis they were killed unceremoniously and to gain indulgences; they were assigned a separate district in Paris, and distinguished by a strip of yellow cloth that they were obliged to wear over their garments. If anyone wanted to fund a church, construct a bridge of raise an army, they drew upon the purse of the Jews, pillaged their shops, held them to ransom; they were expelled and then recalled, only to be expelled again. The invariable pretext for these frequent exiles was religion.

The Jews retained, however, by virtue of taxation, the right of sojourn in Paris in the vicinity of Les Halles, and certain streets were leased to them, as the names of the Rues de Juiverie, des Juifs and de Judas testify. They had a cemetery, a mill and synagogues; they were merchants and money-lenders. In spite of the extraordinary rigors imposed on them by the king, the provost and the bishop, in spite of the insults and the blows that all of them received, they resigned themselves to that ill-treatment, which was compensated by the profits of their money-lending. The love of profit held sway over the dread of danger, and even while they were banished from France they penetrated therein with impunity by representing themselves as Italians, whether Genoese, Venetians or Lombard; it was under that denomination that they were proscribed in 1349 by Philippe de Valois. But they always devised new disguises, and when Charles VI had expelled them for the last time, the richest eluded the ordinance of 7 September 1394 by covering themselves with the name of Lombards, to which the old Rue de la Buffeterie owes its present name.

These Lombards, celebrated in our financial history, were natives of all the states of Europe and received that generic name, equivalent to that of banker, because of their great fortune. Many Israelites borrowed that safeguard, common to so-called Christians who knew no religion but their interest and no altar but their counter. The Israelites in question were identified as much by their predations as their fidelity to the law of Moses, which they practiced in secret. Their ostensible commerce consisted of changing money and transporting it to the Court of Rome, which drew enormous subsidies from France by way of tithes, prelatures and the purchase of pardons, but money-lending and pawnbroking, although forbidden, brought them greater returns. During the ten years that the occupation of Paris lasted, the English showed themselves to be greedier and more pitiless than the Lombards, as attested by a contemporary proverb which employs the term "Englishman" to enhance the significance of "creditor."

The most famous trading-center of the Lombards was known as the Hôtel de la Boîte-aux-Lombards, doubtless because their principal treasury was located there. The house in which, according to the accounts of the Provost of Paris in 1438, the counter of the Boîte-aux-Lombards was customarily located was situated in the Rue Saint-Denis, facing the cemetery between the Rue Aubry-le-Boucher and the Rue Trousse-Vache. Its façade of carved stone is still remarkable today, for its three stories decorated by sculptures, its gables pierced with protruding rounded skylights, the overhanging edges of its roof and, most of all, for the tastefulness of the ornaments that the architect has lavished on the frontons and pilasters of the windows. Italian style can perhaps be recognized in the regularity of the lines and the ensemble of the exterior decoration; did the Lombards import their architects from Genoa and Florence? The house is now occupied by a perfumer.

In a basement, which the smoke of lamps had coated with the color of soot, in the midst of bales of merchandise from the Levant, three Jews were sitting in a triangle on piles of silk cloth. The shop had not been open the day before, the Sabbath, at the risk of incurring suspicion and the corporeal or pecuniary penalties of unemployment on Saturday. They were constrained, to their great regret, to observe the day of rest on Sunday, like good Christians, and they were consoling themselves for that odious necessity by sitting up after curfew on the evening of Palm Sunday, drinking the beer or stout that the English had made fashionable in Paris.

They had three very characteristic Jewish faces. The youngest and most influential, Balthazar Culdoë, the master of the Boîte-aux-Lombards, was about fifty years old. From his bald forehead and patriarchal beard, in which gray hairs were beginning to invade the black, to his austere expression, his small lynx-like eyes traversed by bloody threads, his deep voice and his imposing gestures, everything about him personified experience and authority. The other two listened to his rare and instructive comments as if they were oracles. He was bare-headed, dressed in a linsey-woolsey overcoat from Amiens, lined with cats'-fur, with a leather belt to support a heavy concealed money-bag. The sign of the corporation was a golden balance embroidered on the back and front of his coat, made of ordinary wool but very proper.

The second, Jeremiah Nathan, an associate of Balthazar Culdoë's, was a tall, thin and pale old man with stringy hair, beardless, with an inert physiognomy and a stupid smile. He wore a long mottled robe of jet black cloth, which the sun and the rain had considerably discolored, with numerous stitched-up rips; its sleeves were shiny beneath an impermeable layer of grease, and the dirty collar would have done honor to a mendicant monk. A conical felt hat rested on his tapering skull, and a hempen cord girdled his waist, as if he were about to set forth on a long journey. Its flaccid grip and narrow dimensions would not have tempted the thieves who then excelled in cutting the strings of purses.

The third colleague, Holopherne Croquoison, master gravedigger and cemetery-warden, was another old man, still sturdy although curbed by the infirmities of age. His thick hair and straight beard, ruddy and ashen, framed his rounded face, whose red cheeks, keen gaze and joyful expression did not betray any decrepitude. He was no less than seventy years old, but his naturally cheerful temperament still retained the ardor of youth. He was liberated from the affected rigidity of those of his religion without being a renegade; although his soul remained Jewish, its envelope had effaced his national imprint by virtue of the friction of the society he frequented because of his profession. One might have taken him for a parish church-warden, and the habit of dissembling had rendered him so discreet in matters of Judaism that he offered the pretext of a feverish cough every Saturday in order to celebrate the Sabbath in secret with his neighbors in the Boîte-aux-Lombards—who often reproached him for being more than half Christian, for he had his bench at Sainte-Opportune.

Master Holopherne, being in daily contact with the curés and manufacturers of fourteen parishes by virtue of his profession, incessantly defended himself against the cupidity that tried to force him to stricter economy in the matter of his costume; he levied the expenses of appearance from those of nourishment, and multiplied his income a hundredfold at the expense of the dead. His coat, in good blue cloth, with a large black velvet collar, exhibited no patches or stains, so careful was he to preserve it from them. A cowl of violet wool hung down his back with a long piece of fabric that could be passed under the chin and passed over the shoulder. Tan boots added the height of their heels to his stature. A rosary at his belt was a portable blasphemy.

"By the staff of Moses!" said Holopherne, biting his fingernails, "I'll be quite content for one of the seven plagues of Egypt to fall upon this Nineveh; it will open up the earth in the cemetery many times over, each of which excavations will be worth five sols to me, in addition to the gravedigging fee."

"Balthazar, my friend," said Nathan, with his imbecilic laugh, "we'll earn large sums, thanks to the famine, and it's prudent to store wheat in our granaries right away."

"Elijah advises you!" said Master Culdoë to Croquoison, gravely. "I admire the way you hire out the cemetery, and the secret income that you get therefrom, which I estimate at two hundred gold pieces per year."

"Yes, the advice is solid," replied Croquoison. "The rent of the Tour Notre-Dame-du-Bois certainly isn't worth much, and in order to receive thirty livres eight sols and four deniers on annual income, I lose the trade in winding-sheets, shrouds, coffins, nails, bodies, grease, hair and all the rest, but I'm also exempt from the danger of being burned, hung, broken on the wheel or quartered."

"Enough, brother!" exclaimed Nathan, pityingly. "Is it really necessary to risk a twelve denier silver coin to have a gold crown at 66 per marc? There's no fortune without desire, no desire without peril, but not to have fortune enough is also perilous. Are the Christians spoiling your origins and your credit, Holopherne?"

"Aaron forgive me!" Croquoison interrupted. "I've stolen, refined, pillaged, and pilfered. The circumstance wasn't foreseeable, and that Bohemian bandit Macabre will carry away my fief, my seizures and windfalls. Yes, indeed!"

"The damage might yet be repaired, friend. Let the afore-said Macabre forage in the tombs as he wishes and take the cloth from the dead, but demand your share of the booty, and make sure that the merchandise is exchanged at our counter; we'll all share the opportunity and interest, without fear of being discovered and punished."

"That's the best advice, friend, given that the seamstress-es of the Lingerie willingly buy Flanders and Burgundy fab-rics for a few sols, which they sell on as new at full price."

"Well, the bargain's agreed between the here of us, and the profits will rise with mortality—so Macabre and his wife will work to our advantage and bear the penalty for the crime alone."

After this verbal pact, confirmed by a handshake, they touched one another's beards as a sign of common understand-ing and drew up the clauses of the treaty in writing. There was an assault of calculations and probabilities; numbers and sym-bols accumulated on the paper, and Master Culdoë demon-strated rigorously the pecuniary results that the contagion an-nounced by the physicians and astrologers would bring them.

Finally, a special ledger was opened for the recording of funerary items that would be supplied to the community. The hope of a brilliant affair and an imminent plague had put the three associates in a god mood, and they got drunk on beer, for want of wine. The swigs succeeded one another between the arithmetical calculations, completing the inebriation of the speculators. The subject was not yet exhausted, nor was the pot of beer, when the conversation, having become expansive, strayed into the domain of private life.

The three faces drew closer together, with the three glasses.

"Brothers," said Croquoison, in a low voice, "I spend a great deal—too much—on alms, offerings at mass and gifts to churches, but my poor family still remains devoid of progeniture, alas."

"It's written," replied Nathan, "that according to natural law, one golden sheep ought to engender two twin sheep, not to say three, per year. It's necessary to harvest money as soon as it's sown."

"The holy patriarch Abraham preserve us!" said Croquoison. "Sons are the punishment of fathers, and mine will consign me a dung-heap, like Job!"

"Lord! Is your Benjamin a prodigal son, a Ham, an Absalom? It's said that he hangs around churches and wears a doublet of silk cloth on Sundays and feast days."

"Yes! The ingrate has recoiled from the face of God; he's in love with and is pursuing a noble Christian lady, losing and dissipating the produce of his responsibilities with a vagabond fake leper named Malaquet."

"Hasn't this fake leper taken up his station across the exit from the charnel-houses near the church for two weeks?" asked Culdoë.

"In truth," Holopherne replied, shrugging his left shoulder, "the leper is healthy and fit enough, I can assure you, to put beggars to shame. He knows all the tricks of vagabonds and thieves; his dines on trickery and sups on malice; it's said that he hails from a band of Cut-throats, and was once condemned to death for a crime of sacrilege by the Provost of Paris; still, he's well and truly punished.

"Alas," Culdoë said, "have pity on me, all-powerful Lord, but I'd pay a rich reward—up to five hundred livres—to have that bad leper cured. Send your son to see me tomorrow, Master Croquoison."

"Teach him the wisdom that he's so direly lacking; above all, teach the reckless fool the value of money and self-interest, because if he carries on with this prodigality, I'll disown him, after having adopted him, like the chicken brooding the serpent's eggs!"

"By the Ark of the Deluge!" Culdoë interjected, going pale and sighing. "The child isn't yours?"

"That, my good friends," said Holopherne mysteriously, blushing and coughing, "is a story unknown to anyone, which

58

I'll gladly tell you truthfully. Frankly speaking, Benjamin is not of my blood."

"Who was his legitimate father, then? Who is his mother? Is he twenty-five years old? Was he a foundling, or stolen?"

"Oh! Why this singular emotion, friend?" exclaimed Nathan, shaking Culdoë's sleeve as he repeated vague questions fervently. "Don't you think that Master Holopherne is making fun of us?"

"It was a strange adventure," said Croquoison, collecting his thoughts. "In the year 1415, while King Charles was demented,[20] an honest merchant was accused by denunciation of being a Jew, of practicing the Sabbath and holding in pawn the sacred vessels of Saint-Josse."

"Was that merchant named Schoeffer and did he live in the Rue de Précheurs in Les Halles?" demanded Culdoë, excitedly, trembling in every limb.

"Yes, indeed, friend. You weren't in Paris at that time? I'll continue the story. The unfortunate Jew was beaten with rods, birches and whips all the way from the Croix-du-Tiroir to the Porte Saint-Honoré. During those exceptional cruelties, the lackeys of Queen Isabeau stormed the victim's house, killed his innocent wife and dispersed his merchandise, furniture and money."

"Oh, the miscreants! They prevented him by that means from redeeming the punishment with a fine, and Schoeffer lost a good twenty-four thousand écus as well as his wife and children. He shall be avenged as he hoped!"

"Now, I was living in the town without my status as a Jew being known, and I was employed as a gravedigger by the Hôpital Sainte-Catherine, without having a wife, relatives or

---

[20] Charles VI first went mad in 1392, and suffered numerous bouts of insanity thereafter, adding considerably to the confusion of the Hundred Years' War, as his spouse Isabeau of Bavaria and various other ambitious individuals contended for the authority thus vacated.

friends. That evening, coming back from work, I hear whimpering and wailing under the pillars near the Tonnellerie, so I went to have a look and found a little child, with his side lacerated, his arm broken and his head bloody..."

"God of Abraham and Jacob! Was he circumcised?"

"Certainly, and I apologize if he was subsequently baptized to please the curé of Saints-Innocents. Thus being a Jew and a Christian at the same time, he grew up in my paternal bosom, and everyone took him for my own son."

"Thanks to which I've found mine! Grace be rendered to you, who have saved him from death! This is poor Schoeffer who cries *Hosanna!*"

"Schoeffer," Nathan said to him ill-humoredly, "why that imprudent declaration? Do you want to be whipped, expelled and pillaged again? This time, we'll be boiled in oil or thrown into the furnace."

"Come on, brothers!" said Holopherne, sharply. "Am I an informer, a spy, a calumniator? Oh, the insulting suspicion? I wouldn't remain cool, I think, if you were heated up by a parliamentary warrant?"

"Glory to Jehovah in the centuries of centuries!" repeated Culdoë, weeping with joy and searching for a prayer that his memory refused him. "I made a vow to the Lord who has resuscitated my child from the dead!"

"What vow, friend" asked Nathan, who wanted to share in all his associate's opportunities. "I claim that the vow is common between us, if it brings in good interest by the month or the week."

"To that end, I consent to your vow too, Master Culdoë," Croquoison added, rubbing his hands at the thought of a new source of income.

"It's a vow for divine intervention," said Culdoë, with an inspired expression. "I swear to you that the Lord will make our commerce prosper for the price of the holocaust!"

"Tell us what you have promised, Balthazar!" exclaimed Nathan, whose eyes were shining with hope.

"Master Culdoë is so prudent and dexterous in business," said Croquoison, confidently, "that it is not necessary to know his praiseworthy enterprise in advance, inasmuch as he possesses the patience of King Solomon."

"Friends," said Culdoë, satisfied by this discretion, "mystery is important to the success of our offering, which I shall reveal to you on the Friday of the Passion, at midnight, within the walls of the Cimetière des Saints-Innocents."

"Why that place, that day and that hour?"" asked Croquoison. "Do you know the whereabouts of a buried treasure?"

"Have faith and assurance," Nathan replied, "for Holopherne is having visions from on high. I accept the said vow."

Croquoison did not want to pull out of the treaty, which was, like the preceding one, consecrated by a triple draught of beer and a fraternal touching of the three beards. "But first, what recompense for Schoeffer's son?" he said, delightedly.

"I'll reward you handsomely, Messire Holopherne," Culdoë said, with a dark look, "when we're all three in the cemetery at midnight on the Friday of Easter. Be patient until then."

"Well then," retorted Croquoison, who had held out his hand at Culdoë's first words, "there will be time on Friday to restore you son to you, who is very expert at opening and digging a grave. Be patient until then."

"What! I must wait so long to kiss the dear child! When I believed him dead, I would have paid a large ransom to have him alive, but now it will only cost me a wisp of straw, I'm reluctant to give it."

"Yes, my case is similar; yesterday, I would have thanked anyone who lightened the burden of my old age of such a precious ward, and now I will only surrender him judiciously, and only for great thanks."

"Come the Friday of the Passion, which the Christians call Good Friday, friends," said Nathan, looking into the depths of his empty purse, "we'll know what this fine offering is. Moses and Aaron determine that it will be a buried treasure!"

Culdoë and Croquoison separated, somewhat discontented with one another—the latter, especially, who promised himself that he would be well compensated for his interested humanity.

Culdoë, remembering the immense losses he had suffered, was indignant at the thought of a further pecuniary sacrifice that was being demanded of him for the restitution of his property; as he had ingenuously admitted, the discovery that he had just made seemed to him to be an acquired right, and he was convinced that he had paid enough for that joy with twenty-three years of regrets. Croquoison, who had no liking for sterile gratitude, seemed firmly decided to sell his capacity as adoptive father as dearly as possible, certain of the impossibility of a legal claim.

After exchanging a few bitter words, the master gravedigger went back, via the rear courtyard, to the domicile in which he lived alone with Benjamin, who often did not spend the night in his lodgings and had only come back at daybreak for a week.

The house must be the one that can still be seen in the Rue Saint-Denis, next door to the Boîte-aux-Lombards, six stories high, which extends backwards, as if the houses contiguous with it were rendering to it in height what it loses in breadth, black and degraded, with no other ornament than a naked man standing against a stake, a crude sculpture that can be distinguished above the entrance. Undoubtedly, the interval of four centuries has changed the appearance of the building, which no longer has the inevitable gable over the street.

Nathan, preoccupied with the offering with which he had associated himself without knowing what it was, went to bed groping in the dark. Culdoë sat up for a long time, recapitulating his plans and meditations on the Talmud and the Jewish rabbi, visiting his ledgers, counting and recounting his deniers, until sleep closed his eyes to continue his golden dreams.

The day was beginning to dawn, and distant noises were announcing the arrival of goods in the market as soon as the city gates were open; the ambulant tradesman had not begun their morning cries; the convent bells mingled their carillons, like birdsong on a spring day.

Suddenly, a violent impact on the shutters of the shop woke the sleeper with a start. He did not hurry to respond to that untimely visit, but there was a more violent knocking and oaths reiterated with an irreverence that would have incurred severe corporal punishment in a more peaceful time lent their brutal energy to that singular wake-up call.

Culdoë, making sure that daylight was filtering through the gaps in the shutter, was more afraid of an attack by robbers, as one incessantly dreads a misfortune previously suffered. He waited in silenced again to see whether the racket might cease, war-weary, but the blows redoubled, as well as the insolence of the besieger, who was muttering between his teeth about the whip and the gallows.

"Hey!" shouted Culdoë, raising his voice. "Who's there? What do you want? Go on your way, fellow—it will be daylight in an hour."

"Schoeffer!" interrupted a guttural accent that he recognized with terror. "I'll declare loudly what you are, and invoke the law of Jews against you if you don't hurry up and open your cell. Brrr! Brrr!"

At this formidable threat, Culdoë, having broken into a cold sweat and a universal tremor, swayed momentarily. Then, gathering his strength, he drew the bolts of a judas hole in the middle of the door.

A coarse face smudged by wine and mud was stuck to the narrow grille of the opening at the same time, and two eyes plunged their flamboyant gaze into the interior of the room, while hiccupping laughter harmonized with the clicking of a leper's rattle. Culdoë, suffocated by despair, tore at his beard and clothing, struck his breast and bruised his face.

"Brr! Herod, Sire!" the leper shouted at him, accompanied by the ringing of his bell, "Do you know a man named

63

Schoeffer, who was once whipped and banished in perpetuity, under pain of hanging?"

"Wretch!" Culdoë interjected, launching himself forward to close the mouth. "Are you not satisfied to have caused my ruination and that of my family once?"

"Brrr! Schoeffer, that was to teach you not to scorn lepers and to spread the profits of usury in alms. So, my worthy Jew, you remember little Crespeau, presently known as Malaquet?"

"For God's sake, Crespeau, my friend, are you so determined to harm me? I'll give you what you need to live honestly, if you swear not to disturb me anymore."

"Brrr! Will I not have a share in your confiscated treasures, if I betray you and tell the truth to Messire the Provost or Monseigneur the Bishop?"

"Oh, don't do anything, my dear son; hold me to ransom instead. Listen, Crespeau; I've converted to the Catholic religion; I've received baptism, and, to prove it, I'll found a chapel to the patron saint of lepers."

"Brrr! That will be as well for the repose of your soul, my pretty, when your corpse is hanging from the gibbet at Montfaucon. I've been drinking all night at the Cabaret du Tonneau-Ailé in the Rue de la Barillerie."

"Indeed—was the wine good? Was it Gâtinais, Orléanais or Muscadet? How many bottles were emptied? I regret not having been there to pay the bill for the honest guests."

"I don't care about your riches, Jew—I'd rather be a leper. Brrr! Gambling has taken the last sou from my purse; give me a double tournois. That's all I need to make rose-nobles— just a double tournois for a quarter of an hour."

"Crespeau, thanks to you, once, I lost my wife, children, possessions and honor; thanks to you, I nearly lost my deplorable life; are you going to take away the rest, and everything, by denouncing me again? Have pity and mercy!"

"Brrr! Henceforth, my friend, have respect for lepers, who are the suffering limbs of Christ. My name is Malaquet, not Crespeau, just as Schoeffer has become Culdoë. Adieu, bonsoir and bonjour. Come closer, so I can kiss you before the dance."

Culdoë approached the judas-hole, sadly, and presented his cheek, which was covered with slimy saliva. He bore that insult with mute patience, and only had recourse to ablutions after the leper had gone, singing a popular song at the top of his voice and drawing away hammering the walls of the street. Culdoë listened to the clicking rattle until he could no longer hear it.

IV. The Cimetière des Saints-Innocents

The cemetery in question, which was transformed into a market forty years ago, and has not changed its name after that bizarre metamorphosis, received its first destination as soon as the faithful had chosen their sepulcher around the chapel of Notre-Dame-du-Bois. A vast extent of ground, known as Les Champeaux—the meadows—because of the fertile pasturage still surrounded by forest, was cleared. The Christian cemetery became one of numerous population when Paris had extended its outskirts over the northern bank of the Seine, and once it only had a single religion under a Christian king. The principal market of Les Halles was then established close to the cemetery, outside the fortified wall of the city, which Philippe-Auguste later moved outwards into the countryside.

Before the reign of that great king, the cemetery of Les Champeaux offered a hideous spectacle for religion and morality, as if the living were taking pleasure in insulting the dead; in that integral plain, bristling with crosses, mounds and funerary stones, the filthiest animals came to dig in the ground and wallow in the mud, while horses, cows and sheep fought over sparse and withered grass; the bones lay pell-mell with filth and carrion, which have left the neighboring streets the significant names of the Place aux Porceaux, Fosse-aux-Chiens, Trousse-vache, etc. Boule was played on freshly-recovered graves; there was traffic in prostitution in the shadow of the tombs, and the beacon that lit the night of that profane place did not deter thieves. Philippe-Auguste, indignant at those sacrilegious scandals, had the cemetery surrounded by an elevated rampart in solidly-joined bricks and ordered that the gates be closed every day at the hour of curfew. It was in that epoch that it was blessed under the invocation of the Holy Innocents, or rather of Saint Innocent, in honor of a child named Richard crucified by the Jews in Paris in 1179, of whom historians relate the miracles operated by the virtue of his relics.

By 1438 the Cimetière des Saints-Innocents had been subjected to a further metamorphosis. Philippe-Auguste's enclosure had disappeared, giving place to the charnel-houses that received the overflow of that narrow ossuary. The chapel of the dead had become a parochial church, built with money confiscated from the Jews, and houses, like their inhabitants, had accumulated in the vicinity of the market, which envied the air and light of the tombs. The cemetery—including the church and the charnel-houses—was thirty-two fathoms wide and forty-eight long, bordered by the Rue de la Lingerie, the Rue aux Fèvres or aux Fers, the Rue Saint-Denis and the Rue de la Charronnerie or Ferronnerie. One entered it by four gates situated in the four corners, counting that of the church, which was always open, and, the cemetery serving as a public passage, each gate designated by its name the place to which it led, such as the Porte de la Rue Saint-Honoré, the Porte de la Halle and the Porte de la Ferronnerie.

The church of the Saints-Innocents, whose parish comprised no more than seventy houses, advanced into the cemetery at the corner of the Rues de Fers and Saint-Denis. The sanctuary had belonged to the ancient chapel, whose obscure and stifled work appeared to be anterior to the massive architecture of the twelfth century; the nave, sustained by heavy pillars and the square tower, with walls entirely bare all the way to the platform, had the character of the times of Philippe-Auguste. The second southern wing and the majority of the chapels were of recent foundation. Jean, Duc de Berry, one of the most generous benefactors of the church, in which he wanted to be buried, had had the portal ornamented by sculptures and inscriptions in verse in 1408. The fountain of the Saints-Innocents, alimented by the aqueduct of Mont Saint-Gervais, took its name from the church, to which it had been adjacent since the reign of Saint-Louis.

The charnel-houses that formed a rim around the cemetery only consisted of a vault and a series of garrets; the low vault, dark and damp, constructed and repaired in different eras, had about twenty-four ogival arches, only open on one side; the tombs, the epitaphs, the paintings, the statues and the engraved stones, paved, carpeted, bordered and filled the gallery, which extended its black and monotonous wall along the streets. It was a fashion among the rich to build a charnel-house at their expense in order to give it their name and have themselves buried there; testaments all contained legacies for that purpose, such that the work ran out long before the money, which flowed from all purses.

Money from Nicolas Flamel, who was found everywhere with his fortune when it was necessary to hire masons, sculptors, painters and other workers, built several arcades charged with allegorical figures that have long intrigued the seekers of the philosopher's stone. One group of charnel-houses was due to the munificence of the Maréchal de Boucicaut, who died a prisoner in England after having faced death in a hundred heroic combats. The other known founders were Mathieu d'Hauteville and his wife Martine, in 1396; Pierre Potier, furrier, in 1397; Nicolas Boulard, steward of the royal kitchen, in 1393; Raoul Estable, known as the carpenter, in 1405; Guillaume Tirevaige, royal auditor, and his wife, in 1407; and Dorechies, clerk-notary, in 1412.

The garrets fitted above the vaults to "lodge and harbor" the bones of the dead, according to the terms of the foundation, were covered by a tiled lean-to, and lit at intervals by high frontal skylights that were unglazed. Every time the cemetery was disturbed by opening new graves over the old ones, the bones that the earth had not consumed were transported and arranged by the gravediggers in the lofts, forming strange mosaic designs whose compartments were borrowed from both sexes, all ages and all conditions.

Père Dubreuil says on the subject of the symmetrically-organized death's-heads that they were "Very beautiful and good mirrors to represent the grandeur and impertinence of our human vanity." That sad debris inspired horror and disgust in the middle of Paris until the Revolution had them hidden forever, in the darkness of the catacombs that replaced the charnel-houses, without scriveners, seamstresses and clothes-merchants being able to erect stalls there.

The cemetery, which had swallowed up many genera-tions over the centuries, was cluttered with monuments, stand-ing and fallen, and crosses in iron and wood; old epitaphs, which did not guarantee a concession in perpetuity, were sold as simple materials; large stones were bought for the comple-tion of the Louvre. Green grass nourished in all seasons dis-guised the black color of the earth saturated with corruption, which reduced a cadaver to the condition of a skeleton in nine days.

Four large open graves, where the biers touched one an-other in order to save space, awaited the bodies of four privi-leged owners; that chapter of Saint-Germain-l'Auxerrois had an entitlement to the bodies brought from Saint-Eustache and Saint-Sauveur; the nuns of Sainte-Catherine to those of Saint-Jacques-la-Boucherie and Sainte-Opportune; the churchward-ens of the Saints-Innocents to those of their parish, and the Hôtel-Dieu to those of Saint-Christophe and Sainte-Marine. That division of property was not established without due pro-cess, and each of the parties conserved its jurisdiction over its gravediggers, under the authority of a master of their corpora-tion, a general warden of the cemetery—who was, at that time, Holopherne Croquoison.

Apart from the Tour Notre-Dame-du-Bois, various con-structions restricted the space for public sepulchers. The chap-el of Neuville-Villeroy, the site of which that family had bought, was a Gothic edifice adjacent to the charnel-houses of the Rue de la Lingerie, with a roof and a campanile; the fa-çade, plastered with epitaphs similar to signs, only offered two sound windows and one arched doorway closed with an iron trellis. The Préchoir was a square building opposite the portal of the church, a short distance from the charnel-houses of the Rue aux Fers; it had pilasters supporting a pyramidal roof and a balcony overlooking charnel-houses of the Ferronnerie, for preaching and blessing the people. The Loge-aux-Fossoyeurs was a building half-cellar and half-ground floor, emerging from the ground like a cadaver along the wall of the church; its name indicates its usage. Beneath the vaults of the charnel-houses, the tomb of Pernelle, Flamel's wife, that scrivener's hieroglyphs, the Calvary, and other pieces of sculpture have survived intact until our day, and disappeared with so many other historic monuments amassed during so many centuries into that funereal museum.

On the Monday after Palm Sunday, at seven o'clock in the morning, the gates of the cemetery were opened by the guardian; the strong-limbed and hirsute gravediggers immediately commenced their daily work, singing. Men and women passed through the abode of the dead on their way to the market, and came back by the same route with their alimentary provisions. A great circulation of comings and goings was stirred up in the populous and commercial quarter, pierced in all directions by passages and back-streets that had their attributions designated by distinctive names: the Rues de la Friperie, de la Chausseterie, de la Poterie, de la Lingerie, de la Cordonnerie, each one being the center of a particular genre of commerce. What produced a contrast scarcely sensible to coarse minds, however, was that concern for life alongside death, that animated buzz juxtaposed with the eternal silence of the tomb. Lepers and beggars warmed themselves in the rising sun, sitting and lying on stones, cleaning their ulcers, and easting whatever they took out of their sacks with a keen appetite.

The terror inspired by Macabre's abode was considerable weakened because of the curiosity excited by the preparations for the *danse macabre*. For several days, carpenters had been erecting a stage ten feet high, accompanied by two boxes, alongside the charnel-houses of the Ferronnerie. The location of the stage had been let by the Bishop of Paris, who permitted at that price the performance of pantomimes; pecuniary indemnities were also paid to the four landlords of Saints-Innocents, who ceded the right to occupy the cemetery during the course of the performance. Macabre directed all the works,

70

and supervised all the preliminary measures through the intermediary of Holopherne Croquoison, who had smoothed over all the difficulties by means of negotiation and money. "The last dance of the celebrated actor and musician Macabre" had already been advertised on placards at the gates of the cemetery and the doors of churches, and cried in the streets, fixed for Holy Thursday at one o'clock in the afternoon.

While the various and bizarre cries of vendors and mendicant resounded confusedly around the cemetery, passers-by paused to consider the progress of the stage and talk about it, with the idlers' bonhomie that is still characteristic of the inhabitants of Paris; merchants of hay, butchers, students, serving girls and bourgeois exchanged a few words from neighbor to neighbor.

"The workers aren't making much progress," said a paralytic who was very assiduous in visiting the theater. "The foreman's asleep on the job, and won't get it finished until animals can talk."

"To hear you talk I'd have thought that time had come," put in a pupil of the Quatre-Nations. "I'd be willing to pawn my bonnet and my books to see the marvelous spectacle."

"Ox-guts!" said a horribly bloodstained butcher. "The farce was played under the government of Monsieur de Bedford, and at carnival the Masters of the Great Butchery formed Death's cortege."

"Damn!" added a chambermaid on her way to wash linen in the river. "As long as the fête lasted it cost five tournois per day, and I saw Death playing his rebec so perfidiously that one felt drawn to him; it was thus that he lured and set to dancing a Reverend Father saying his paternosters, a housewife getting dinner ready, an amorous lover, and many others."

"Saint Nicolas aid our good city!" cried a grocer-apothecary, putting his hands together. "It's abominable impiety and diabolical invention! This Macabre burns candles made from the fat of the dead."

"So he's the Antichrist, Père Moutard?" retorted a pauperess of Saints-Innocents. "Still, it's obvious that his viol

71

was extracted from the bones of some hanged man, as canon who provides the church candles says."

"By all the Holy Innocents," replied the night-crier, "he was dancing the Sabbat with the souls of purgatory last night, and I plugged my ears in order not to hear his infernal music."

"What, Silverbeak!" interrupted a sauce-cook carrying a pot of thyme mustard. "You've heard the ball of the damned and Satan's hautboy? Your hour is nigh, my son!"

"No, crier of hot sauce," said the public crier, "for ten years and more I've been accustomed to that perilous harmony, which would send you to brew mustard for the companions of Death within a year."

"May the good God excuse me for swearing," exclaimed a churchwarden of Sainte-Opportune, "but Monsieur the Bishop ought to do a good and charitable deed and excommunicate that pagan, who's about to light the fire of Sodom and Gomorrah."

"A pox on that old church rat!" murmured a carpenter who had mingled with the group to enjoy the eulogies given to his work. "Isn't it a praiseworthy thing to give work and wages to poor people?"

"Truly, Master Gougibus; strike as hard with your tongue as with your hammer," said a newcomer from the Porte-aux-Peintres. "These avaricious churchwardens would like to tax a blue sky as their image of Our Lady."

"Certainly, whoever spends a Parisian sol merits good work and merchandise," said a clothmarket employee, "for money is retiring to the depths of purses, as in the times of the English."

"Those English swine have made money and good will disappear," grumbled a fishmonger returning to her stall. "Since the departure of the king, fresh herrings are rotting in the barrel."

"God's blood!" replied the butcher, caressing he hilt of his cleaver. "There was more joyous cheer in Paris when Messire Saint-Yon, the syndic of butchers, was Privy Councilor to Monseigneur de Thérouenne; when the good sire de

Willeby, the English captain, ordered two cows and six sheep killed every week for his house; when we had the red cross of Saint André..."

"Down with the Burgundian!" cried a barber, fleeing. "If I weren't afraid of being bloodied by that cut-throat, I'd have him taken to the Châtelet prisons."

"By the white cross!" said an inhabitant of the Porte-aux-Meuniers, "Messire Ambroise de Loré, Provost of the city, ought to annul the ordinance that forbids any transport of foodstuffs to Mantes, Creil, Rouen and other places held by the English, who have gilded money-bags and long teeth; a sack of flour will be worth twenty sols a seventh in the market in Paris and sixty outside the walls..."

"That's mill talk, straw promises," retorted a baker red from the heat of the oven. "On the contrary, the Provost would be prudent to amass a mountain of wheat to prevent imminent famine."

"What famine?" asked a wage-laborer devouring his brown bread greedily. "Happy is he who abstains from eating and fasts daily?"

"The price of wheat has gone up to six sols eight deniers, Maître Courlebois," the baker went on, addressing a salt-porter, "there won't be a harvest this year because of the maneuvers of the men of war."

"May the late King Charles V protect us, from paradise!" Courlebois said, who remembered having carried the body of that wise king to Saint-Denis, in accordance with the privileges of his trade. "Will peace never come?"

"Peace is further away from us than Paris from Bourges," said an archer of the watch discontented with his pay. "It's possible that the city will be retaken and sacked; there isn't a single man-at-arms on the ramparts."

"So, Monsieur Bowman," enquired a ribbon-maker in a low voice, "if the English come back and launch an attack, we're at risk of being taken by force, without mercy?"

73

"Damn! What's King Charles been doing in Bourges," said a washerwoman, her fists on her hips, "since he went there with his entire court on the third of December?"

"Ha! He's kissing his darling Agnès Soreau, the lecher!" riposted a prostitute, combining speech and lewd gesture.

"May Saint François be merciful and favorable to him!" said a fat shoemaker, simultaneously. "He's holding an ecclesiastical council and proposing pragmatic sanctions for the liberties of the Gallican church."

"As if the war and the famine weren't enough," Courlebois went on, shaking his white-haired head, "the plague's coming back to frolic among us, as it did in the memorable year 1434."

"The plague!" someone cried, anxiously. "What are you saying? Are you joking? What a dream! May the plague take you, you old impostor!"

"Children," said the salt-porter, lowering his voice, "be certain that within two months, many will have perished of the contagion that is taking root at the Hôtel-Dieu and the hospitals; in the meantime, let's live cleanly."

"Crazy talk!" said the barber, laughing. To a gravedigger leaning on his spade, he said: "My dear tailor of clothes for all seasons, how many deceased did you dress yesterday at Saints-Innocents?"

"Twelve coming from the Hôtel-Dieu," the gravedigger replied, coldly, "Six from the hospital Sainte-Catherine and twenty-five from various parishes. The crowd will be even larger today."

"My great patron Saint Nicolas keep us safe and sound!" said the grocer, with a groan. "That accursed sorcerer Macabre is the sole cause and author of these calamities. I invite you to seek your drugs in my apothecary."

"Everyone bare heads, right away!" the cry went up on all sides. "On your knees and pray! Here comes the brotherhood of the Holy Trinity."

The Brotherhood of the Father, Son and Holy Spirit, instituted with a devotional objective in imitation of the associations then founded in several churches for guildsmen, held a procession every Monday around the Cimetière des Saints-Innocents. That procession, the origins of which are unknown, although it can be linked to the Brotherhood of the Passion and the Resurrection of Our Lord based at the Hôpital de la Trinité, filed silently beneath the charnel-houses, while the onlookers, including the carpenters on their stage, knelt down and made the sign of the cross.

The crowd moved forward to follow the procession, which, having accomplished its duty, returned slowly to its point of departure, banners and cross at the head, led by its masters and governors, drawing in its wake another procession of curiosity-seekers.

The well-turned out young man who had pursued a lady into the church of Saint-Jacques-de-la-Boucherie the day before was standing still and leaning pensively on a tomb opposite the Porte de la Rue Saint-Honoré. He was not paying any heed to what was going on around him, and he alone remained standing while the procession filed past. He was gazing incessantly outside the cemetery, and a clap of thunder would not have extracted him from his preoccupation, which, sad and cheerful by turns, brightened ad darkened his face, pale with fatigue. Expectation and anxiety were interrupting his breathing, veiling his eyes and seething in is soul.

He emerged regretfully from that painful and passive state when he felt a clutching hand obstinately shaking his arm. With a gesture of impatience he recognized Holopherne Croquoison, who had noticed the absence of his natural representative while carrying out an inspection of the gravediggers' work, and had perceived him in the distance, in that nonchalant pose. After the passage of the procession, before which he had prostrated himself, grumbling, he had hastened to catch up with the bad lot, who had not yet returned to the paternal dwelling to hear the customary insults.

Holopherne paused momentarily to examine, angrily, the cloth of the garments that Benjamin was wearing, in the hope of disguising his status. He felt his son's sleeve, with a scowl that was augmented by virtue of the quality of the fabric. Then he burst into indignation and shook the arm that was abandoned to him as if he were trying to ring a bell; the other still did not turn his head.

"God of Israel!" Croquoison said, in a muffled voice. "Are you trying to ruin us, body and soul, malign child? Do you dare to refrain from rendering honor to processions, son of a Jew?"

"In truth, I didn't notice the procession," Benjamin replied, without changing the direction of his gaze."

"Will you be content to see me hanging from the gibbet, and will you laugh when they burn you for heresy?"

"In truth, I'm burning and consumed in a very different way. Go back to your graves, Father, and keep your eyes on your dead, in case they escape."

"Oh, I wish I could lay you down, to be better assured that you won't damage my settlements! Let's see: yesterday, forty-three new graves were opened, on which my fee..."

"Which fee was spent by me on trinkets and adornments, not to displease you."

"By the generation of Abraham! Am I not your father, you miserable thief? Are you conspiring wickedly to throw me on to Job's dung-heap? That sum belonged to me, and it was only permissible for you to reserve the cost of the gravedigging. Forty three graves worth six sols eight deniers apiece! Will you murder me, then, infamous seeker of amorous adventures?"

"It's you who've reduced me to these extremities by withholding my patrimony, if you are my father; if not, I'll go wherever my whim takes me to earn my living or go to the dogs."

"Ingrate! Do you imagine that you're the son of some noble baron and the issue of an ancient lineage? Well, you'd regret the change, and I advise you to keep your gravedigger's livery instead of those gentleman's garments. Benjamin, my son, the summer won't pass without copious profits, thanks to the malady that's running riot; take up your spade and work harder."

"No—I'd rather take up a rope to hang myself and a dagger to kill myself! Watch over your men, Father; I have an appointment elsewhere, to which I shall go shortly."

Benjamin had stood up precipitately at the sound of a leper's rattle, which was clicking relentlessly; satisfaction shone in his smile. He ran into the street, leaving the old man irritated and surprised by that sudden disappearance.

V. The Women's Steam-Baths

The Romans, who appropriated the customs of con-
quered lands, imitated the baths of the Orientals, which they
spread throughout the Occident and into Northern Europe.
Those baths of hot water and steam, initially reserved for
sybaritism and patrician luxury, soon became necessary to the
people, who adopted them as a new need in the warm climate
of Italy; Rome then became effeminate along with its emperors, and the eight hundred and fifty-five public baths that were
counted there passed for as many places of debauchery.

Roman civilization had marched in the wake of Julius
Caesar's armies, and in spite of the mild atmospheric temperature in Gaul, baths were introduced there with the proconsuls.
The only antiquity that Paris has conserved of the sojourn of
the Romans is a great vaulted hall of the Julian baths. The
custom of almost daily ablutions and sudorifics gradually became fixed in local customs, and penetrated as far as the lowest classes, less as a measure of health and cleanliness as by
routine and idleness. In fact, the variations of the air and the
influences of the seasons were to change that often salutary
habit into a constant source of disease. The Romans did not
take back with them the benefits of their government and the
traces of their occupation; the conquering Franks, in their turn,
gladly accepted the example of the Romans and the Gauls.

Thus, for centuries, baths were an essential part of the
hygiene of citizens, who nonetheless lived in filthy and noxious streets. It is believed that the fashion almost fell into neglect under the kings of the Carolingian dynasty, but it was
revived at the beginning of the crusades with a splendor that
lasted until the middle of the 17th century, when medicine
recognized the danger of sweats produced too frequently or
inappropriately.

Undoubtedly, the crusaders, who brought back many unknown things from their voyages overseas, renewed the

fashionability of bathing, and especially the steam-baths in which they had delighted in the Orient; in the subsequent era, steam-baths became so commonplace in Paris that there was one in every street; people went there in the mornings and the evenings, because bathing, which played an allegorical role in chivalry as in all religions, was a quotidian preliminary to dining.

Two streets have kept the proof of their ancient destination to the present day in their names: The Rue des Vieilles-Étuves, in the Saint-Eustache quarter, was dedicated to men's steam-baths; the Rue des Étuves in the Saint-Martin quarters to women's steam-baths. Old charters still indicate the situation of several steam-baths in the Rue Pierre-Sarrasin, the Rue de la Huchette and the Rue de l'Arbalète. It was in vain that the sexes were separated and isolated in these public establishments; lax morals took advantage of the facilities procured by an institution so favorable to mystery; the baths of Paris no longer had anything to envy those of imperial Rome.

Amour, prostitution and libertinage attracted the greatest numbers to the bath-houses, which covered everything with the same discreet veil; the male and female attendants of those sanctuaries assisted correspondence, meetings and pleasures; often, secret passages connected men's and women's stream-baths that were honest branches of infamous places. Nevertheless, in spite of the scandal, the declamations of preachers and the prohibitions of old men, everyone went to steam-baths, the poor pell-mell in vast terraced sweat-rooms, the rich in private booths; as for baths, every town-house had an apartment prepared for taking warm baths at midday.

The barbers-cum-steam-bath-attendants, a corporation of whom who served those warehouses of impurity did not, it is true, limit themselves to the role of go-betweens and brokers of gallantry; they were artful wielders of the razor and lancet, caring for hair and beards, bandaging and cauterizing wounds, selling various unguents and practicing a little non-professional medicine; at daybreak they made tours of the vicinity of their establishments, ringing their bells and shouting at the top of their voices: "Lords, go to the baths and steam-baths right now, without delay; the baths are warm, and that's no lie!"

Benjamin followed the leper, who continued to rattle two bones between his fingers in conformity with the law; the passers-by, warned by the sound, waited for him to draw away or put their hands over their mouths, careful to turn away from the direction of the wind.

Malaquet, who had gone into the Rue des Fourreurs, interrupted his repulsive music when he reached the cloister of Sainte-Opportune, still deserted and silent, because the canons were lying in bed after the fatigues of the day before, leaving the morning services to the junior clergy. He stopped behind an exterior pillar of the church and leaned against the wall, closing his eyes, as if to finish brooding his nocturnal wine. When the empty barrel that he carried at the end of a curved stick fell off and rolled in the gutter he woke up, shook himself, stood up, yawning and tottering, extending his arms.

Benjamin, who tapped him on the shoulder, dissipated the fumes of his intoxication momentarily. Benjamin would not have been afraid of the approach, contact or breath of a veritable leper.

Malaquet, formerly Crespeau, whose rubicund and shiny face was less suggestive of the hospital than the tavern, and who only had the rattle and barrel of the lepers of Saint-Lazare, had enrolled in that hideous company in order to share in its numerous benefits without difficulty or labor, at the risk of also sharing the incurable disease the desolated populations in the Middle Ages.

No one had ever attempted to cure or wipe out leprosy, and the leprosaria founded at the gates of cities, enriched by alms, protected by priests only served to encourage idleness and mendicancy; all beggars were lepers, because all lepers were beggars, and the hereditary horror that they generally inspired was mingled with a superstitious pity that prevented their separation from society; thus, those odious beings came to display their sores and scars in squares and marketplaces, with no other significant signs than the small barrel to staunch their ardent thirst and the rattle made of bone or wood to announce their contagious presence.

A large number of fake lepers usurped the right to the charity and respect of the poor people, who venerated them no less than cretins in Switzerland. Woe betide anyone who maltreated or insulted a companion of Saint-Ladre! He would become a leper himself within a year.

Women, for whom novelty has always been a powerful recommendation, accorded to lepers what they refused to healthy lovers of paler complexion; leprosy was handed down from father to son.

Malaquet, who had no appearance of leprosy, but much of drunkenness, belonged to the category of "white" or "hidden" lepers, whose disease was internal, and in consequence rather doubtful; such white lepers could have clear faces, healthy mouths, even lead a joyful life, drinking incessantly, making love frequently, justifying the saying "as happy as a leper."

Malaquet enjoyed the privileges of the estate that he had embraced for a month since hazard had brought him to Paris and installed him under the charnel-houses of the cemetery; he had much for which to thank his lucky star and the profession of leper, for money, blessings and presents came to him in abundance, filling his barrel and his ladle. Every procession, every interment and every market convoy paid him a tribute that he demanded with an imperious cry; merchants and maidservants did not pass by without smiling at him, interrogating him and annoying him; he replied boldly, and pursued the nymphs more ardently than a satyr of fable. He had long had a trusty mistress unaffected by fear of leprosy: Guillemette, Madame de la Vodrière's chambermaid, a mature and experienced woman.

The fake leper rarely remembered his forty-five years and his gray hairs, which he also caused his feasting-companions to forget. He was short in stature, with a large head and disparate limbs; his swollen legs seemed characteristic of the deformity known as elephantiasis, which gave certain lepers the monstrous proportions of an elephant; he did not wear the costume of any hospital, and did not exchange his liberty for the rule of a religious house; his sackcloth robe only came down to his knees; a hooded cape in green cloth protected his neck and shoulders from damp; strips of cloth wound around his calves and feet like the shafts of columns; his hands were thin and jaundiced; his purse, hung by a cord from his belt, still reeked of the part of a ram that was used for that purpose in those days, without taking away its true name.

"Well, friend," Benjamin said to him, impetuously, "is everything all right? Have you done what I asked? What is it necessary to do now?"

"My son," relied the leper, in his hoarse voice, "in order to speak more moderately, learn to take a sip of wine between each sentence, and swallow a little between every sip; it's a sound principle."

"Malaquet, my friend, tell me the result of your crusade. Is Madame Jehanne going to the baths? In which street can I join her? Has Guillemette decided to help me? Which is it? Is it necessary to weep or rejoice?"

"Brrr! To what, and how, shall I reply first? Tell me, in your turn: is sleep still clutching your eyelids, from having stayed awake last night and the preceding ones under the windows of your sleeping lady?"

"Oh, no idle chatter, my dear Malaquet! Don't hold back my hope and my joy any longer! Will the rendezvous succeed? Go on, I beg you."

"Brrr! Let's sing a *de profundis* for the virtue of that rebel, my dear Benjamin, for I love you like a father, and I do what I can to amuse your amours. Brrr! Shall I see you this evening at the Cabaret de la Grand-Pinte?"

"I will remember your incomparable services forever; I would give you Nicolas Flamel's Great Work if he had left it to me; I would crown you if I were king—so stop teasing me in this fashion, friend.

"Brrr! What more do you want? Have you eyes more open than your belly, and a thirst more capacious than this barrel? It's not enough to make you content for a day? Excuse me, Messire—you need a better servant."

"I thank you, on the contrary, my beneficent Malaquet, but I still need to know the time that awaits me, and the means of carrying your prediction to a conclusion."

"Brrr! I predicted, in accordance with the wine lees, that you would marry Madame de la Vodrière; that horoscope will begin its accomplishment this morning, at the steam-bath. In the meantime, I shall sing a song at table, with a full throat."

"For God's sake—or rather the Devil's—have you seen Guillemette and told her what I want? I'm drying up with impatience—get to the point! Doubtless Jehanne is unaware of the plot? Who will keep watch on the husband's threshold? Which steam-bath? Rue de l'Arbre-Sec? Hôtel des Étuves-aux-Femmes? Accursed leper, have you sworn to ruin my fortune? This precious time will be lost without return; my friend, my father, my savior, give me this terrestrial paradise at the expense of the other!"

Malaquet, who desired to oblige Benjamin, had stayed half-awake and had kept his promise, struggled against the assaults of a heavy sleep the fumes of which were rising to his head. His red eyes could no longer distinguish the objects that his intelligence no longer perceived; his mind was wandering in the vertigo that nocturnal libations had imprinted on his faculties; he tried to give a direction to his ideas and meaning to his words, but his thick tongue remained stuck to his palate and his voice expired in a prolonged yawn. The wall and his staff were insufficient to sustain him, and his head fell forwards, heavy and inert.

Benjamin, in desperation, begged, swore and implored, until the leper, noticing the absence of his barrel, bent down to pick it up and fell into the gutter with it. He adapted himself to that bed, for want of a softer one, and did not budge, in spite of the cries, supplications and nudges of his companion, who sadly gave up trying to get him to his feet and dragged him into a heap of mud along the wall of the church, making him a pillow with his barrel. The sleeper rid himself of an enormous weight that he had on his stomach and snored more loudly than the knell sounded at an interment.

Cursing the drunkard, who might perhaps have robbed him of an irrecoverable opportunity, Benjamin struck himself on the head with a closed first, as if to bring forth an inspiration, and then made his way, via the Rues Trousse-Vache and Saint-Martin, toward the Rue des Étuves-aux-Femmes, which has only changed half its name in changing its attribution.

That little street, less dirty than the others because of the overflow of hot water, was full of bath-houses, steam-baths and barbers' shops. Odorous fumes escaped from the doorways and the chords of musical instruments invited penetration into those secret refuges to which women of all ages and ranks flocked; crudely painted signs swayed above the doors, and toothless old women stood guard to ensure the persons of the wrong sex did not get into the bath-houses.

The young man walked slowly along the street, looking in at every window, in the hope of seeing someone appear, stopping at every door in the hope of seeing a veiled woman emerge whom he would recognize by the sound of her footsteps and the rustle of her dress.

He was beginning to curse the author of his disappointment from the bottom of his heart when the memory of the leper suggested an ingenious expedient to him. At the corner of a street he picked up two potsherds, which he placed between his fingers in such a way as to imitate, by agitating them, the sound of a rattle, and without worrying about the strange opinion that it would arouse against him, he shook the shards against one another with so much eloquence that devotees came running to give him alms, and were not a little surprised to encounter a leper looking so well.

The trick succeeded, for almost immediately, a frightful sibyl, as yellow as parchment and as tanned as an old boot, decked out in dirty linen, came limping along. She gave him a sign to stop the music of Saint-Ladre and follow her; he obeyed with tacit gratitude.

His guide, whom he overtook in the impatience of his amorousness and interrogated without obtaining a satisfactory response, went out of the Rue des Étuves to go along the Rue Beaubourg as far as the Rue de la Courroierie, and then the Rue Baudrairie. The duenna then went into a dark alley, into which Benjamin did not hesitate to plunge.

A stiff hand gripped him in the opaque obscurity of the haunt and drew him under the wan radiance of a reeking lamp; he found himself face to face with Guillemette, who peered at him slyly, with the most agreeable grimace she could contrive.

Guillemette, Madame de la Vodrière's chambermaid, was no longer young but not yet old; the obesity that overloaded her soft and discolored flesh served to falsify her age, which was betrayed by wisps of variegated hair escaping from her conical bonnet. She did not seek a luxury of costume that would strike a balance between her and her mistress; a green woolen dress fell straight all the way to her ankles, and allowed her bosom to hang down over her stomach like an avalanche ready to slide.

Benjamin, accosted by the two duennas, who were tickling his arms urgently to attract his attention got the impression that he was listening alternately to vice and virtue, so fat was the one and so thin the other. In the depths of the lair, the panting of bellows could be heard, along with flames crackling in ovens and stoves, water running into tubs, songs, voices and murmurs; one might have thought it the mouth of Hell.

"God protect you, and your amours too!" Guillemette said to him, in a bittersweet tone. "How come my friend Malaquet isn't accompanying you? I thought, by the rattle, that it was him coming to clutch me in a loving embrace."

"No," said Benjamin, intent on cutting the digression short, "I can assure you that, at present, he's stuck to the cobblestones of the cloister of Sainte-Opportune, sleeping sounder than a bishop in his palace."

"Saint-Ladre grant him the mask of a church candle!" replied the second duenna. "Guillemette, my pet, are you not weary of loving that vile vagrant, who'll render you leprous, if your old affair with Crespeau hasn't done so already."

"Shut your mouth!" said Guillemette, blushing like a virgin. "What's this talk of Crespeau? I don't have such a long memory, lady of yesteryear. Peace to the dead above the ground!"

"Damn! Don't you remember, lazar-lady, that we were both in our prime in 1415, when your gallant Crespeau, having denounced Schoeffer, the Lombard money-lender, drank and ate in the sacred vessels of Saint-Josse, then ran away after the sacrilege and was condemned in his absence to the heretics' torture, or to die unconfessed in a pilgrimage to Rome or the Holy Land."

"You can talk, dealer in philters and poisons! I wouldn't finish until tomorrow if I were to draw up an account of your misdemeanors, and the least of them worth a hundred bundles of straw and sulfur."

"Truce for today, if not tomorrow!" cried Benjamin, who was hoping to obtain an opportune enlightenment from the discussion and was seething with impatience. Why quarrel so bitterly about nothing? Let's talk business, and help me in this fortunate chance. My lady is at the steam-bath; enable me to see her, to converse with you, and I'll abandon my life to you if you want to take it for a sacrifice."

"Christian faith, he's right!" said Guillemette, whose anger evaporated before a pecuniary accommodation. "He's restoring things to their time and place; we'll continue our altercation another time—for now, let's attend to the more pressing matter."

"Yes, indeed, Guillemette," said Benjamin, in a tender tone. "Malaquet commended the care of my joy to you, and now, in his name, I require you to keep your promise and conduct me to my darling..."

"Assuredly," the old woman replied, putting put her hand more insistently. "Genteel lover, the beautiful lady shall be delivered to you stark naked and sleeping a propitious slumber..."

"Oh, my dear sisters!" he cried, seizing the hand that was offered to him. "I shall not forget you in my prayers. Don't delay my transports, and deliver me incontinently."

"Gladly," Guillemette replied, consulting her companion's eyes. "Simply cough up ten gold pieces, and the same for Dame Caillebotte, to cover the expenses of the mystery."

"Twenty gold pieces?" repeated Benjamin dolorously. "I'm neither a Lombard nor an Englishman, and it would be necessary to bury an entire city in a day to raise such a vast sum with the price of graves."

"By the Devil! The soporific beverage costs as much and more," objected Caillebotte. "On top of that, there's the bath-house-keeper's fee, the danger of the enterprise and the hire of the maid on watch. You owe us the rest."

"Oh, Guillemette, who has helped me so much and so well, will you leave me in their pitiful embarrassment? Will my sovereign desire sink within sight of port? You're not so miserly, so cruel, so contrary, my guardian angels?"

"Crack open your money-bag, darling," said Caillebotte, inflexibly. "Your father has more gold pieces in his coffers than corpses in his cemetery. Can't you borrow twenty écus from the Lombards."

"I'd sell my salvation to all the devils in hell. You won't tell my lady what would harm me too much—my birth and my employment—will you, ladies? I'm expecting an inheritance that will make me rich!"

"Make sure you don't take too long, proud pursuer of amours," said Guillemette, pretending to withdraw, "for my mistress becomes bored when alone, and is always in haste to return to the cradle of her little boy."

"Hurry up and get hold of the money, darling," added Caillebotte, grumbling, "for it's necessary to make the preparations, get rid of the importunate, mix the drug, post the sentinels and not leave anything out..."

"Well then, by the blood of Christ, I'll go in quest of the twenty écus and bring them back as soon as I can. In the meantime, be indulgent, excellent ladies; the bargain will be concluded without delay when I return, so get to work."

Benjamin, suspended between hope and encouragement, having passed from extreme happiness to extreme displeasure, convinced himself that he would succeed in acquiring the money necessary to pay for the interested services of the two old trollops, and disappeared at a run, like a madman, into the streets, along which he went at hazard, knocking down passers-by, colliding with carts, causing dogs to bark and women to scream.

In a private booth in the steam-baths, the frescoes of which represented the Biblical subject of the chaste Susanna,[21] and which was feebly lit by a round opening in the ceiling with a mobile shutter, a charming semi-nude individual sitting in a niche, like the white marble statue she was replacing, with her hair undone and her head tilted back, was taking a steam-bath in accordance with the Oriental method. A brick oven where a metal brazier was incessantly alight was giving off a penetrating heat and an atmosphere condensed by means of hot iron pipes under the floor and in the walls; an ardent iron ball connected to the furnace rose up in the middle of the room, thickening the vapor when perfumed water and scents were poured over it, which were received by the dilated pores of the skin.

The bather, who was streaming with salutary sweat and breathing in the inebriating delights of the bath, while plunged in a dreamy somnolence, did not notice that her garments were some distance away from her and that the transparent veil, all that she had conserved, outlined in its damp pleats the most secret forms of her faultless body. Her sturdy bosom beat the measure of her thoughts, falling back with tender sighs. Her thighs, to which the transpiration had given a rosy tint, white

---

[21] In chapter 13 of the apocryphal *Book of Daniel*.

as they were; her capriciously rounded hips; her arms, folded over her breast, and her fingers, splayed as if to replace the gauze fabric that had fallen damply at her feet; the mysterious graces emphasized by the indiscretion of the fabric that clung to her flesh; the furrows of blue veins; the quivering of modesty at the slightest sound; the picturesque abandon of poses: what charms and provocations those details of a chaste and unassuming nudity would have had for a lover! Indifference could not have resisted that spectacle, in which nature indulged in a studied competition with coquetry. One recalls the sudden passion that the sight of Bathsheba in her bath ignited in the heart of King David.

But a passion more violent and more stable would have been born in the contemplation of that angelic figure, worthy of a body as beautiful. Black and lustrous hair flowed around a majestic neck; black eyebrows, which a paintbrush could not have arched with such finesse, crowned dark eyes with a velvety gaze and penetrating radiance: those eyes, which would have been burning without the fan of lashes that shaded their lids; those eyes, which could make and unmake destinies, which, once seen, would pursue you incessantly. Her slender nose, scarcely open at the nostrils; her small mouth, cleaved by a habitual smile that loved to fix itself upon those reddened lips, between those pearly teeth; her delicately chiseled ear and her oval chin with a dimple in the middle: each of those beauties would have been sufficient to awaken a sentiment of admiration, a frisson of amour, a flash of joy. The heart would be half-involved in an examination in which the mind stopped *en route* or voyaged beyond the real. The old poets imagined an emblazonment of the female body in order to express the various types of beauty, which, in imitation of heraldic symbols, had a fresh skin for a field, odorous and satiny: a marvelous escutcheon more noble than the nobility of kings.

Jehanne de la Vodrière, whom the vapor lulled into a drowsy reverie, screamed at leapt up at the unexpected opening of the door; she smiled at her fright on seeing Guillemette, her chambermaid, who had the only key to the steam-room and had advertised her coming by her heavy tread on the flagstones of the corridors. The latter was carrying a warm beverage in a silver cup, very carefully, and appeared to be meditating the infallible effects of that drink, which her friend Caillebotte had concocted especially. Jehanne was distractedly occupied in rubbing her limbs with a silky sponge.

"My dear lady," Guillemette said to her, lowering her eyes and her voice, "Take and drink this marvelous julep, which would restore your strength, vigor and health, even if you were debilitated and vexed, from which God has preserved you."

"Vexed! I need something to reinforce the strength of the heart," Jehanne replied, taking the cup. "The jealousy of Messire my husband is making me suffer great distress, and I haven't recovered from the annoyances of yesterday evening..."

"The Devil cuckold the elect of his association! That old man is reducing you to annoying and untimely slavery. He murmurs against your paschal devotions and scolds the venerable Père Thibault."

"I excuse that folly, nevertheless, which arises from his extreme amity. In return, I honor him as a daughter does her father. I was thinking about that young and gallant sire again, you know."

"I can believe it, by Our Lady! He spoke to you lovingly yesterday in the church of Saint-Jacques, and last night, he remained standing like a spy outside your house in the Rue des Bourdonnais."

"To be sure—I looked through the window when Messire de la Vodrière was fast asleep. The gentleman is very personable, and seems to come from a good family. Do you not know his name and status?"

"No, but if one judges by his appearance, no house would be too noble for him; I suspect that the said Benjamin has his honors in King Charles' court. Please Madame, drink this precious balm."

"We've been away from home for a long time," said Jehanne, handing back the cup after having emptied it. "Monseigneur will complain of waiting too long for me. My dear child will fret, not seeing me return!"

Already weakened by an abundant sweat, Madame de la Vodrière was fully disposed to feel the influence of the narcotic influence of the preparation; she pronounced a few vague and halting words, tried to stand up and fell back into her seat, closing her eyes and tilting her head; her hand wandered around momentarily, searching for the clothes she had taken off in another room. Then she succumbed entirely to the sleep that number her brain and her senses; an easy respiration testified to the calm of the artificial oblivion that the juices of plants was causing to circulate in her veins; her smile and her posture revealed a kind of intimate bliss whose source did not seem to be of the earth.

Guillemette considered her briefly with an equivocal grimace, and then went out, with her index finger placed over her mouth.

VI. The Two Pacts

Benjamin walked at random, unseeing and heedless, like a somnambulist isolated from exterior objects and following an idea blindly. He passed through the same streets without perceiving that he had returned to his starting-point. Finally, the memory of the promise that had been extracted from him caused him to wake with a start. There was a fit of rage that was immediately extinguished, leaving a profound depression.

He considered his happiness, the price put upon it, and the unlooked-for term put on his amour, dependent upon a few miserable gold pieces. He cursed his birth, his rank, his religion, and most of all his father's avarice; he resolved to obtain, one way or another, the money necessary to the accomplishment of his desires, but when he foresaw the impossibility of collecting such a sum with the shortest possible delay, his head spun and he settled on the premeditation of a crime that her would have rejected with horror in any other circumstance.

Uncertain of what he was doing, after having wandered around in the vicinity of the steam-baths, he found himself in the Rue Saint-Denis, opposite the cemetery, though which the crowd was trailing that as going to see the burials and Macabre's theater. He plunged an avid gaze into the depths of the shop of the Boîte-aux-Lombards and lent an ear to the metallic sounds that were reverberating in his heart; he drew away, sighing, on the brink of succumbing to an invincible temptation to theft; his eyes interrogated the capacity of every money-bag that he would have liked to attach to his own belt.

During those minutes, which went by without changing his cruel situation, stifling the final glimmers of his hope, he remained standing at the foot of the Tour de Notre-Dame-du-Bois; he ground his teeth and bit his fists. Holopherne Croquoison, absent from his dwelling since the morning, would not go back there until the evening, but one would not have found a stray lamb out of a fold that hid such thick-fleeced sheep.

Suddenly the door of the *guifs* that seemed eternally closed, like that of a tomb, moved soundlessly, letting out a woman of tall stature enveloped in a cape of brown cloth with a red domino, ample over the shoulders, with a horn and tail of similar fabric above the head.

That costume and coiffure were too common among the women of the people for make the woman who wore it notice-able. Curbing her stature figure and veiling her face, she slipped so rapidly beneath the charnel-houses that no one no-ticed her passing, any more than her emergence from the tow-er. Benjamin alone was torn from his preoccupation by a me-chanical instinct, which led him to that door, left ajar, which was bolted behind him as soon as he had crossed the thresh-old.

The treasures that public opinion attributed to Macabre had seduced him in his discouragement, and he had advanced like an inexpert thief who does not provide himself with a means of retreat. He knew the inhabitant of that retreat, how-ever, and even suspected the kind of commerce for which that lugubrious habitation might serve; that is why he was not afraid of the darkness that surrounded him, nor of the cold hand that pressed his own.

He followed his invisible guide, descended the spiral stairway and was introduced into the cellar, whose poisonous air even shocked the sense of smell of a gravedigger. Macabre, who could be distinguished between his skeletons by the dubi-ous light of the lamp alimented by human fat, cracked all his limbs and made a rattle of bones audible; he sat down with a dull sound on a cenotaph and gestured an invitation to his guest to sit beside him.

Benjamin, who was suffering from every further delay, repented of his action on examining the horrible poverty that was displayed in that cesspit. He was tempted to go back without articulating the motive for his visit, and without color-ing his dishonest departure with an excuse. Macabre's eyes were, however, fixed upon him like two ardent coals, and he felt his arm bruised by long gnarled fingers; a groan of joy escaped the throat of the Bohemian, whose knees knocked together and whose ribs shook in cadence as he swayed like a serpent ready to launch itself at its prey. Benjamin, fascinated, did not budge.

"Friend," said Macabre sniggering, "I'm glad you've come to spare me anxiety in this circumstance; Giborne, my prudish wife, has gone to search for you at the Loge-aux-Fossoyeurs, for I was expecting you this morning."

"You certainly merit your reputation as a prophet," Benjamin replied, with astonishment. "Being warned of my coming in advance, I imagine that you doubtless know the reason for it as well?"

"I ought to know, undoubtedly; nevertheless, I beg you to tell me frankly, for fear of a misunderstanding; afterwards, I'll tell you my case. One word: many dead are being brought to the cemetery. The plague is spreading through the city, then?"

"I don't care about the plague. As for the dead, they're short of money, and I have no business with them. But are you, friend, the possessor of a large treasure, as everyone believes: some enormous hoard of écus?"

"That's an abominable calumny—don't believe a word of it, my friend. You can see the paltry abode that testifies to my poverty. Oh, the treacherous liars! I have no other treasure than my rebec and my actor's pantomime."

"God of Abraham and amour! I regret to see that you're not money-changer enough to oblige me with a considerable sum. Oh, twenty gold pieces would be worth more to me at this moment than paradise!"

"Twenty gold pieces! The sum isn't small, my dear son, and it would require a good pledge to borrow such a sum from the Lombards. Nevertheless, you'll have them, on one condition."

"What?" demanded the young man, putting out his hand. "I accept in advance anything that it pleases you to command of me."

"Your hand is as hungry as that to hold them, those precious royals? First of all, it's necessary to earn them; that's why I'll promise you five per month, if your work is honorably accomplished."

"Well, my excellent friend, who can tell where you and I will be, come the end of May? The said twenty écus will lose their effect for having waited. Oh, lend me those twenty écus, I implore you."

"Listen to our treaty first, my friend. Myrobolan, my valet, who played the dance of men in my pantomime, was killed in a brawl at the Cabaret des Gueux, and my play has been interrupted by that..."

"God absolve me! Monseigneur, there's no need for this rambling: just give me the twenty écus, and save the rest of your statement for tomorrow."

"This is my proposal: will you agree to replace Myrobolean, who was a good player of farces, and learn his character, which I shall teach you in outline, for the performance on Thursday? I'll give you ten écus in advance."

"Not ten, but twenty, in cash. At that price, I swear and certify that all the clauses of the treaty will be faithfully maintained."

"What saint and sacred oath are you invoking? Isn't fifteen écus enough for you right away?"

"Twenty, I said, and that's enough. I take as witness of my faith pledged to you the god of Abraham and Jacob, in the Jewish fashion, and the blood of Our Lord Jesus Christ, in the Christian fashion."

"My opinion is that you worship several gods, including money. So, I require you to come every evening to my dwelling, in order to learn your character. Oh, I forgot the fifteen écus—which is to say twenty, if I have them."

Macabre was careful to lock Benjamin in, who, doubting the result of a bargain so lightly concluded, listened to his footsteps fading away over his head, and addressed ardent prayers to Heaven for the prompt arrival of twenty gold pieces.

He was incapable of any thought foreign to the impatience that was boiling his blood and gripping his heart; a suspicion passed through his mind that Macabre was abusing his credulity and would leave him imprisoned here for a day, an hour, or a few minutes; anger caused a cold sweat to break out on his brow, and, hearing nothing more, he thought that the écus would never come.

He prowled around the cellar like a lion captive in a cage; he knocked on the iron-clad door, and called out to his jailer with a superfluity of epithets; he shivered at the thought of arriving at the rendezvous too late.

Finally, discouraged, he put his ear to the keyhole, ruminating a vengeance that he augmented from one moment to the next, beating the floor and the walls, breaking what he encountered beneath his feet.

"Pecker of cadavers," he shouted, accompanying himself with reiterated thumps on the door, "robber of shrouds, thief of tombs! Skeleton-face, grimace of the dead! Will you free me from this ambush! If not, I'll dig your grave and nail your coffin shut. Do you know the harm you're doing to my amours? I'll fashion flutes with your bones, and make a ladle of your skull, you Bohemian bandit!"

The steps of the staircase resonated again, and the footsteps that had drawn away approached again; hope moderated his irritation; he softened his voice, and passed suddenly from threats to pleas.

"My dear Seigneur! Venerable Macabre! Have pity on my anguish! Please, the twenty gold écus! I resign myself to being your servant and exceedingly docile pupil, but first, acquit your promises. Oh, tell me whether you have laid out a false lure! If so, I would pardon your malignity, provided that you render me my liberty immediately. Release poor Benjamin, who is dying for want of twenty écus!"

Macabre, who had paused to listen to these lamentations, did not want to prolong the anxiety of the actor that he wanted to recruit; the latter threw himself into his arms, stunned him with caresses and took possession of the money he had brought.

As soon as the sound of the gold was succeeded by contact, Benjamin, drunk with joy, kissed the coins that the obscurity prevented him from seeing. He counted them by pressing them to his mouth, and without thanking, other than by crazed laughter, the Bohemian who was pursuing him with mistrustful instructions. He fled, groping his way, and found himself once again at the tenebrous issue of the labyrinth.

His first impulse, on seeing daylight again, was to devour with his gaze that which was shining between his fingers; joy stifled him. He launched himself like an arrow through the streets that separated him from the steam-baths. He recognized by instinct the black alley to which the old woman had led him, and fell exhausted, dazed and out of breath at the feet of Guillemette, who was already repenting of having been too hasty and talking to Caillebotte about waking Madame de la Vodrière.

The gold pieces changed hands, and the young man was introduced into the steam-bath.

The counter of the Boîte-aux-Lombards was open, and the affluence remarked at the door was composed of merchants of various goods exchanging news relative to their commerce; there was much talk of the plague, the high price of food, the absence of the king and the probable return of the English.

The main room of the shop was overflowing with merchandise, money-changers, borrowers and strange faces; shrill voices and foreign languages mingled confusedly with the sound of money being counted, bales being lifted, balances being loaded and crates being broken open; everyone was speaking on his own account; everyone was defending his deniers; bargains were being struck, pledges being negotiated, interests-rates being set; eyes were opened wider than purses; people were smiling, touching hands and kissing beards, in order to deceive one another mutually.

Jeremiah Nathan was directing the transport and inspection of silk fabrics, linen sheets, leather, canvas and all the objects bought at a rock-bottom price in order to be resold for their full value. Balthazar Culdoë, graver than a Roman senator in his curular chair, was sitting at his counter, his brows furrowed and his mouth closed; he weighed, assayed and appreciated the gold and silver items that were presented to him; he accepted or refused coins with movements of his head, most of which were clipped or degraded; he judged at first glance the false coins that the misfortunes of the times had multiplied; he gave the impression of sniffing the metal.

A woman whose red cape rose above the greasy felt hats and bald heads shoved her way through the busy crowd with difficulty, all the way to Master Culdoë's counter, who was muttering in a low voice about a coin whose value had been altered by removing half of its weight; he measured the diminution of the coin, struck in the reign of king Jean, and calculated the alloy that it might contain, but an olive-tinted hand, with reached out between the gold and his line of vision extracted him abruptly from his meditation.

He thought that the Bohemian woman wanted to interrogate the lines of life and fortune in the palm of his hand and was tempted to have her thrown out by his employees, but fortunately recognized Macabre's wife. Remembering the association he had formed the night before, he got up silently, handed the care of the counter over to his associate, and indicated by a gesture that the woman should go up with him to the upper floor.

That obliging welcome astonished the person he was addressing, who was not accustomed to it. Giborne melted into salutations and apologies, already hoping for the complete success in the objective of her visit that the good omen promised.

98

"God protect you, my daughter," Culdoë said to her, when they were in private. "You've doubtless come with regard to our secret agreement with Maître Croquoison."

"I don't know what agreement that is, Monseigneur," said Giborne, hoarsely, "but all will be well with such a generous party; I've come to you about the matter of the *danse macabre*."

"Yes—it's on the Thursday of this week that we shall see that beautiful mystery. Monsieur Macabre will reap handsome profits if he charges a fee of five tournois for each spectator."

"Argot-speaker's honor, my good seigneur, the avaricious fellow won't be content with the riches of a Lombard, and I fear that he'll leave his body and possessions in this country, in accordance with my prophecy."

"It would be wise to invest his wealth with the Lombards, who would return copious interest on the capital. In any case, tell me your proposal when I've told you mine to your advantage."

"Faith of a Bohemian, your probity and glorious generosity are known throughout the world, my noble seigneur; Macabre would entrust his soul and his finances to you as if you were our father."

"That's good judgment on his part. Hear the conditions: Master Croquoison, the warden of the cemetery, will continue to rent you, without augmentation, the tower in the middle, in exchange for your selling to our counter the clothing, linen and sheets of the dead, which have been taken to the clothes-dealers."

"What are you proposing, Monseigneur? Is this is a trap set to cause us prejudice? Whoever commits the sacrilege of violating the tombs of the dead is buried alive!"

"Whoever devotes himself to that traffic is flayed alive, and Master Croquoison does not care to take the risk; hence, the spoils will be purchased at my boutique, or he'll require you to vacate the place in favor of a better occupant. Macabre won't want to withdraw, when the contagion is multiplying the chances of profit a hundredfold."

"It will be done as you command, Monseigneur, so I beg you not to diminish our returns, in order that Macabre does not condemn me to perish of hunger; I fast more than two Christians put together."

"By Moses' staff, your plumpness accuses your mouth of lying. So don't fail to deliver the week's booty henceforth, and be joyful as you leave."

"Hear me out, Monseigneur; Macabre sent me to ask you, by way of hire, for the costumes and masquerades needed for the performance of his play."

"That means dresses, livery and baubles to dress an emperor, king, pope, bishop and all the estates in the world? I'll gladly sell those things at the lowest price, or lend them on a sound pledge."

"Macabre doesn't have the wherewithal to buy them, my indulgent Seigneur, and you won't get any pledge from his poverty save for his word or his signature."

"Certainly, my dear, Sieur Macabre's word is worth that of the king's silversmith, and his signature is a delight; nevertheless, I can't do anything in this matter."

"What! Monseigneur, do you realize that the interests and expenses have to be met? The dance cried for Thursday next will offer more than a hundred pleasant mummeries."

"It will be a marvelous spectacle, and from this window the stage is visible without rent or toll. I shall applaud the farce charitably."

"Oh, Seigneur, if you were not engendered by a Jew and a she-wolf, give me a little help, for if I don't obtain a favorable response, Macabre is going to kill me."

"Not at all; the good man will send you back soon with an honest ransom—six hundred écus or more."

"Six hundred écus! Death of my life! Six hundred blows with a stick, six hundred quartan fevers! Oh, my gentle Seigneur, you don't want to seal my doom!"

"By the Ark of Noah!" Culdoë cried, suddenly, remembering his tacit vow. "there is a expedient that I would take for a sufficient and agreeable pledge."

"What, merciful Seigneur? Nothing seems impossible to me except for extracting a denier from Macabre's hidey-hole. What is it? Speak, and I'll obey."

"Swear and protest before the Lord God that you won't reveal this formidable pact, in spite of the efforts of threats and torture?"

"I swear and protest to do as you desire and keep the secret devotedly, whatever it might be."

"Then, I consent to release without guarantee the accoutrements, robes, suits and jewels, for as long as the dance might last, provided that you deliver me a newborn male infant on the Friday of Easter."

"By the head of an old wolf! What are you going to do with that child? Where can I find and procure it? Be patient until I fall pregnant, in order to have my progeniture."

"Promise to satisfy me, or I'll excuse myself from our agreement; while awaiting the child that you'll bring here on the due date, I'll give you what you need to put on the dance for the first day."

"It shall be as you wish, Monseigneur; I commend to you the child that I shall steal from his mother or his nurse. May the Devil ensure that you adopt him for your son!"

The Bohemian woman, who recalled her former trade, reiterated the promise to steal an infant, and did not ask what would become of the child in Culdoë's hands. The latter, glad to have an opportunity to acquit himself of a fanatical vow made a long time ago, sent Giborne away with more regard than he gave to his debtors, and returned to his counter radiant, without the sight of his balances laden with money changing the course of his preoccupations: the thought of his son, alloyed with thoughts of blood and vengeance.

Suddenly, a dull rumor, which rose up in the groups outside at the signal of a rattle, spread into the interior of the Boîte-aux-Lombards, where everyone moved aside, covering their faces, to avoid contact with Malaquet, whose violet face and soiled vestments penetrated into the shop with all the dignity of the master of the house.

No one dared manifest aloud the surprise and indignation that the brazenness in question inspired, but there was a general exclamation of reprobation when the leper chose from among the merchandise on display a piece of scarlet silk cloth, which he threw over his shoulder and carried away tranquilly, while the witnesses sent jeers and insults after him. Nathan tore out his last few hairs.

Culdoë, immobile at his counter, did not think of pursuing the thief; a tremor of rage ran through his entire body, and although he tried to appear calm, he was pale and haggard. He smiled and ground his teeth. "Don't be bewildered by that, friends," he said, in an emotional voice. "That leper bought the scarlet cloth from me, which is worth three écus a yard; I fear that he'll make a Cross of Burgundy from it. Did you think he was an insolent thief? The cloth will revert to whoever cares to get him hanged—although he might be mistaken for a leper!"

"Alas!" added Nathan, more sensitive to the loss. "Nevertheless, I'd accept the cloth from the hands of the leprosarium. Three écus a yard, that fine Venetian cloth! My purse would be glad to have them!"

VII. The Sire de la Vodrière

The door of the steam-bath had not been opened for an hour since Benjamin had entered that refuge impenetrable to men via the intermediary of Guillemette. A double bolt, which Madame de la Vodrière had neglected to draw, protected the feeble door from any sudden surprise. Two people occupied the steam-bath, whose ordinary destination had been changed by amour: Jehanne, whose voluptuous sleep still overwhelmed real pleasures, her breast beating, her mouth swooning, unaware of her disorderly nudity, was lying back, unmoving, indistinct words murmuring on her lips; and at her knees, Benjamin, begging forgiveness and burning her with his kisses, for he was reproaching himself for his joy, stolen by surprise, and remorse was redoubling his love.

He dreaded awakening the woman he had outraged, and yet he was pronouncing her name drunkenly; he was contemplating his beautiful conquest audaciously; he was weeping with simultaneously sorrow and joy, anxiety and hope. Then he wanted to redeem a culpable violence with all his blood, and only to owe to love what he owed to odious machinations. He was waiting, in a supplicant posture for his arrest and punishment.

Jehanne, who had been assailed by sharp sensations through that artificial slumber, was beginning to recover consciousness; the soporific power of the beverage was still acting on her senses; she had lost the memory of the past and the perception of the present; a cloud enveloped her mind and her eyes, which she opened slightly only to close them again heavily.

Soon, however, the ardently-impressed kisses and the caressant sounds of a familiar voice dissipated the residues of her lethargy; she saw, she thought.

A cry of alarm announced her return to existence. She proudly rejected the caresses that were being opposed to her rigors. She ordered Benjamin imperiously to withdraw. Then, perceiving that she was nude, she lowered her head to hide her tears and her blush; she made a veil out of her extended hands; she implored her lover for pity.

"Go, Messire," she said, in a faint voice. "At that price only will I pardon your dishonest treason. For my good reputation, I beg you to go without anyone seeing you!"

"I'll go in a little while," Benjamin said, drawing closer to her, "for I would die rather than displease you; so is it true that you will pardon my insult, if not my mad love?"

"May the Holy Virgin forgive me! Oh, wicked abuser, what have you done? Don't say that you love me again, since it causes me such grievous harm. Benjamin, my friend, what have you done?"

Jehanne, to whom reflection gave only-too-certain proof of her misfortune, choked on her sobs and struck her head against the walls. Her despair was deaf to Benjamin's consolations. He was humiliating himself at her feet and distributing hisses at random. She was nearly deprived of consciousness for a second time, and the imprudent young man prevented that faint, although he wanted to take advantage of it.

Finally, the tumult of futile regrets gave way to a more peaceful chagrin. Jehanne understood that it was necessary to resign herself, and her tears, which continued to flow silently, mingled with those of Benjamin, who was ready to expiate his fault by recidivism. Jehanne however, tormented by the scruples of confession, forgot the dangers of a tête-à-tête that was gaining terrain by the minute; she was still lamenting and persisted in the pleas that her gaze belied involuntarily.

Benjamin agreed to everything and obeyed nothing; the awakening was about to absolve the slumber. An almost intolerable heat was exhaled into the chamber by the pipes and the iron ball, which became red hot because the bath-attendants had lit the furnaces and boilers to prepare new baths.

"Benjamin," she said, with a veritable anxiety, "the venerable father in God Père Thibault, knowing my mortal sin, will refuse me absolution, and I will be unable to take communion."

"Is it an unparalleled dolor, dear beauty," he said, with frequent distractions, "to confess this amorous mystery? I have played my part in this sin as well, and would not exchange it for a plenary indulgence."

"It's adultery, Messire, and I thank you for lightening it for me; so avoid meeting me again and go; I don't know how long I've been away from home, and Monseigneur is irritated by the slightest lateness."

"Jehanne, it's me who will be your seigneur henceforth; it's me who will love you; I am the spouse of your heart and the body, the other being only your church spouse, your domestic tyrant and deplorable enemy."

"Oh, no, my friend; the Sire de la Vodrière, a noble man and chevalier of the king, holds me by right of marriage, and I honor him as such, in spite of his malign jealousy, from which the good God preserve us!"

"My God! That jealous villain who frightens you, my darling, will not attempt anything against our noble amours, or I'll lay him in the dust, in such a way that he won't emerge again till the last judgment. I'll dig his grave tomorrow..."

"Don't talk like that, Messire. He'll he furiously perturbed by my undue absence; he'll come to seek news of me. Adieu, my dear friend—go at once."

"Do you think, false friend, that I would go, and leave you at the mercy of that old man, who will threaten you and draw his sword on you, poor lady? If he discovers our frolics, is it possible that he'll kill you?"

"Assuredly, Benjamin; he's already thought of killing me for the great love he has for me, saying that it would prevent me soiling my robe of chastity and defaming conjugal law."

"May the demons of hell rip the soul from the madman's belly! So, I must arm myself with a sharp dagger in order to repel his attack and halt his pursuit, for I'm taking you with me out of Paris."

"Don't say that, my friend, and cease this jesting. A wife and mother, I don't want to leave my husband and my child. Oh, my God! Let me call my chambermaid and don't stay here any longer."

"You're mine, Madame, and I'm taking you under my protection. Jehanne you are the most becoming, the most delightful, the most beautiful, and hence the most esteemed, most beloved woman in the world! Oh, hurry up and get dressed, and let's get out of here."

"Messire, I can't do that, I assure you. Remember that my poor child is not yet two years of age, and that Monsieur de la Vodrière would avenge himself with our spilled blood! Grant me mercy, and let me return to my house."

At that moment, the leper's rattle became audible in the distance. Benjamin, attentive to that abrupt and urgent clicking, which was drawing nearer, made no response to the last invocation made by Jehanne, whose heart was beating faster than the rattle; she composed her face in accordance with her lover's.

He had risen to his feet; she rose to her feet; he listened; she listened. She was the first to recognize the cracked voice that harmonized with the leper's music; she did not have the strength to pronounce a name, but, with her index finger directed at the door, she exchanged an expressive glance with Benjamin, who searched for a resolution that the animated conversation did not inspire in him right away. He groped for his clothes, in order to find weapons there.

"Accursed leper!" cried an angry old man. "I, Sire de la Vodrière, a nobleman and chevalier, command you not to get in my way, under pain of being banished by the Provost and Vicomte of Paris."

"Unpleasant Seigneur," retorted a hoarse voice, "I, a very noble and very powerful leper, invite you to listen to the advice of my rattle and to retreat from the pestilential air that I exhale in this vicinity."

"Back, putrid lazar! I require passage into this house, where I have urgent business. Get back, or this slim blade will become leprous in perforating your entrails, filthy purveyor of Bordeaux!"

"Pity, Reverend Seigneur! I'm a poor sufferer, who has made the journey from Palestine and Rome on foot; give me a denier of alms, for the love of crucified Jesus, the twelve apostles and Saint Lazarus, who founded our estate."

"By my white beard! Does this malign orator and musician think he can vanquish me by stubbornness? Here's a Parisian sol as a pure gift, in order that you go and bray elsewhere, and I offer you an angelot to tell me what you know."

"Grace be granted to you on high, worthy and magnificent chevalier! Certainly, I know that you are the most generous, the most amiable and most glorious sire; everyone knows as well as I do what you are."

While growling a panegyric in a slow and bittersweet tone, Malaquet, without discontinuing his monotonous clicking, lay down across the alley in the Rue de la Baudrairie, parted his robe, rolled up his sleeves and scratched himself with frantic activity; his skin, however, seemed white and healthy, devoid of asperities, blisters and ulcers.

All the passers-by fled at the sight, and even the Sire de la Vodrière, whose fury was increased by these obstacles, recoiled in order to preserve himself from the contagion that flakes of leprous skin might communicate. He foamed at the mouth, blaspheming; he bunted his sword on the cobblestones; he turned and leapt, like a dog around a wounded boar; but he did not pounce. Guillemette had hidden when her master arrived, and Caillebotte dared not liberate the lovers, who were shaking the door, locked from outside.

The Sire de la Vodrière, whose first marriage had been to a Demoiselle de la Trimouille, whom Jehanne Coutanceaux had succeeded, was a high-ranking officer of the late King Charles VI, whom he had served in an exemplary fashion until his death, and since then, he no longer attached his fortune to princes. He had refused the honors with which the King of

England wanted to heap upon him; he did not associate himself either with the dauphin's party or that of the Duc de Bourgogne; he did not come to any understanding with popular factions—and that prudent insouciance had served him well during the troubles that had desolated the capital. He was not exiled; he was not imprisoned; his property was respected, and the Hôtel de la Trimouille, which had been confiscated by the English in 1421 from his wife's family, had even been returned to him by special favor.

Louis de la Vodrière was one of those egotistical and despotic old men who turn everything to the profit of their own wellbeing at the detriment of others; he profited from revolutions and public misfortunes; the dementia of Charles the Beloved had made his fortune. After the death of his first wife, whom he had persecuted cruelly, he got married again, in spite of his sixty years, to an orphan whose extraordinary beauty compensated for the mediocrity of her birth. Père Thibault, the canon of Saint-Jacques-la-Boucherie, was to repent of having sacrificed the woman he had the right to name his daughter, even without the justification of his white hair and his capacity as her confessor.

That marriage, which counted three years of painful ordeal, had not realized the happiness of two individuals so different in age, character and tastes. Jehanne, gentle and naïve, would have needed a heart that understood hers, and existence in which her own was reflected; but, far from that, young and ardent, she had become the companion of cold old age.

Her gaiety so frank and playful, took on the somber color of the walls that imprisoned her; nobility, rank and wealth saddened her condition, by regret for the joys that they could not procure her. The jealousy of her jailer increased from day to day, with her despair, and the son that she had brought into the world prevented her from dying in tears. She only went out rarely from her house in the Rue des Bourdonnais, accompanied by her husband or Guillemette, a female Argus whom cupidity had recruited to her party; it was her soon who consoled her in her chagrin, who encouraged her to live; she spent days and night by his cradle, while Louis de la Vodrière stood sentinel, his ears pricked, keeping watch on his wife's honor.

Several times, his suspicions had led him to ill-treatment of that unfortunate woman, who appealed for death at the point of a naked sword. For a month, in particular, Benjamin's prowling in the vicinity of the house had been noticed, and the division of the spouses had been envenomed by daily quarrels, as Jehanne, weary of such harsh slavery, had been drawn toward a sentiment of her choice—not without remorse or terror.

The day before, on emerging from the confessional, she had promised herself in a whisper to avoid any dangerous encounter with the young man to whom she had imprudently listened, but she had retracted her oath when, on her return, the Sire de la Vodrière, with no regard for the respectable ecclesiastic, still present and weeping, had threatened her, insulted her and almost killed her.

The day after that scene, which Père Thibault had terminated with a paternal allocution that appeared to move the odious and jealous individual, Jehanne had obtained permission more easily to go to the baths, but her absence of several hours had reignited a dormant rage, and the Sire de la Vodrière, to whom officious advice vaguely informed him of what he incessantly feared, ran to wash away his dishonor in the blood of the two accomplices.

The old gentleman's stature had not been curbed by the weight of armor or the fatigue of war; his thinness stemmed from the incandescent jealousy that was consuming him. His bulging eyes were flamboyant as they rolled in their bloodshot orbits; his thick blue-tinted lips always protruded in a silent pout; his sparse hair seemed to stand on end, and his pug-nose dilated in a nervous grimace. He was dressed like one of the fops of the era, who adopted a ridiculous frivolity of costume. His shaggy felt hat, turned up at the front, shone with clusters of pearls and a plume of rubies; his tightly-fitting hide jerkin was hidden by a green satin doublet, serrated around the neck loose about the hips, with a leather belt and wide ragged sleeves, trailing to the ground. His leggings of amaranthine wool outlines thin forms that a tailor's art had tried to hide, and his feet were uncomfortable in laced shoes that bruised their calluses in order to make them longer and slimmer. His empty scabbard hung down over his left thigh.

Malaquet held firm and blocked the passage, agitating his rattle, scratching his body and singing popular songs in a quavering voice to drown out the imprecations of which he was the impassive target. A crowd was beginning to gather at a distance, and the Sire de la Vodrière, torn between the fanatical respect accorded to lepers and the dread of the malady, dared not make use of his sword to cross the threshold of the house. Nevertheless, the blood flowed back to his brain, darkening his vision, buzzing in his ears and exciting his furious preoccupation.

The leper, thinking that he had given the lovers enough warning and the time to separate from one another, judged it prudent to quit the place rather than remain there dead; he drew his head back into his shoulders, and launched himself, by means of a cleverly planed tumble, out of range of the sword, whose wind he felt chill his cheek.

His adversary did not linger for a second thrust, and disappeared into the alley, to the clamors of the idlers, who were no rare or less tenacious than they are today in the streets and at crossroads. The leper, who was no longer scratching himself, was surrounded by a circle of questions and besieged by gazes, but he remained obstinately silent.

Meanwhile, Benjamin had divined the imminence of the peril, and the mute discouragement of Jehanne, who was wringing her hands, added a dolorous distraction to the necessity of the moment. She threw herself into the arms of the imprudent author of that critical situation, of which her death and shame would be the denouement; she sought a supreme support from the man who had doomed her. She did not proffer and reproach or any plant; her voice might guide the sword that she saw suspended and ready to strike. She even dissuad-

ed Benjamin from breaking down the door, as he had attempted to do. She knelt down and prayed with a delirious fervor.

Benjamin could not resign himself to surrendering his
life and that of his mistress without resistance; he wandered
around the room like a captive tiger, clenching his fists,
scratching the walls, bumping his head against the corners of
the walls, stamping his feet, surging forward, stopping, listening, sighing, sand contemplating Jehanne's bleak dejection.
She had wrapped herself in her veil as if in a shroud, and was
waiting for the inevitable catastrophe.

Suddenly, a hope of salvation glimmered in Benjamin's
mind, when he burned himself by accidentally the iron ball
reddened by the action of the fire; the atrocious pain of the
burn was simultaneously tempered by an idea as fortunate as it
was unexpected, which he put into execution.

He poured water slowly over the ball, which condensed
as an opaque vapor; he could not even make out his companion through the cloud, which he deliberately thickened. Then,
confident and joyful, he hastened to reassure the trembling
Jehanne, who was wishing that she were already dead in order
to escape the insult of a public scandal.

"Jehannette, my lady love," he said into her ear, deafen-
ing it with kisses, "this will save us both; your jealous husband
does not have the visor he needs to see through these fumes."

"Alas! Good God! Say your prayers," she said disengag-
ing herself from his embrace. "Confess your sins. My friend,
for I sense the death-blow coming, and you will plunge into
the utmost depths of Hell."

"Have heart and courage, Madame; prepare yourself for
the assault. For my part, I shall put your honor in surety: and I
shall not kiss that dear mouth again, if I'm seen making my
exit from here. Adieu, as you command!"

Benjamin threw more water on the iron ball, which quiv-
ered in deploying swirls of vapor, and stationed himself behind the door, whose bolts he withdrew cautiously.

Jehanne had no other sentiment than that of her doom;
she redoubled her prayers and signs of the cross.

The Sire de la Vodrière, who had traversed the alley blindly, ran into an animate mass that emitted a groan; it was Caillebotte, whom fear had caused to fall in a faint, and who was stammering a confession of her crime. Fortunately for her and the lovers, the offended husband did not deign to listen to her and shook her brutally, shouting at her in a terrible voice.

"Filthy crone, concubine of Beelzebub, tell me where I can find my whore of a wife and her audacious gallant! I'm certain that they're not expecting me. Hurry up and open the door of the steam-bath!"

Caillebotte, who had closed her eyes in order not to see the glint of a menacing sword, dragged herself to the door on her knees, and opened it with a slowness that was in no way accelerated by the blasphemies of the Sire de la Vodrière, who hurled himself into the steam-room like a madman.

Benjamin had time to slip out silently before the new-comer's eyes could become accustomed to the vapor that enveloped him and rendered him invisible to himself.

The Sire de la Vodrière closed the door to intercept the retreat of anyone who was in the room, and probed the corners with his sword, which grated against the wall, but the vapor began to condense into water, and became more transparent.

"What is it, Monseigneur?" Jehanne hazarded, convinced of the flight of her lover. "What do you want? Can I not bathe and steam without incurring your displeasure?"

"By Heaven and Hell!" cried the old man, who could not discover anyone but his wife. "Where is he, then? Is he a sorcerer who can vanish? You were certainly not alone in this hovel, so I'm told. Don't lie, when you're about to die."

"Die! My good seigneur! I've seen in a dream the new ambush that you have set for me, and I shall feel an extreme joy in going from life to death to complete my martyrdom. Kill me, if it pleases you, and I shall thank you for it."

"Yes, by God, I shall kill you, Madame Lover, but first I want to kill your handsome darling, so tell me where he's hiding. False and rascally Jehanne, what have you been doing in this place for three full hours?"

"What! Has time gone by so quickly? I was taking a bath, Seigneur. Guillemette having returned to the house to see to my dear son, I was asleep when you woke me up."

"Jehanne, you have betrayed conjugal faith; woe to me, woe to our child, woe to you! When we are together in the grave, you young and me old, at least no lover will envy me my faithful bed."

Absorbed by a somber presentiment, the Sire de la Vodrière, replaced his sword in its scabbard, and coldly ordered his wife to get dressed.

They left the steam-baths together, she troubled and red-faced, he severe and pale. The crowd that had gathered in the Rue de la Baudrairie served as their escort all the way to the Rue des Bourdonnais, with grimaces, jeers and laughter.

VIII. The Hôtel de la Trimouille

In the Rue des Bourdonnais, which was known in the thirteenth century as the Rue Adam Bourdon et Sire Guillaume Bourdon, the house of the Couronne d'Or, at number 11, which, inhabited today by tradesmen, still attracts the admiration of artists, has successively borne the names Hôtel de la Tremouille and Hôtel de Bellièvre. It was the seigneurial domain and fief of the Trimouille family, which included several houses in the neighboring streets. The house is mentioned in various places in the history of Paris: Guy de la Trimouille, the head of that illustrious family from Poitou, lived there in 1393, after having bought it from Philippe, Duc d'Orléans, the brother of king Jean; the bishop of Liège lodged there with his officers in 1409, when he brought an army in the service of the Duc de Bourgogne; later, Anton Dubourg, Chancelier de France, occupied it; and afterwards the Président de Bellièvre transmitted it to his descendants. In 1438 it belonged to Louis de la Vodrière, chevalier, who took possession of it as a result of its confiscation by the English in 1421 and paid the rent for it to the direct heir of Jean de la Trimouille, Seigneur de la Jonvelle, *maître d'hôtel* and chief steward to the Duc de Bourgogne.

The large house, far from being enclosed by party walls, had plenty of air and sunlight then, its grounds extending to the Rue Tirechape and along the Rue de Charpenterie, now the Rue Bétisy. A gallery, a pasture, a garden and fountains alimented by the city's waters completed the replastered and distempered walls that made up three sides of a square courtyard that one entered through a somber arch opening on to the Rue des Bourdonnais. Arched arcades, which formed the peristyle of the ground floor, have been walled up and pierced by bourgeois windows, but modern architects, who make department stores out of palaces, have forgotten to destroy the projecting rims of the arches, the delicate sculptures of the

114

ledges and entablature of the ancient edifice. Five days of masonry-work would suffice to efface what remains of the Hôtel de Trimouille and bring it in line with the neighboring houses, which Philippe-le-Bel had the bad taste to visit in spite of the proximity of the Fosse-aux-Chiens, a hideous and stinking refuse-tip, now the Cul-de-Sac des Bourdonnais.

Perhaps the arts, however, in default of the government, will protect the almost-intact Gothic tower that rises up at the corner of the courtyard; that precious jewel in carved and sculpted stone, more than six fathoms high, which terminates in a lead cap that hides the ornaments of the architecture from view. Two arcades with sharply pointed arches lead to a spiral staircase that climbs to the top of the tower and communicates with a new wing; the first floor, illuminated by a single arched window, only contains one oval room, and the garret-window on the second floor does not indicate that the tower has changed its aspect or its usage; the stairway it enclosed ought to connect to several buildings that no longer exist. What is most noticeable of all are the embossed figures of humans and animals, flower-designs in relief and ornamental lintels that decorate the exterior of the little tower like fancy metalwork.

It was in the room on the first floor that Jehanne de la Vodrière was weeping or kissed her son, who did not understand her tears and smiled at her, on the morning of the Thursday of Holy Week. Since her return from the steam-baths, she had not left the house, whose coaching entrance seemed condemned never to open; the apartment that she had occupied in the wing overlooking the Rue des Bourdonnais had been abandoned on the pretext that the air was bad there, and the closed shutters intercepted the view of the surroundings.

Jehanne, imprisoned by her husband in that narrow cell, had found a means to inform Benjamin of her rigorous captivity, begging him not to take the risk of showing himself in the vicinity for fear of being recognized; she was watched night and day like a state prisoner, and her husband, who had lost sleep along with his peace of mind, prowled incessantly in the gallery, in the courtyard, and even on the roofs, like a soul in torment. He proffered frightful oaths, sharpened his weapons and put himself *en garde* every time a cat slid along the gutter, a bird flew from one gable to another, a rat gnawed a skirting-board or a ray of moonlight danced in the shadows.

Guillemette put on an act of assisting him and enriching herself on his suspicious tyranny, but she was devoted to her mistress to the extent of the value of a rosary enriched with gems that the latter had given her to ensure her fidelity.

Jehanne had shed many tears without exhausting them; to begin with, she had bemoaned the crime committed on her person, but she soon deplored the absence of Benjamin, who had, if not consoled, at least helped her to support her misfortune. She was still ignorant of the birth and rank of the young man, whom she imagined as one of the noblest and most honored lords of the court, although he did not wear around his neck either the order of the Étoile or that of the Toison d'Or. Sometimes, on the strength of a few words dropped into their conversations, she convinced herself that he was linked by vows to some religious and military community that prescribed an austere chastity; that apprehension added to her remorse, and the dolor of not taking communion at Easter was moderated by the secret contentment of sparing herself a difficult confession.

"Dear and beloved child," she said, without interrupting her maternal caresses, "when you're a grown and mature man, you'll weep at the story of my suffering, which only death can alleviate and cure; Oh, I am badly married!"

"By the passion of Christ!" shouted the Sire de la Vodrière, who was listening at the door, "if that little one could hear you, you'd soon succeeded in turning him against his father, and toward the father of lies."

"Monseigneur," she said, rocking her son, who had been frightened by that thunderous voice, "do you see this poor thing, who is disturbed and bewildered by your harsh words? He is asking for mercy with clasped hands, so fearful is your manner!"

The Sire de Vodrière, who had come in spontaneously, his face surly and his naked sword in his hand, as usual, rocked the cradle in order to silence the infant's redoubled cries, but his train of thought was abruptly interrupted by the sound of the knocker on the main door.

Hoping that the unwelcome visitor would get tired of knocking in vain, he stayed where he was, but the hammer resounded again with such perseverance that he lost patience and went away, cursing, to the door, which Guillemette had just opened without waiting for orders.

Père Thibault, who was introduced after a conversation through the keyhole, wore a distressed expression, and the soldierly countenance of the Sire de la Vodrière, who welcomed him under arms, darkened his venerable face even further. A similar operation was effected on the jealous face of his host.

"My dear son," said the priest, with melancholy bounty, "What is going on here? Windows shuttered, bolts shot, and still that naked blade. Is Jehanne ill? I have not seen her at confession."

"She is grievously out of sorts," the other replied, placing himself in front of the monk to stop him advancing. "The physician has forbidden anyone to disturb her, so I beg you to return at a better time."

"Bonjour, my excellent Father," said Jehanne, showing her pale face at the window. "How glad I am to see you! Messire de la Vodrière would not permit me to come to confession yesterday."

"What, Messire!" said the Dominican, astonished and annoyed. "The physician has counted without his patient, and Jehanne, so far as I can judge will not feel any worse because of my presence."

"To be sure, it does not please me that a confessor has that authority," the old man murmured, as the ecclesiastic moved past him. "I don't trust this fine bird-trap who has caught me in the lime of marriage."

Jehanne threw herself, weeping, toward Père Thibault, who had intelligence of her woes; he spoke to her about her mother and providence, in order to appease the sobs that she hid in her confessor's bosom. The child was agitating and crying in his cot, over which his mother's face was no longer leaning. The husband, suspicious and bleak, contemplated uncertainly his wife's effusion in the arms of a man. A chair that he knocked over in a fit of anger caused Jehanne to shiver, and Père Thibault, who was speaking with his eyes raised to heaven; there was a conflict in the priest's soul.

"My dear daughter," he said, squeezing her hand to encourage her, "since the holy day of Palm Sunday, have you experienced some injurious quarrel with your husband, to whom you are honestly submissive?"

"Enough of that, Messire," cried the latter, who did not want an explanation. "Last Sunday I suffered because you sharpened the argument, but I invite you not to insert your finger between the tree and the bark any longer."

"By Notre-Dame-de-Bon-Secours!" exclaimed Jehanne, indignantly. "Remember, Messire, that I'm an orphan with neither relatives nor friends, save for this venerable father in God, in whom I have entrusted my supreme hope."

"I only remember that you're my wife and servant," retorted the Sire de la Vodrière. "As such, I order you not to associate anyone with our quarrels resulting from your impudicity and infamy."

"Hola! That is manifest falsehood," interjected the Jacobin, stepping out of his habitual character. "Jehanne is pure and intact of any soiling; I have the evidence of her confession. The young seigneur has solicited her to sin in vain."

"Damnation!" cried the husband, whose face became violet. "She has confessed it now! Who is this young seigneur, that I can carve him into pieces? O false woman! O infidel! O malign beast! Are you ready to die, Madame?"

"And you, Messire," retorted the monk, openly siding with Jehanne. "Have you a yen, however noble, rich and powerful you might be, to be condemned and sentenced in the parliamentary court, if not by the Provost? Tell me?"

"Enough of your monastic impertinences, Messire; get out of the house of your master, Louis de la Vodrière, chevalier. It displeases me that the affairs of my household are the booty of the confessional. Get out, for fear of coming to grief."

"May Saint Dominic aid me! Messire, I have the right to remain, to respond to your cruelties, and to retain this honorable woman under my guardianship; so, I forbid you to do any harm to the woman I have given you for a wife."

"Lord God absolve me if I commit any sin! Get out of my house, old monk, or I shall be driven to some extremity! Out, confessor of women abuser of innocence, spoiler of marriage!"

"O divine Savior, forgive him as I forgive him. Cease, sinner, cease your slander; I, whom am her father, order you to treat this poor martyrized woman worthily!"

"Heaven be blessed!" cried Jehanne, who, trembling at this altercation, sought refuge in Thibault's arms. "You, my father and lord! I ought to have suspected it, from the love I bore you in recognition."

"Yes, truly," the priest went on, wiping tears away from his cheeks, "I am the one who engendered you, my dear Jehanne; give me the name of Father henceforth; I am the one who will defend you against any insult, who will cover you with a buckler, surround you with a rampart! I blame myself for maintaining the mystery, since the church has given me absolution for having sinned in my youth. Oh, my little one, you shall not invoke my natural authority in vain—do you hear that, my son-in-law?"

"So I've espoused the bastard of a Jacobin," murmured the Sire de la Vodrière, who dared not misconstrue the character of Thibault. "Messire, I beg you to advise Madame better, either as confessor or father!"

"Oh, Monseigneur, the good Lord is a witness between us that I have never spared my good advice! Jehanne holds you in high esteem and venerates you, in spite of your habitual quarrels; would you not prefer to employ tenderness and indulgence?"

"I would Father, and the anger that I enter into derives from my violent love. Jehanne has opposed my desire many times and falsified my hope; if I loved her less I would be less jealous and more credulous."

"From now on, I beg you to love me less, Monseigneur," said the young woman, becoming bolder on seeing her husband's anger decline. "I do nothing but weep from morning till night, and am nourished on pears of anguish."

"My dear children," said Thibault, in the hope of cutting the matter short, "I recommend you both to imitate Christ, who prayed from his cross for the forgiveness of his tormentors, and put aside your unfortunate resentments."

"Alas, my Father, I do not see any possibility of reconciliation; Messire de la Vodrière has too cruelly threatened to put to death this innocent child, who can do no harm and can only smile at my lamentations!"

"He makes you whine and complain, Madame!" said the old man, whose grievances were still raw. "Have you confessed the adventure of the steam-baths, which is perhaps worth all your blood—for the young seigneur was there, so I've been told."

"Why reignite this untimely dissent?" Père Thibault interjected again, pushing his daughter toward his son-in-law and smiling at them both. "Messire, chase away these imaginations, which I refute; Jehanne, excuse the wrongs born of error."

"Listen, Jehanne, my darling," said the Sire de la Vodrière, looking at her hypocritically, "I'll consent to pay no heed to my suspicions and to neglect seeking more ample information, provided that you can name the said seigneur for me."

"I only know the first part of it, I swear to you," said Jehanne, blushing, "and what I do know, I shall not pronounce; for I declare to you, Seigneur, that his amorous pursuit has been discontinued."

"How glad I feel to see you thus, my children!" the good monk concluded, forcing them to embrace. "Louis, let your hand be not so quick to draw your sword; and you, Jehanne, let your tongue be quicker to justify yourself!"

The Sire de la Vodrière, like all jealous men, had suddenly passed from extreme anger to the most easygoing bonhomie, either because he was weary of the life he had been leading for three days and three nights, spying and keeping watch on his prisoner; or because the absence of any intelligence with the outside had entirely rehabilitated his wife in his mind; or, finally, because he feared establishing a difficult conflict between paternal and conjugal authority.

Père Thibault, who had not kept his vows any better than the majority of monks, without staining his virtue as a priest and honest man, rejoiced in a declaration that had brought union into a household in discord; he caressed his daughter and son-in-law tenderly; they retained a hint of melancholy in heir features and an embarrassed stiffness in their gestures. Naively, he recounted the story of his amours with a penitent that he had rendered a sinner and a mother; then he stopped, sobbing, to recommend the soul of the dead woman to the mercy of Heaven.

Jehanne asked questions about her mother, whom she had never known, and wept at another memory, avoiding the piercing gaze of her spouse, who frowned periodically. Père Thibault seemed disappointed that his daughter refused to receive communion at Easter; nevertheless, he went away joyful and rejuvenated to go to Saint-Jacques-de-la-Boucherie, where his confessional was continually full during Holy Week. The bells of all the parishes were ringing the sequence known as the "howl of death" to announce the universal mourning of the anniversary of the Passion; at midday, rattles would replace the bells.

The criers of the church of the Saints-Innocents, who had the exclusive employment of crying the dead with the knell of a hand-bell, were going through the markets, the streets, the crossroads and the squares, making the solemn cry, to which the idlers listened open-mouthed, and which was followed everywhere by a popular announcement:

"The great *danse macabre* will be played and celebrated in the Cimetière des Saints-Innocents by the actor and musician Macabre, playing Death in all his works, from the sovereign emperor to the worst of wretches, with the permission of Monseigneur the Bishop and the churchwardens of the church of the Saints-Innocents. This play of noble instruction is performed for the last time, in that the inventor will depart for Germany after the duration of the mystery, which will take place on the stage in the said cemetery, every day at one o'clock in the afternoon; during that time, no one shall enter that place, man or woman, except to be buried, without paying at the gate six Parisian deniers. The first day will commence today, Thursday of the week when Our Lord was passioned and crucified for the redemption of the sins of the world. Amen.

"Arise, bourgeois and honest people of Paris, and go at once to the aforesaid cemetery, for that very pleasant and genteel spectacle in pantomime, acrobatics and music of the rebec; arise people of the church, of trades, of merchandise and household, come see how Death, lord of the Earth, sets paltry humans to dance and laugh at their fortunes. They are the vigils of the living."

Jehanne, who had heard the story of that lugubrious performance, lent an ear to that cry and sighed.

The Sire de la Vodrière, possessed by an impulse of gallantry, noticed his wife's sigh, which he attributed on this occasion to the most natural cause, and proposed that they should go to see the opening of the *danse macabre*, on condition that she wore a veil and only looked at the theater.

Jehanne, tormented by a vague desire for liberty, with which was mingled, involuntarily, the thought of Benjamin, accepted almost with gratitude an opportunity to get out of her narrow room, to breathe in the open air and see living beings, but she would gladly have dispensed with the supportive arm of her husband, who would submit the slightest of her glances and each of her thoughts to the most scrupulous inquisition.

She hid her red eyes and fatigued physiognomy beneath a transparent veil; then she commended her son to Guillemette, who remained alone with him, and as if by virtue of a presentiment she brushed the sleeping infant's pulp cheek with a kiss. The latter woke up crying and holding out his arms to his mother, who drew away with a heavy heart.

As soon as Guillemette had seen her veiled mistress disappear with her master—who had only left his sword behind because Père Thibault had taken the precaution of making him put it away—she leapt to her feet, after which her body-fat had difficulty recovering its equilibrium. Without paying any heed to the redoubled cries of the child abandoned in his cradle, she visited the kitchen and he cellar to steal a ham, a pâté, a loaf of white bread and three jugs of wine, for which she had a liking. The child, however, whose despair increased in crescendo, cried so loudly that she ran to him, swearing, struck him brutally and carried him away in her arms to calm him down by movement and distraction.

She opened the door to the Rue des Bourdonnais by a crack, and looked as far as she could see in the direction of the Lingerie, in search of her friend the leper, who arranged a rendezvous with her every day in the Fosse-des-Chiens, but there was no sign of the leper as yet, and the rattle was not advertising his approach through the noise of the people crowding the Cimetière des Saints-Innocents. She cursed his lateness and sat down on a stone bench, which retained a funeral inscription, her eyes fixes and her ears pricked, with the child on her knees, who was calling for his mother; Guillemette frightened him with her coarse voice, and even gave him slaps capable of breaking him like glass.

A woman in a red cape, dragging her deformed obesity, was coming along the Rue de la Place-aux-Pourceaux. She was extending her head in every direction to assure herself that the surroundings were deserted, the shops and doors closed; she was listening with her head bowed, and turned to move alongside the houses of the Rue des Bourdonnais. It was Giborne. She headed straight for Guillemette, who was no longer distracted from her amorous preoccupation by the infant's cries.

"My good and compassionate lady," said the Bohemian woman, in her sepulchral voice, "for three entire days I have been suffering a raging hunger; will you give me, to end my fast, a dog's pittance, may God reward you?"

"I only give alms to servants of religion," Guillemette replied, distractedly. "If you fast by day, you gargle by night with your fellow vagabonds, Mesdames the beggars; drink better."

"That's a fine way to talk," the other replied, in a deliberate tone, affecting to be agreeable. "Let's wager, for a slice of ham or even a piece of sausage, that the lines of your hand promise no less good fortune than they hold?"

"Aha! You know the Bohemian custom, friend," said Guillemette, touched by the flattery. "My friend is coming to dinner, and I invite you to remain to have a share in the cheer, and also to look into our hands."

"Thank you for the honor you do me, Madame; I'll pay for your hospitality with fine tales, but in truth, my guts are howling with famine, and I'll die without remedy by dinner time."

Giborne would dearly have liked the chambermaid to entrust the child to her while she went in quest of aliments, but Guillemette, in her haste to oblige the adulatory beggar, did not think of asking her for that service. She ran off, in spite of her inconvenient burden, and returned with the bread, the wine and the ham, which she laid out on the bench by way of a table.

Giborne, whose insatiable stomach was deeper than a monk's pocket, did not wait for permission from her hostess to attack the solid and liquid fare; she comported herself so gluttonously that the morsels succeeded one another in her mouth more rapidly than words emerged from that of Guillemette, who admired that prodigious appetite without paying any heed to the fact that the bewildered infant had remembered not having eaten and was agitating for a small piece of bread that the Bohemian woman was showing him.

That famished individual reached for the knife, the glass and the napkin; the wine had run dry; the ham was no more than a bone and nothing remained of the bread but imperceptible crumbs. She could easily have recommenced that experiment in voracity, Macabre limiting her to the mot frugal diet. She tipped up the neck of the bottle, gnawed the ham-bone and gathered up the crumbs, all the while eyeing the infant, who was terrified by her green-tinted face and red-tinted hair.

Guillemette delighted in observing the rapidity with which the preliminaries of the feast that she had offered the fortune-teller had been swallowed up. She narrated her amours, her intrigues and her profits, while Giborne's eyes devoured the infant—who, to escape that fascination, was writhing in the arms of the insouciant chambermaid.

Suddenly, Guillemette saw her leper coming along the Rue des Déchargeurs, without his rattle or his barrel. He went into the Fosse-aux-Chiens, the noxious depository of everyday ordures and occasional carrion. She called out his name, but he did not turn his head in her direction. She forgot that the cul-de-sac in question had no other exit, and became excited to the point of wondering about its scarcely-equivocal cause.

She handed the infant, blue with convulsions, to the Bohemian woman, and ran in haste toward the Fosse-aux-Chiens, where Malaquet had adopted a stance. Giborne wrapped the child in her dress to stifle the cries he was uttering. Making sure that no one could see her, she set off toward the Boîte-aux-Lombards via the Rue de la Charpenterie, hastening her steps, holding her breath and lowering the hood of her cape.

Guillemette soon reappeared with the leper, who had blossomed like an oyster in the sun and was smiling to himself as he walked. He had came from a tavern in which he had left his leper's attributes as a pledge against the payment of his

bill; he was so luminous that he seemed to have a vinous leprosy; he had, however, only saved half of his reason in losing
his baggage, which the rubies of his nose had been unable to
redeem; he was risking prison and a fine, even banishment.

His sensible chambermaid was reproaching him so
sharply for his imprudent drunkenness that she had not the
slightest memory of the child and the Bohemian woman; she
took Malaquet into the Hôtel de Trimouille and closed the
door behind him, for fear that the neighbors might offer rough
treatment to the rattle-less leper. The latter was only talking
about eating and drinking, sniffing around like a dog following a trail.

"By the way" he said, as an idea occurred to him, "my
Benjamin's annoyed by not seeing his lady, and says that he's
going to steal her by force, killing the husband and whoever
gets in his way. Tell that to your mistress."

"Damn!" she replied, disdainfully. "I don't know why
you're so fond of that gravedigger, who doesn't have what's
needed to reward our good offices. I'm often ashamed of serving his amours."

"Shut up, you vile trollop! I like Benjamin better than
you, and I wouldn't like him any more if he were my own son.
It's reciprocal affection; he takes an interest in my good
health, drinks from my glass, and has chosen me the sunniest
place in his cemetery. He puts his hand in mine, obliges me
with his purse, listens to my follies, laughs when I laugh, and
has no fear of my leprosy—although, in truth, I have no leprosy save for the rattle and the barrel."

"My God!" cried Guillemette, tearing her hair and running to the door. "Monseigneur! Madame! The Bohemian
woman has stolen the child!"

"By Lazarus!" said Malaquet, putting his lips to a jug of
wine, which he emptied in two swigs. "It's only a baby. If the
mold's still there, Benjamin will work in it."

IX. The Danse Macabre

Since daybreak, when the sun had risen bright and re-
splendent, the crowd had been pressing around the Cimetière
des Saints-Innocents, into which no one would be admitted
except the dead and their corteges until eleven o'clock; gravediggers, priests and relatives hurried to fulfill their duties in
order to give way to the spectators who were flooding from all
points of Paris and the surrounding area. The *danse macabre*
occupied minds and conversations, to the extent that no one
gave any thought to counting the biers that were being brought
in procession from the four gates. The toll for fifty corpses
was received by Maître Croquoison, who, not so much an enemy of Christians as a friend of money, congratulated himself
on the progress of the contagion. From a high window of the
Boîte-aux-Lombards, Nathan recorded the number of shrouds
that would come to him to be sold, astonished that a single
man could rob that many cadavers in one night.

Around the cemetery there were outbursts of mad joy,
insensate cries, songs in various dialects, oaths, proverb relative to every profession, grimaces and laughter. No one was
giving any thought to the fact that the plague was ravaging the
hospitals and the Hôtel-Dieu; that the Saint-Denis and Sainte-
Opportune quarters had been afflicted; that the Provost of Paris, Ambroise de Loré, was having the victims of that mortality
secretly buried or thrown in the Seine every night; that the
Cut-throats, a rabble of brigands of all lands, were recom-
mencing their atrocities in the countryside; that English caval-
rymen were pillaging convoys of foodstuffs under the walls of
the capital; that the great city had no garrison but the watch;
that the king had no intention of leaving Bourges; that the
famine of 1434 was about to reappear with all its horrors; that
there had been no wheat in the markets the days before; that
the money-lenders were coming out of their lairs like flocks of
crows; that the sentries were run ragged attending to public

calamities. No one was even thinking about Holy Thursday, otherwise known as Maundy Thursday.

The mud of the population had risen to the surface, so much had curiosity been stirred up, all the way to the depths of Paris, immobile and dormant for two years. The Cours des Miracles had vomited their hierarchies of vagabonds and thieves more horrible than their horrible names, the majority drunk, all clad in filthy rags, displaying their fake infirmities and imploring alms with the aid of sores, convulsions, indecencies and skillful tricks. Money-bags, jewels and mantles were already furnishing easy prey for cutpurses. The sham lame, the sham mute and, most of all, the sham blind were in the greatest hurry to get into the cemetery, which was guarded by the sergeants of the Châtelet, to whom Macabre paid a tax and the price of a meal.

The streets of prostitution had unleashed their dissolute women, guided by matrons clad in silk and furs, sparkling with gilded ornaments, in spite of ordinances fallen into desuetude, with low necklines, carrying missals and rosaries. An innumerable variety of ambulant vendors ventured into the crowd with their trays and bizarre cries, but the moment was not favorable to their commerce, and even the relic-merchants could not capture attention, in spite of their pilgrim's robes, their staffs, their sea-shells and their marvelous tales. The only ones who found takers were the pâtissiers hawking hot tarts, hot pâtés, hot cakes and biscuits; the mercer, who was selling a singular variety of baubles and trinkets, also saw his merchandise surrounded by a triple circle of customers.

Students, who accompanied disorder everywhere, were annoying wives, tickling daughters, hitting husbands and, perpetually shouting, perpetually striking out, piercing the densest parts of the crowd like wedges driving into wood; they climbed on to the charnel-houses, helping one another up, and arranged themselves at the summit of the roof without paying the price of admission to the spectacle. The sergeants had enjoined them in vain to get down or pay; they responded by showing their teeth, their fists and the rest.

When eleven o'clock chimed, the gates were opened and the criers of deaths, whom Macabre employed for preference in his service, had as much trouble collecting the tax of six deniers a head as salt-tax collectors in a market. The sergeants dared not make use of their birches in order to stop those who dispensed with putting their hand in their money-bags to pay the fee, and the confusion became so great that everyone got in gratis.

The solid barriers that protected the collectors' counter was continually creaking under the vague swell of the multitude that was engulfed by the cemetery. Attempts were made to close the gates that served as dikes against that flood, but the gates were wrenched from their hinges and carried away by the popular tide. Tranquility was restored, however, when all the people who like to take their pleasures at public expense had taken possession of the best places.

The barriers were reclosed; the inoffensive mass was driven back with blows of the birch; the tollbooths were reopened and the bourgeoisie, who were uninfluenced by the bad example and unoffended by the brutality of the sergeants, for love of order, paid scrupulously, while twelve hundred good-for-nothings who had got in ahead of them by the force of their muscular arms or the suppleness of their hams, mocked all the newcomers.

The collection encountered no further obstacles, although the cemetery was not large enough to contain fifteen thousand curiosity-seekers of all ages, professions and ranks, even though the dead were less numerous there than the living. The peaceful influx was so considerable that the collectors thought of moving their location on to the street to make more room and ended up changing their counter into a private stage, while other intelligent speculators made their shoulders into an amphitheater.

The honest criers, convinced that it would be impossible to take one denier more unless the terrain were enlarged, went to the Rue de la Ferronnerie in order to hand over the day's takings to the impatient Macabre and then go into the nearby tavern to wet their desiccated throats. The sergeants soon joined them, renouncing the possibility of policing the compact and moving crowd, which had a mortal grip so far as they were concerned.

It was a spectacle stranger, more picturesque and more animated than the *danse macabre* itself that the Cimetière des Saints-Innocents presented before the performance. The surrounding houses were the terraces of the theater that deployed its confused and tumultuous circus at their foot; those houses, which gave the impression of hoisting themselves up to look over one another's shoulders, were bristling with heads and illuminated by eyes; the windows gave passage to thousands of gazes of which the stage was the unique focal point; the attics, chimneys, gables and gutters all had their spectators sitting, lying, standing or suspended like the statues of saints and devils of a Gothic cathedral.

In the neighboring streets a river of people circulated slowly, struggling against the reflux, rolling from one wall to the other, only waiting for an issue to launch forth in a torrent; colors, forms and faces were confused in that floating chaos, and a noise emerged from it like that of a blazing furnace; the sun's rays, metallic reflections and the silken hues of fabrics combined in sparkles that ran over the undulating surface of the crowd.

As for the cemetery, it offered a mobile mosaic of faces, hair, bonnets and other head-dresses, beneath which the trampled tombs had disappeared, knocked over, broken and buried. The interior crowd was less turbulent, less changing, less vivacious that than outside, which passed by and was incessantly renewed. Here the anxiety, the anger and the disappointment were manifested by kicks, insults and unusual efforts; there, the hope of pleasure, gaiety and contentment, expressed by songs, conversations and a placid attitude. People then gave no thought to the fact that they were walking on the bones of a father, a mother or an ancestor; the cult of the dead had only been invented for the great and the rich.

The auditorium had settled down, and everyone had chosen his place according to the order of his arrival; the unevenness of the ground did not render the choice irrelevant, and the stone crosses, monuments and chapels had been the first to be invaded, along with the galleries of the charnel-houses, the cover of which was sagging under the weight of besiegers; the tomb of Saint Richard had not been respected and served as a pedestal for twenty young women reckless of their physical safety. The church of Saints-Innocents bore men like a tree laden with fruits; some were astride the buttresses, others hanging on to the ledges in the fashion of the sculpted larvae they embraced; some were looking over the heads of gorgons, others hiding between the projections of the bell-tower. The integrity of Macabre's abode in tour de Notre-Dame-du-Bois, immune to climbers, owed its resistance entirely to its iron-bound door.

The Sire de la Vodrière soon regretted having ventured with his wife into the middle of that crowd, which nudged them in all directions, forcing them forwards or backwards, rumbling around them like a distant storm; but it would have been necessary to march over a pavement of moving heads to get out of that turbulence, which grew by degrees and slowed its movements; the cemetery was so full that the dead were less cramped in their sepulchers, and the walls of the charnel-houses seemed ready to be parted by that living lever.

Jehanne was less frightened than women ordinarily are by an apparent and continuous danger. The rude pressure of the crowd, the verbose insolence of the vulgar, the repugnant contact of the populace, and even the bruises inflicted by certain hooked fingers had no power to distract her attention, which wandered in long glances over the dazzling face of that multitude.

The Sire de la Vodrière, by contrast, experienced an increasing anxiety which took on the most churlish and morose expression; he cursed the *danse macabre* and Jehanne's imprudent whim in a low voice; he tormented her with recriminations, injunctions and caprices addressed by every glance

131

and every gesture, by his silence as well as his words; he watched her with a meticulous jealousy, to make sure that she was not suffering from any coarse proximity; he drove away a sharp elbow, turned aside an officious hand, intimidated excessively bold eyes, studied the thoughts behind physiognomies and produced the effect of the mythological Medusa on all those charmed by the grace of his veiled wife.

He felt a trifle reassured when he had succeeded in clearing a passage to the *petit guifs*, where two vagrants backed up against the wall ceded their places to him for money; they were directly in front of the theater, able to see over the tallest heads by virtue of the elevation of the ground at that point. The Sire de la Vodrière, congratulating himself on being secure, in that a rampart of stone provided better protection than an Argus, established the Tour de Notre-Dame-du-Bois behind Jehanne and planted himself in front of her in order to defend his property on all sides.

He perceived, with a groan, that during the trajectory he had lost her veil, and that her beauty was awakening a flattering murmur that was going from one person to the next, attracting all eyes toward a single target; he went pale with anger but strove to put on a brave face. Jehanne had not blushed, so far from her mind was that universal admiration, which was not worth as much to her as a single glance from Benjamin.

"On your soul," he said to her in a low voice, "do you have to dress so immodestly? Look how these peasants are blinding themselves looking at you. What have you done with your veil?"

"It must have slipped off my head," she replied, searching for it, blushing and excited, "or someone stole it in the crush; excuse me for the negligence, my dear seigneur."

"What an angel!" said a voice in a nearby group. "That's a noble lady—she's as gorgeous as a crowned princess."

"Saint Guerlichon help her! She'll die a virgin with that old spouse."

"No, friend; she has masculine progeniture by the Sire de la Vodrière."

"Oh, the evil wolf, biting the sloe! He's scolding his wife for being so pretty."

"Believe me, if I had such a nasty husband, I'd make him sorry, one way or another."

"Right! You can be sure that the lady doesn't go short of amorous oats."

"Yes indeed, she gets her revenge on the tyrannies of that tanned stag—I hear she has a lover, or two, if not more."

"Holy Easter! I'd like to spend my purgatory reigning over that tasty tidbit!"

"Swan's beak! Resign yourself to having nothing but the appetite."

"Hell's bells! Devil take the wretch who's blocking my view of that masterpiece!"

"Messire, your plume could serve as the King of Castile's fly-whisk!"

"What's that? You can't see?"

"God's blood, what have my ribs done to you that you should break them thus?"

"Hey, friend, you'd be more comfortable if you tucked your belly in a bit."

"Shit! I don't give a fart or a tinker's curse!"

"Hey! Start the dance!"

"By the Cross of St. André, has Macabre gone back to the English? Why is he so late starting the dance?"

"Give him time to say a paternoster to the Devil."

"You—take that hat off!"

"Silence, popinjay in a cage, or I'll shut your gob with cow-shit!"

"May the sworn tormentor cut off those heads that are held too high!

"My tongue's peeling with thirst."

"Start the play, or give us back our money!"

"Let's hear the rebec! Bring on Macabre! Noël! Noël!"

The Sire de la Vodrière, who was pretending not to hear any of the impertinences offered on his account by the crowd, changed his posture and face continually to hide his embarrassment, until the sound of the church clocks chiming one redirected all gazes in the direction of the theater. He recovered from the visible disturbance that the words of the audience had caused him, and took advantage of the brief tumult that preceded the spectacle to scold Jehanne pitilessly, accusing her of having provoked the insulting scene deliberately.

She responded with large tears, which had only been waiting for an opportunity to flow; she had only encountered unknown faces; Benjamin was not there.

The Sire de la Vodrière thought she was subject to repentance, which he judged to be real by her moist eyes and the profound sighs that were agitating her bosom; he consoled her in a tone calculated to redouble her sorrow, and promised to continue the quarrel when they returned home, which he wanted to accelerate, although Jehanne was submissive to a severe rule of conduct, which demanded his pardon with her gaze, if not her thoughts.

Jehanne was looking without seeing, listening without hearing, enjoying the unalterable liberty of soul that rendered the memory of Benjamin present in the presence of her odious despot; she found happiness in her imagination.

The performance commenced, at the signal of a lugubrious and solemn symphony executed by an invisible musician hidden in a box to the left of the stage. Silence was demanded everywhere, with a prolonged noise that would scarcely have been dominated by a clap of thunder, but the most attentive calm settled by degrees over the assembly, which was no longer living save through the eyes. Vague imprecations were still circulating against tall statures and bonnets; people stood on tiptoe and stretched their necks; half the spectators could see very little or nothing at all, but they resigned themselves to it, promising themselves that they would come earlier to the second day, which was to take place on the Tuesday after Easter.

More than fifty thousand people were there, mouths open, ears pricked and pupils dilated; a buzz of impatience ran without interruption through the obstructed streets, from which the lamentations of women and children rose up. The colorful and heterogeneous cemetery had resumed its mute immobility, and that artificial terrain was compressed by the immense weight, with dull creaking; ten centuries were trampled underfoot.

Macabre's stage was uncovered, with neither canopy nor curtain; the decoration of the backcloth, half-effaced by usage and damp, combined the indications of places necessary to the changes of scene. The painter had hurled pell-mell on to the canvas, without observing the principles of design and perspective, churches, palaces, fields, houses, forests, meadows and mountains, with a scroll emerging from the mouth of the sun to announce that the painting signified the "earthly world."

While the symphony, suave and terrible by turns, imitated laughter and sobbing, angelic singing and the cries of the damned, two men disguised in burlesque fashion as demons, with bearded masks, bull's horns and a cow's tale, held up two placards, one of which bore the composition of the dances of the first day and the other four lines of advice to the public, in which Macabre showed himself to be a poet and a philosopher:

> The danse macabre calls
> Which for men and women to learn
> Is quite natural for all
> Everyone taking their turn.

When these diabolical heralds had withdrawn, a grave and formidable voice, like a trumpet of the last judgment, called three times for the Pope. Macabre immediately appeared, rebec in hand, playing a tune of religious exultation, which would have sent the seraphim into ecstasy, prancing in such a fashion that his harmonious bones beat the measure.

That apparition was followed by a rumor of surprise and fright, which was communicated with a spontaneous electricity even to those unable to see its cause; one might have thought that the actor's bony rattle had echoes at the Porte Saint-Denis and the Pont-au-Change. Women covered their eyes with their hands, but curiosity immediately parted their fingers, between which the horror seemed more bearable. Everyone expressed astonishment, some aloud, questioning their neighbors, some signing themselves, some adjuring God and his saints, some laughing, some shivering, all feasting their eyes untiringly.

Macabre was, indeed, a frightening corpse, for the dead do not usually dance while playing a rebec, and Macabre had realized such a hideous illusion that people suspected that he had quit his coffin to play his role. He was entirely naked, save for a winding-sheet gathered around his loins by a futile decency and hanging loosely over his shoulders; a shred of bloody leather hung down in imitation of an open belly and the visible entrails, in accordance with the conventional characterization of Death. That fantastic nudity put in relief the acute forms of the skeleton, the earthly parchment that enveloped it, and the bizarre alliance of death with life.

Without being disconcerted by the noisy welcome he received, Macabre drew strains from his rebec so majestic that the members of the audience, gripped by respect, would have prostrated themselves had they been able to budge. They forgot the cadaverous ugliness of the musician who was expressing with three strings the magnificence of the Court of Rome, the sublimity of Jesus Christ's successor, the power of the Christian Church, the gnashing of teeth of Hell and the indescribable joys of Heaven.

That was the introduction of the Pope, who obeyed the summons, emerging from the box to the right, richly dressed in a gold chasuble, a tiara on his head and St. Peter's keys in his hand; he advanced with dignity to the edge of the stage, where he extended his slipper toward the audience, while Macabre insulted him with a burst of laughter so piercing, so prodigious and so satanic that the most intrepid felt an icy chill in their veins and a prickling in their hair.

"By the shade of Samuel!" exclaimed Balthazar Culdoë from a window in the Boîte-aux-Lombards, "That's my son I can see! Oh, the denier of the God of Abraham, he has lent himself to these profanations!"

"It's our son, you mean!" said Holopherne Croquoison, who recognized Benjamin under his papal disguise. "That's why he's been sleeping in the Loge-au-Fossoyeurs for three nights running!"

"I'll wager one écu against twelve," added Jeremiah Nathan, "that the child has been spoiled in the company of Christians. My opinion is that this character acting will be worth a moneyed absolution to him."

"Benjamin!" repeated Jehanne de la Vodrière, who had hesitated to recognize her lover thus decked out. "It's him! An actor and player of farces! I thought he was a noble and gallant seigneur!"

"God's truth, Madame, what are you muttering?" interjected the Sire de la Vodrière, who had allowed himself to be drawn into a reverie, in conformity with the nature of the spectacle, and had only heard an echo of the exclamation.

"Oh, nothing, or less than nothing, I swear to you," Jehanne replied, her voice and features distressed. "I was admiring that marvelous player of farces, and feeling compassion for the poor seigneur that Death will cause to dance."

"Shut up, chatterboxes," murmured someone nearby, to the satisfaction of the young woman, who was almost fainting. "Death will grab you by the beak, tame magpies! Whoever jabbers will go to the land of the moles."

The Sire de la Vodrière, forced to postpone the explanation that his wife's pallor and emotion caused him fervently to desire, feared that he had paid too much attention to Macabre and not enough to Jehanne, who had been able to deceive his surveillance. He turned his back to the theater and observed the interior turmoil of his victim, whose palpitating heart he interrogated with the careful barbarity of a sacrificer.

Benjamin had perceived the movement that his presence had provoked at a single point in the assembly; Jehanne's voice had struck him with a bitter discouragement, and when he met her gaze, which was still considering him wild-eyed, a cold sweat broke out over his entire body, a nervous tremor agitated his limbs, his face turned crimson, and his pitiful countenance begged for mercy with so much verity that there was applause for a performance so very appropriate to the circumstance.

He remained so long in that supplicant posture that Death set down his rebec and armed himself with a gravedigger's spade to caress the soft spine of the holy pontiff, who had the leisure to make his reflections. Then the Pope, rid of a false shame, knelt down before Death, offered him his tiara and keys, attempted to give him a blessing and his slipper to kiss, threatened to excommunicate him, and ran around the stage in order to avoid the thrusts of his spade, taking refuge in Macabre's box, while the latter celebrated his victory on his rebec.

The people laughed wholeheartedly, and applauded the pantomime as much as the music, without noticing that the sun's rays were weakening by the minute.

"Friend," said Nathan to Culdoë, pensively, "your son is subjecting our richest accoutrements to wear and tear, soiling the fabric and spoiling the decorations; will he be a prodigal and dissipater of the Lord's wealth?"

"Moses pardon him!" said Culdoë to Croquoison, who was considerably amused by that comedy. "I want to retract my beloved son from the gentiles' den; and as soon as we have accomplished our vow together, at midnight tomorrow, I shall buy Benjamin back, no matter how high the price might be. Nevertheless, friend, don't tax your honest hospitality too dearly."

The entr'acte was brief, and the Pope, who had returned to his own box by means of a stairway, had soon undergone a complete metamorphosis. The magical voice was calling upon the Emperor.

Macabre reappeared, with no other change of costume than his winding-sheet falling to the ground; he whistled in a strange manner and plied his bow with so much vivacity that he imitated twenty instruments and twenty musicians; he reproduced in his extraordinary chords the sounds of tambours and clarions, the gallop of horses, the rhythmic marching of battalions, the collision of two armies, hymns of triumph, war and peace.

The enthusiasm captivated those ignorant masses, who understood the eloquence of the inspired chords in which the genius of the artist overflowed. It was an entire musical poem, didactic and picturesque, on the pomp and grandeur of the empire of the Caesars, with all the episodes of a glorious reign. Macabre identified himself with and incorporated himself into his rebec; his grimaces and contortions might have made one think that he was an instrument himself, like the statue of Memnon, and that each new intonation drawn from the depths of his entrails caused him physical suffering.

Unanimous acclamations accompanied the entrance of the Emperor.

Him again! thought Jehanne, who could not suppress her displeasure. *I have a poor actor for a slavish lover! He's played a trick of his trade on me! Nevertheless, he looks handsome in that get-up!*

"By Jerusalem the Holy City!" said Culdoë to his associates. "I'd give ten yards of scarlet cloth to put an end to that mummery, along with the impiety of my son, who is perjuring his God."

The Emperor bowed humbly to Madame de la Vodrière, who dared not return the salute, and blushed more than was necessary to arouse a suspicion in the spirit of the malign old man. She feigned a violent headache augmented by the ardor of the sun—which, however, was diminishing sensibly. She took advantage of that excuse, suggested by the necessity of furnishing a pretext for her blush, her agitation and the indiscreet revelation of her gaze. Her husband rubbed his hands, with an expressive grimace.

Meanwhile, Benjamin, coiffed with the sealed crown of the emperors of the Occident, clad in purple and brocade, holding the scepter and orb of Charlemagne, commenced imploring Death, who laughed like a roaring tiger. He tried to tame him with his scepter, he offered him half of his imperial mantle; he took off his crown in order to bargain with it; he made a sign to his guards, mounted his throne and clung to it hard. But Death, leaping and shaking his skeleton, showed him the finger, stripping him of his ornaments, kissing his forehead and according nothing but scorn to his terrestrial power, and danced away to fetch a coffin, and forced him to get into it, while he held them hem of the purple robe, without interrupting his joyful clowning.

The spectators were taking an increasingly lively interest in these allegorical scenes, and no one had noticed, as yet, the progressive variation that was taking effect in the light of day.

"Brothers," said Culdoë, shivering, after having raised his eyes toward the sun, half-hidden by the moon's shadow, "an eclipse is beginning; it's a presage of incomparable evils!"

"Is it the coming of the Messiah?" cried Nathan, squeezing his empty purse in his hand. "As long as our goods and money escapes the peril, may the Lord's will be done!"

"Hurry up and pay the ransom for your son, my friend" added Croquoison, half signing himself, "for by St. Elijah and St. Joshua, plague and famine are drawing near."

The voice of Death was inviting the Cardinal to the dance when the contemplative attention of the crowd was disturbed by the ringing of bells, and people turned toward the Préchoir.

X. The Solar Eclipse

It was the famous Franciscan preacher Brother Richard who, under the domination of the English, had had the privilege of making the people, overwhelmed by misery and taxes, dying of hunger and disease, flock to his sermons; his ministry of pious imposture and holy wrath warmly supported the cause of the English, of whom he was the vile agent, like the fiery preachers of the League hired by the Spaniards a century and a half later. The Bishop of Thérouenne and his adviser Saint-Yon, the head of the butchers' faction, employed Brother Richard every time the leavens of discord were brought into Paris, ever ready to return to the authority of its legitimate master.

Then, Brother Richard, dressed in sackcloth, his head soiled with ashes, his feet bare, beating his shoulders with the disciplinary rod, went to the Cimetière des Saints-Innocents with a crowd that he gathered as he passed by, went up on to a balcony of the Préchoir or a stage constructed for his usage in 1429 opposite Macabre's theater, to which he turned his back out of professional jealousy, and, with his energetic improvisations, played the parts of God the Father, God the Son, the Holy Spirit, the Virgin, the saints, the angels, the demons, the impious king in Bourges, his ministers, his priests and his libertine court, all of it seasoned with mocking oaths, equivocal coarseness, Latin citations and bawdy allocutions to the audience. The acrid and mordant hyperbole gained support for the English tyranny, which defamed the mores and intentions of Charles VII via an impure organ of the Christian religion; his sermons were thrown to the populace of old Paris like gladiatorial combats to that of ancient Rome.

Since the retreat of the English, however, whom he had initially followed, like Saint-Yon and the principal rebels, whom the royal pardon had then brought back to the capital, Brother Richard had participated in the forgetfulness of the past. The Provost had put a ban on all public sermons in his jurisdiction; in any case, public opinion had changed so much that the most furious of Brother Richard's listeners would have stoned him instead of applauding him.

However, the love of the flesh consumed the Franciscan as much as the love of money. and those two unfortunate loves increased in the solitude and poverty of the cloister that had kept him prisoner for three years. He had therefore resolved to persuade the Provost and Bishop of Paris to return his former privilege, and, knowing that the cemetery would bring together the most brilliant assembly for which a preacher could hope that day, he had hidden in the Préchoir in order to show himself at the moment he judged favorable.

He had renounced political harangues, for fear of encountering a peremptory response in every stone that could be raised against him; he wanted an oratorical triumph to signal his reappearance and pecuniary offerings to supplement the expenses of his lubricity. The *danse macabre* presented him with a text for satires and declamations in the superstitious vein of the day; and, to complete his joy, the solar eclipse came along to support his predatory quest. A total eclipse was then reckoned as a sign of celestial malediction.

The high window of the Préchoir suddenly opened to the sound of the bell that was ringing in the campanile, and Brother Richard came out on to the uncovered balcony where the regiment of butchers and fishmongers from the market had once greeted him. He was still young and vigorous, replete and rubicund; good wine and lust, rather than fervor and zeal, inflamed his puffy face, dilated his nostrils and made his eyes sparkle.

This time, he had only modified his Franciscan costume by the addition of a cord around his beck and a coating of ash on his head; in any case, his robe of coarse grey cloth, his hooded cowl and mantle of the same fabric, his sandals and his thrice-knotted rope girdle, were eloquent arms for the majority of penitents of that indefatigable order. Brother Richard, who heard a dull rumor rumble, knelt down facing the East, struck his breast and prepared to address his partisans edified by those demonstrations of devotion, while his assistant, a fat and clumsy lay brother, having ceased his carillon, began to sound a rattle no less loudly to inform the faithful that the chest of the poor awaited alms.

Voices went up in the crowd:

"It's good Brother Richard!"

"He's resuscitated between the death and the English."

"Praise Montjoie and Saint-Denis!"

"He no longer has the cross of Saint-André?"

"Oh, the torturer of honor and religion!"

"Good God! What's he doing here?"

"Friends, is the fox of Thérouenne lodging in the Hôtel Saint-Paul, sending his ambassador forth to sing his praises?"

"A waxen mask for that handsome confessor of women!"

"Thank God! The poor holy man has come to the dance—don't be displeased!"

"Five hundred thousand chariots of the Devil, how he could swear!"

"God forgive him if he's got some sermon in his belly!"

"Can't you see that he wants to sell us England's pardons? I'll pay him with money struck with good coin and good weight."

"May Saint Anthony's fire rack the guts of that swine of nature! He was the one who solicited the Burgundians to loot my shop!"

"Carimari, carimara! Throw him to the dogs; if he wields his tongue, we'll wield daggers!"

"Oh, shut that clacker-mill up!"

The spectators turned away from the stage, where Macabre was announcing the Cardinal's dance with voluptuous Italian music in which all the delights of sensual life took on an intoxicating voice: there were the feasts of the conclave, courtesans, horse races, sacerdotal slumber and idleness; but infernal laughter annihilated that dream of sybaritic enjoyments and the Cardinal, in a red robe trimmed with ermine and coiffed in his tasseled hat, prostrated himself before Death, who took his pulse, examined his tongue and condemned him medically to die of indigestion, without deigning to taste the dish of kid with artichokes that the gourmand had been unable to finish. Macabre, whose laughter succeeded the rebec, danced around the unfortunate Cardinal with a bony creaking that did not drown out the Préchoir's rattle; the daylight was darkening as if thick clouds had veiled the sun.

Still him! thought Jehanne, who was becoming accustomed to the idea of finding her lover in all the costumes of an acrobat. *He's certainly a skillful actor: the pope, emperor and cardinal couldn't match him in gentility.*

"By the fire that consumed the accursed cities!" exclaimed Culdoë. "It will take no less than my vow to expiate the folly of my son, who's spoiling and corrupting his faith with this Christian mummery. May the Lord have mercy on him!"

"Yes, indeed!" added Croquoison, in a bad temper. "I had no idea that my son had that rare science, for which I too intend to seek redemption. Say, friend, isn't that the wailing of a child coming from your room?"

"You're mocking us, friend," said Culdoë, swiftly, frowning and biting his lips. "How can you hear anything from here, with that monk playing the rattle and Macabre crumbling his bones?"

"Madame," said the Sire de la Vodrière to his wife, whose eyes were riveted to the theater, "That dance pleases you, it seems to me, and you won't have to wait a long time to dance it."

"Brothers and sinners!" cried the Franciscan Richard, striding back and forth on his balcony and shaking his first over the balustrade, "by the five hundred thousand chariots of the devil, sin and damnation! It is written: in that time there will be signs in the sun and the stars; now, that time has come, I assure you; the new year will not pass without great calamities, *id est*, those calamities will engender worse and more numerous evils, as children surpass the perversities of their parents. You laugh, quaffers of rime, students of thornbushes? Damnation! Your Seigneur Satanas will give you what you need to cackle and fry! In truth, I tell you this: *Vigilate et orate*, gird your loins and purify your souls. Jean, open the alms boxes and announce the indulgences."

There were more cries in the crowd:

"Hurrah! Descend from your calvary, accursed thief!"

"Soon you'll be preaching to the dead in the cemetery, handsome monk!"

"Jacquet, lend me your cattle-prod, which I gave you as a wedding present."

"Give us a rest, Messire Franciscan; that English gray has some evil spell in store for us."

"Hey! Boo! Silence, monk and rattle! Oh, what an annoying interruption!"

"Is Macabre going to dance that importunate drooler?"

"I'm damned if we can hear the rebec!"

"Enough! Let him go preach in the desert!

"Bleed him like a veal-calf in the butchery!"

"Marmari, marmara, tarabin, tarabas!"

"Spare me a grievous concern, Madame," said the Sire de la Vodrière, who was suffering all the more because he was allowing less to show. "That actor is wearing a golden cross on his cardinal's hat similar to the one you lost during mass at the church of Sainte-Opportune; is it possible that it was extracted from your paternosters by that cutpurse?"

"Monseigneur," Jehanne replied, having noticed the same things on the quiet, "do you see that Franciscan in the Préchoir? His sermon is being greeted with an outrageous lack of respect. The daylight is withdrawing its brightness from us!"

Jehanne, who was in quest of a composure that it was increasingly difficult to maintain, looked mechanically at the sun, which, having been bitten into by the shadow of the moon, resembled the latter's crescent. The Sire de la Vodrière, to whom she hastened to point out this phenomenon, was too much of a gentleman to be insensitive of it; he shook his head as if the fatal augury applied to him alone, and his neighbors,

145

alerted by his gestures of despair and raising their own eyes, were seized by the same consternation, which spread in all directions with a bleak and quivering silence. The vicinity of the Préchoir was enveloped in a tempest of cries, threats and projectiles, which Brother Richard sent back to his adversaries in thunderous speech.

Benjamin having informed Macabre of the reason for the sudden preoccupation, so closely was he following Jehanne's movements, they both retired to their boxes, which were locked and barricaded from within, as were the exits from the stage. An instant later, Benjamin, having shed his cardinal's robe, slid like a serpent through the uncertain and fearful crowd.

"As for that, I ask you why?" shouted Brother Richard, who had just been struck on the arm by a tile thrown from the charnel-houses. "Am I a Saint Étienne, that you should stone me in that manner? Do you want to shed my blood, because I want inform you charitably? Maître Courlebois, you're a man of age and prudence, draw up this proclamation: whomsoever throws a stone at me will be boiled in oil in Gehenna! Hear this, good people: I hold you to blame and vituperate against you for having deserted the offices of Maundy Thursday to frequent a profane, unhealthy and heretical farce in which the pope is defamed."

"Brother Richard is thrice justified," said old Courlebois, flattered by the direct eulogy, "so I prefer the sermon to the dance. Maître Moutard, launch a volley of kicks up the back-side of that impious individual who's mocking."

"Jehanne," said the Sire de la Vodrière, with profound dejection, "I apologize for my unworthy treatment of you, and I pray to God that he will keep you under his holy protection, with our little charge, if I should happen to die."

"I shall doubtless die before you," said Jehanne, who thought she could distinguish at a distance someone resembling Benjamin. "It distresses me to be so crowded, and to be away from my dear child."

Meanwhile, everyone had already forgotten the *danse macabre* for Brother Richard's sermon. The latter was no longer being assailed by a hail of insults and debris; the habit he was wearing had conciliated general respect, and there were not a few women wishing secrets to be confessed by him. The bloody color of the sun seemed to be slowly dying away as the shadow eating away the globe of fire reduced it to the proportions of a slender crescent; stupor and prayer were making the multitude seethe, their eyes fixed on the eclipse, which was about to become total.

Brother Richard judged the power of his eloquence by the tinkling sound that emerged from the alms-chest like the murmur of a lively spring; he picked up the thread of his discourse, which his shrieking voice caused to penetrate the ears, while his animated gestures caused it to reach the mind through the eyes. The adroit charlatan calculated the degradations of the light and founded the climax of his speech on the dramatic quality of complete darkness.

"My dear brothers in Jesus Christ and in Satanas!" he howled, like a man possessed, "what grave lesson do you take from that dance of figures and worldly villainies? The knowledge that man and woman are serfs and subjects of death? Ha! Whorish dolls, who show your two teats on a meat-stall, you will be laid on a bed that can neither be bought nor sold! And you, Maître Gougibus, who have shaped and built these players' stage, nothing will remain to you but a bier of your own carpentry. As for what will become of you, my friend Moutard, your apothecary will not save you from dying before chickens lay golden eggs. *Ecco desolatio abominationis*. Fortunate are those who give their wealth to the Franciscan fathers! For the doors of paradise will not open to the rich, and the plague will reap a rich harvest within our walls."

"The plague!" lamenting voices repeated.

"It's all over with our lives and our souls!"

"Excellent Brother Richard, is it necessary to buy masses and burn candles in the churches?"

"The Lord God receive us in his bosom!"

"The plague has already commenced, and fifty bodies have been laid underground today."

"Is it not the end of the world?"

"Good Lord, deliver us from contagion, and we will dedicate chaplaincies in each of our parishes!"

"Alas! Messire, will the sun lose its glare? One might think it a slice of lemon!"

"Has that evil sorcerer Macabre conjured the demons, scourges and sores of Egypt? May the plague take him first!"

"Plague, by the hundred and twenty thousand chariots of the devils!" said the Franciscan, counting his profits in his imagination. "Famine will come to keep you company, sharpen your teeth and plant a legion of demons and colics in your stomachs. The wheat will not grow and your granaries will be empty, and I do not know what will be ground on the Pont-aux-Meuniers. Then the war of the English will make that destiny worse, by which more than forty thousand will discover whether purgatory is a desirable abode, and if access to heaven is still permitted to the elect.

"Mesdames, will your beautiful accoutrements, dresses with trains and gilded belts, serve to hide your filthy stains and mortal sins? Bourgeois sire, it would profit you to look less at the sun and more at the poor that are recommending you to my almonry. I warn you that Hell is a vile cul-de-sac stinking of sulfur and smoke, from which one does not emerge either by prayers or the dedication of charnel-houses; make haste while you are alive to practice fasting, piety and alms-giving; sow down here before harvesting on high. These veridical prophecies are ascertained for you by celestial and terrestrial signs; the day is darkening and veiling its face; darkness will frighten the sons of men, as it is written. To the sixty million chariots of the devils, hardened sinners, spoiled, gangrenous, scabby and pestiferous!"

"*Miserere nobis Deus!*" the most undevoted were saying. "Have I not heard the trump of judgment?"

"Mercy of God! That detestable Macabre must be the Antichrist!"

"Ohe! Admire the dragon that is eating the sun! It is the night of tears and the gnashing of teeth!

"The earth is giving way beneath me!"

"By the merits of the true cross!"

"By the passion!"

"By the resurrection!"

"By the ascension!"

"O fatal day!"

"Brother Richard, confess us and say the absolution! The world is exploding into smithereens, and the sun will fall!"

"My wife!"

"My husband!"

"My son!"

"A *De profundis!* I'm dying, I'm fainting, I'm damned!"

"Ah!"

"Oh!"

"Ohe!"

There was a single cry of inconceivable terror when the disk of the moon entirely covered that of the sun and intercepted its last rays, which, pale and rare, overflowed the opaque body placed in front of it. The cry, prolonged in echoes and redoubled echoes to all parts of the city, expired in a silence of expectation and stupefaction, troubled by the monotonous rattle of Brother Jean and the superb absolution of Brother Richard. The wan twilight that struggled with the obscurity resembled the imminent dawn of an eternity of pain and recompense; that belief, so frequent in the centuries of superstition and ignorance, was rapidly accredited among the people by reason of the duration of the eclipse; the crowd floated and undulated like the Ocean at the approach of a tempest.

Suddenly, harsh and increasing clamors rose up from a corner of the cemetery, and a horrible catastrophe unfolded; the beams and joists forming a ceiling over the ditch of Saint-Germain-l'Auxerrois had given way under the weight of the multitude, and a gulf five fathoms deep swallowed up the living along with the dead. General confusion became the inevitable sequel to that partial disaster, which continued and grew: the void that the abysm had opened up in the crowd was immediately filled in, and every movement of that animate sea dragged down new victims, stifled, crushed and torn against a reef of piled-up bodies.

Disorder was everywhere, and knowledge of the danger nowhere; everyone create a more or less fantastic image of the end of the world that was dominating all minds. Some twisted their necks in looking upwards to see the Son of Man appear, seated on a cloud, the stars fall and the heavens open to deploy their myriads of angels and saints; others imagined that the sepulchers were about to render their inhabitants, and that the ground was already alive; while the blind mêlée was racked and rattled by an atrocious mixture of prayers, plaints and imprecations.

That effervescent chaos growled and roared in the shadow; the instinct of self-preservation because the sole cause of the ruination of all. The crowd, which fear precipitated at hazard, raised insurmountable obstacles to flight, agglomerated instead of dispersing and incessantly heaped the wounded on top of the dying; the crowd, unruly and blind, surged, ran, fell and halted, like an element more redoubtable than water and fire combined.

People called out without seeing and replied without hearing, embraced and were violently torn apart, struck out and were struck; rage, despair, dolor, terror and distress shared that mobile stage of horror; efforts, blows, bites, grips and convulsions spared neither rank nor age nor sex. Tears, sobs, moans, screams, sights and howls: the human voice ran through all the tones of physical and moral sufferings at once. Limbs were broken, ribs cracked, faces mutilated; an irresistible force bent iron railings, uprooted monuments, smashed crosses and epitaphs, ploughed the soil, shook stone walls and tipped over walls of human beings.

No one had retained the power of reason in that frantic conflict, save for a few incorrigible thieves who prepared for death by stealing purses, jewels and objects of value useless in the other life.

As soon as that sudden panic began, the Sire de Vodrière had put out his arms in front of him to contain the irruption of the crowd, but he was carried away by the current and lost sight of his wife, whom Benjamin had drawn in another direction, cleaving through the swelling waves of fleeing people in order to clear a passage for her. Love tripled the power of the young man's fading strength, who was not dragging anything after him but an inert and passive body, while the old man roared like a lioness in search or her cubs.

Finally, Benjamin, harassed and almost unconscious, succeeded in reaching the Porte de la Ferronnerie with his burden, which he had slung over his shoulder. Beneath that black vault, a stairway led up to the charnel-houses, which he climbed on a momentary inspiration; he felt his heart beating with joy on finding himself the possessor of the woman he had saved, but he could not believe that his happiness was secure in those long galleries of bones, which the crowd might inundate. The floor was juddering beneath his feet, the roof trembling above his head.

He applied his burning mouth to Jehanne's icy lips, and continued on his way through heaps of skeletons, along the garret that ran along the Rue Saint-Denis. Then he went down into the Loge-aux-Fossoyeurs, where he gently laid his unconscious lover down, who recovered her senses in response to the evocation of his kisses.

XI. The Loge-aux-Fossoyeurs

The disaster and the panic that it had caused only came to an end with the eclipse. The crowd, on seeing the sun reappear, more luminous, as it emerged from the shadow of the moon, understood that eternal darkness had not commenced, and that the world would continue living that day.

The disordered, seething, irresistible crowd stopped, suddenly calmed down like lava cooling outside the crater; but the *danse macabre* had been so completely forgotten that even the most miserly did not think of demanding the refund of money that Macabre, locked in his box, trembled at the thought of not being able to add to his treasure.

While Brother Richard withdrew into the Préchoir, dazed by his own eloquence and Brother Jean's rattle, both bewildered before a pecuniary result that the eclipse had enhanced so vastly, the cemetery gradually disgorged its crowd into the adjacent streets, which were emptying through every issue.

When the floods of people flowing in all directions, with a rumble like retreating thunder, had laid bare the broken and furrowed surface of the cemetery, the casualties of that day were exhumed from beneath the feet that had trampled them, the masses that had hidden them and the earth that had buried them.

Six hundred people had been killed or injured in that fatal fête, and the dance of the dead had become a frightful reality.

Ambroise de Loré, Provost of Paris, went to the cemetery, whose gates remained closed for the clearing of the corpses, which had not been completed by nightfall and continued by the light of torches. The living were separated from the dead, all as mutilated and disfigured as one another, but those who were still breathing were taken to the hospitals, and that triage was carried out so rapidly that more than one unfortunate woke up among those who were sleeping forever.

Relatives were permitted to identify and take away a few of the wounded to care for them in their homes; as for the dead, or those judged as such, they were thrown pell-mell into a deep ditch, in which three hundred found places under a shroud of lime. Ambroise de Loré, assisted by Adam de Cambrai, the first president of the parliament, and Simon Charles, the president of the Cour des Comptes, the sole depositories of the safety of the city, adopted that prudent measure in order to destroy the infection that would serve to propagate the plague, and to disguise the number of victims, which renown had already exaggerated.

Brother Richard, the principal author of that deplorable event, had the further profit of blessing its effects, and officiated in the nocturnal ceremony that torches illuminated with their funereal gleams. All the gravediggers were employed extraordinarily, at the Provost's expense, and Master Croquoison waxed indignant at the absence of Benjamin, who was the only one not devoted to the task. He was not found among the living or the dying.

The Sire de la Vodrière was about to be buried like a tradesman, a vagabond or some unimportant peasant; fortunately, he was still breathing, and opened his eyes just as he was about to enter the bed of quicklime; he felt himself liberated from the mound of cadavers under which he had been lying, breathless and unmoving.

His return to consciousness was so swift and so complete that he called to his wife, begged all those present to bring her to him, tore at his white hair, rolled on the ground and ran hither and yon crying like a bacchante, giving signs of frantic madness. He wanted to die; he wanted to immolate for his vengeance the provost, the presidents, the priest and the gravediggers, whom he suspected of having abducted Jehanne.

He was only mastered by being tied up and gagged; then, out of respect for his nobility, he was transported without difficulty to his house, which Guillemette had abandoned immediately after the disappearance of the child, in order to avoid the dolor of the mother and the fury of the father. She returned to the Hôtel de Trimouille as soon as the desperate state of the moribund man became known, at the same time as the absence of Jehanne, but her care and mercenary zeal were limited to a false demonstration of tears and sobs, when the Sire de la Vodrière, who was writhing in his bonds and shivering from head to toe passed suddenly from frenzy to the most absolute lethargy.

His limbs stiffened and froze; his pulse and respiration died away; his heart, whose beats could have been counted through his doublet, ceased to beat; the pallor of death jaundiced his face and distended his features. It was thought that he was going to die, and the physician who had been summoned arrived just in time to certify his decease.

Guillemette had him buried, after waiting in vain for news of the mother and the child; an ordinance from the Provost required the dead to be buried immediately, in view of the contagion.

The Loge-aux-Fossoyeurs, where Benjamin had taken refuge with his lover was only composed of two vaulted cellars, one of which communicated with the garret of the charnel-houses, the other having an exit to the cemetery itself. The former, dark and fetid, was the arsenal of gravedigging; spades, picks and ladders hung on the walls, scarcely rusting in spite of the perpetual damp. The second cellar, which only partly merited that name, could pass for a habitable room, thanks to a narrow opening some seven feet above the floor, fitted with bars that did not intercept the air or the light.

That second room, which Benjamin had appropriated to make into his rest-room, would have been painted entirely black if saltpeter had not caused the color to peel away in places. Its only furniture consisted of a rickety bench, an empty dresser and a camp bed neater than one might have presumed in such a sepulcher, which retained something of its primitive state. It was there that Jehanne and Benjamin were ensconced.

The combat had been violent, in both attack and defense, when Madame de la Vodrière, recovering consciousness, had remembered and foreseen; she tried to employ prayer, force and determination to go back to her husband, whom she was in no hurry to see again; she had recourse to tears and the power of a noisily-expressed dolor. Benjamin refused to set her free, while always appearing to consent to it. He dissuaded her more by caresses than words; he raised the objections, in turn, of the increasing danger of the crowd, the difficulty of not being seen together, the scandal of such a public step, and then the impossibility of getting out, the cemetery being closed, the darkness.

Every moment, in fact, added to Jehanne's embarrassment; constrained rather than convinced, she only replied to the more specious reasons with silent tears and desolate gestures. Benjamin exhausted himself in testimonies of love in order to distract her from the lugubrious ideas that she embraced by inspiration, at the distinct noises of ground being dug and bodies being brought.

She listened with an anxiety that made every blow of the pickaxe resound in her heart. She thought she heard someone calling for Benjamin; she thought she could distinguish the tearful voice of her husband. She felt a bitter, poignant and insurmountable remorse; she launched herself toward the door; she tried to reach the window; Benjamin retained her in his arms; she uttered a cry, which Benjamin stifled with a kiss.

That long struggle was succeeded by a defeat, which sacrificed the past and future to the present; Jehanne forgot that she was a wife and mother; the torchlight that wandered over the wall like specters, the voices intersecting in the darkness of the cemetery, the echoes of footsteps and tools, all failed to extract her from the intoxication that annihilated her entire being; she thought she was going to sleep in a world of ineffable delights that would have neither awakening nor morrow; she was mad with love—and the light of dawn that entered through the opening in the vault surprised the secrets of the gravedigger's miserable bed.

She threw herself to huddle against the bosom of her lover in response to the racket that went up from the neighboring cellar when the gravediggers, weary from having worked all night, deposited their instruments before going away. Benjamin, who knew that the door was securely locked, reassured the culpable Jehanne with a tender gaze, while she lowered her own, blushing and not daring to examine the present situation.

The noise did not last, but the calm that was reestablished around them no longer existed in the heart of Madame de la Vodrière; she wept abundantly.

"Where am I?" she asked, with a plaintive softness. "Where have you brought me, Benjamin. Oh, Jesus my God, how will I ever be able to return to the Hôtel de la Trimouille? How can I pretend and lie, wicked friend?"

"It's not the time to think about that, my darling, and we have leisure until tomorrow; in the meantime, kiss me, soul of my life and life of my soul!"

"Truly, Benjamin, you have doomed me, without any resource! Do you know of any expedient that might save me? Here's dawn breaking, and I've been away far too long!"

"There's no reason to despair, Jehanne, and in an hour, at the most, I'll take you back to your house. I shall say, honestly, to your husband, that I saved you from imminent peril and hid you in my poor domain."

"Certainly not, if you value your life and mine! Have I not told you, my Benjamin, that Messire de la Vodrière has often unsheathed his knightly sword against my person? He would kill you without mercy."

"Unless I kill him first—but God preserve me from a needless murder at this time when we are content, with the same contentment. Rather aid yourself with a lie, the sin of which I take upon myself in this world and the next."

"To be believed, it's not sufficient to hide the truth, alas! And Messire de la Vodrière is by nature very perceptive of the false. Benjamin, I'm going to beg him to kill me and avenge himself, while you take to your heels."

"No, Madame! One doesn't have to be a gentleman to do one's duty, and I would give my blood twenty times over to preserve yours. Thus, I propose to say that you were locked in the charnel-houses by mistake."

"No! The charnel-houses are not a place of residence, and he would rebuke me for not having shouted for help to the people in the cemetery. Player of farces as you are, support me with your imaginative dexterity."

"I'm not an actor by profession," the young man interjected, in a chagrined tone. "That was my pledge, and madness. Could you not offer the pretext of a faint, from which you were brought round by Giborne, the wife of the musician Macabre?"

"Alas, my beloved, sin has led us into this predicament, and only repentance can get us out of it. Thus, I shall go to my father and confessor, Thibault, who can absolve me of my sin and punish me in a convent."

"Yes, good! That reverend father in God, who is your true father, will gladly strive to deliver you from this uncertainty and claim that you have been received in his house; that way, your honor will be safe and our amours secret."

"Upon my soul, Benjamin! Can you believe that my venerable father would agree to support that deception and conceal our adultery? I would rather die of shame. No, I say. Penitence requires me to become a cloistered nun; I shall care for the sick and pilgrims in the Hôpital Sainte-Catherine; I shall assist the patients and condemned, like the Filles-Dieu of the Rue Saint-Denis. I shall fast, pray, mortify my flesh and redeem our sins."

"God forbid, my darling! Worry not about sins that I shall bear alone. But if there is no means to disguise your undue absence, if your excessively rigorous husband is inclined to punish you, I propose that you come with me, away from Paris and from France."

"What! Would you leave behind your dignities, your fiefs and the king's court? No—I was forgetting that you're an actor; that's not a cause to love you less, but I excuse myself from departing without further ado."

"You have taken to heart my public performance in the *danse macabre*, and I'm sorry to have offended you; nevertheless, I'm not an actor, I assure you, and I do not live in the Rue Saint-Julien-des-Ménétriers. Remain in this little hovel until tomorrow."

"I shall not remain here for a single hour, for daylight has come and I have not seen my dear child since yesterday, who will be distressed by not seeing me. Don't keep me any longer, Benjamin, and tell me how to get out without being seen."

"By the Lord God of Israel, Jehanne, you're asking me for more than I can do. I won't put you back under the yoke of a deplorable marriage. I require and order you to remain under my protection as my wife and lover,"

"I beg you to let me go! I certainly intend to come back, Benjamin, if only after death. Permit me to return to my son and retire into a convent for the expiation of last night, and of the mystery of the steam-baths."

"No, by all the kingdoms of heaven and earth! I shall return your child to you this evening, whom I cherish in your image, and we shall leave together tomorrow for some distant country, where we shall live in great and naïve amity. Henceforth, Jehanne is mine! Jehanne is no longer Madame de la Vodrière, Jehanne is Madame Benjamin. Oh, don't take away the good fortune of my paltry destiny, which might not last long! If it must expire soon, let it be by the force of accolades and pleasure!"

Jehanne, already wavering in her resolution to leave, had nothing to oppose to these arguments, more persuasive than those she had been unable to resist the previous evening. Once again she forgot her husband, her child and herself. Benjamin redoubled his eloquence to subjugate the mother as he had the wife; he succeeded in gaining time, and when Jehanne thought again about escaping from the arms of her seducer, she recognized by the exterior noise and the living rumor of the city that it was too late, and that she would have to wait for nightfall for her exit to pass unnoticed.

She knelt down in a corner of the cellar and said her prayers with a melancholy fervor; she prayed for her son, for her lover, for herself; and when she came to think of the Sire de la Vodrière, she found nothing in her memory and on her lips but a *de profundis* surrounded by funereal presentiments.

Benjamin respected her prayer, which was long and punctuated by tears, She got up more tranquil in her soul and countenance; she listened to the plans and hopes of the young man, who was deluded regarding his precarious position and created an existence for himself more in conformity with his desires. He hid both the Jew and the gravedigger in him; he maintained his mistress in the high opinion that she had conceived of him by virtue of his distinguished manners and elegant costume; he recoiled before an inevitable confession, and almost regretted not having limited his pretensions to the title of actor, which she had lent to him so benevolently.

A more urgent idea began to pursue him, however, with more pressing spurs; for if the amorous lose appetite, lovers gain it. Their hearts were, therefore, more satisfied than their stomachs. Jehanne complained of hunger long after Benjamin had been racked by it—without, however, daring to absent himself to go in search of the nourishment of which he felt the need. He dreaded not finding Jehanne when he returned, scarcely being able to retain her by his presence. He could imagine nothing better than making her swear on the head of her child that she would not quit the lair under any pretext.

She swore.

As soon as he had slipped out of the Loge-aux-Fossoyeurs, however, he retraced his steps and pricked up his ears anxiously; there was the noise of a crowd in the cemetery, and the voice of Master Croquoison dominating the popular rumor, the singing of priests and the shrill screech of a rattle; it was the numerous funeral cortege of a gentleman being laid to rest.

A procession of mercenaries and curiosity-seekers accompanied the corpse, but the gravediggers who had worked so hard all night had relaxed in the tavern, and not one of them wanted to tear himself away from his bed or his table. Master Croquoison was blaspheming Moses and Chris between his teeth, and he promised to punish the negligence of his subordinates, who had the special nomination of the cemetery's leaseholders. He send his men urgent promises and threats, stamped his foot on his funerary domain and rejuvenated his strength to run from door to door, to go through the charnel-houses, up to the garrets and shout the names of all the absentees. Jehanne believed she heard Benjamin's. Only the dead man did not become impatient with the delay.

Finally, Master Croquoison, hoarse, choking and beside himself, took the only course that his ever-increasing embarrassment left him, so much did he appreciate the respect owed to the dead. He carefully took off his hat, his coat and his chaplet, which he confided to the beadle of Sainte-Opportune, who was leading the procession; then, his anger corroborating his muscles and his bones, he launched himself into the Loge-aux-Fossoyeurs to select the instruments he had once plied. He perceived that the second cellar was locked, and heard the movement that Jehanne had made in precipitating herself fearfully into her lover's bosom; he conceived suspicions that envenomed his bad mood, and, throwing back the tool he held into the heap of the others, he attacked the door with his feet and fists, with a fury that Benjamin's silence increased.

"Gentile!... Philistine!... Idolater!... Amalekite!..." he cried, in cadence. "Oh yes, the vagabond is wrapped up in his sheets and sleeping luxuriously, idle and bored—or is he with some whore from the Rue Brisemiche?"

"Good God, let's be careful!" murmured Jehanne, bursting into sobs. "Who is that man? Is it possible that he's come on behalf of Messire de la Vodrière? We're going to be caught together in this place!"

"Jehanne," said Benjamin, detaching himself gently from her frantic embrace, "Don't worry about that brute; I'll send him packing—but I implore you not to leave this place in the meantime."

"Accursed Benjamin!" Croquoison continued, exultant with rage. "Benjamin of all the devils! Serpent's son! Aren't you going to help me with the work? Indeed! The ingrate, the traitor hasn't dug a grave for a fortnight!"

"Here I am, malign old man," interjected Benjamin, who, fearful of Croquoison's indiscretions, appeared in front of him, closing the door abruptly behind him. "What do you want? I'm ill, with a high fever."

"Damn your fevers!" Croquoison said, slightly appeased by the sight of Benjamin. "Is it not a scandal to be asleep at this hour! It's a matter of laying to rest a noble lord, so get your pick and follow me right away, good sire."

A conversation in low voices was established between them, without Jehanne being able to connect up the meaning of the stray words that she seized with avidity. After a short argument, which Benjamin sustained weakly, they both drew away—in accord, so far as Jehanne could tell from their even footfalls and softened voices. She was less astonished by her lover's retreat than the mysterious circumstances that accompanied it.

Prayers for the dead were sung, and the audience replied devotedly to the priests. Jehanne was curious to cast an eye over the burial, which seemed to have attracted a considerable crowd. Her heart was beating as if to burst. She put the heavy dresser on the bench and was able by means of that tottering platform to raise her head to the level of the ventilation-hole.

At first her sight was vague and cloudy, she could only make out, confusedly, a crowd of the people on their knees and at prayer; then things became sharper and three-dimensional; she saw the clergy in black ornaments carrying the cross, the blessing, the gospel and the offering. She saw the poor and the hired mourners with their lighted torches; she saw the officers of the city, magistrates in livery; she saw the grave that was being dug, the bier surrounded by candles.

Suddenly, however, that indifferent spectacle became a horrible dream, an incredible vision; she scarcely recognized Père Thibault, who was leading the mourning and presiding over the ceremony. The man who was busy digging the grave, in which he was already waist-deep, bare-armed and without a doublet, was Benjamin!

Jehanne could not see any more; a veil had covered her eyes and a buzzing filled her ears; she stumbled, and dragged down in her fall the dresser that was supporting her. She did not have the strength to cry out, and her arm, extended forwards, attempted to drive away the odious phantom. She leapt to her feet, searched for a way out, groping, and encountered the one that led to the garrets; she dragged herself up there and tried to advance through the bones that rolled beneath her feet. She opened her frightened eyes to see nothing around her but emblems of death, walls of tibias, pyramids of skulls; feeling faint, she leaned against one of those strange monuments, of which the cemetery had furnished the materials.

"Bourgeois and manual workers of Paris," repeated the criers of Saints-Innocents, agitating their hand-bells, "hear this, good people, pray for the soul of the noble man, Chevalier Louis de la Vodrière, who has died; pray that God should receive him in His holy paradise. Pray!"

Jehanne de la Vodrière had fallen unconscious, still alive, in the midst of the scattered fragments of skeletons.

XII. The Violator of Tombs

Macabre was profoundly afflicted by the lack of success of his dance, which he dreaded being unable to continue on Easter Tuesday, so much had the progress of the contagion been favored by that prodigious influx. The number of the dead was twice that of the previous day, the day of Holy Friday, and all the quarters had shared in the mortality that was spreading less rapidly than the consternation. The rich inhabitants were beginning to leave Paris under the pretext of visiting their country houses, and the price of food was increasing in proportion to the likelihood of famine. The streets were deserted, the houses closed and the churches full. The Provost had several ordinances of sanitary precaution cried to the sound of the trumpet, which redoubled the anxiety imprinted on every face.

An hour after curfew on the evening of Holy Friday, which the raucous rotation of rattles had saddened further, Macabre and his wife Giborne were not asleep in their subterranean lair, hung with damp linen which the latter was detaching and folding carefully. Macabre was not taking his eyes off the operation, over which he was presiding, for fear that a sheet might go astray without his noticing it. Giborne was wearing her red domino, her patched shoes and her Sunday dress, as if she were going to show herself in public. Macabre was counting on his fingers the profits that the week's dead would bring in; he was bent over by fatigue and need.

"Wife," he said, in his sepulchral voice, "a hundred and twenty winding-sheets of new cloth, ninety shrouds of old cloth, and a hundred linen items of various sorts, the total worth at least ten francs of good money."

"Do you suspect that I'll clip them on the way?" said Giborne, ill-humoredly. "I've a strong desire to go and not come back, to join the zingaris, the companions of our race and our fortune, far away from the plague and the famine."

163

"Content your desire and go right away, malign and tyrannical gargoyle. Get out of my house and cease eating my bread. You're as avid for food as the grave-worms, and your nourishment cost more than twenty."

"By our mother earth, swallower of treasure, would you be content to repudiate your loyal wife Giborne? Who would go to sell change the booty of the cemetery, buy food every day and play my part in the *danse des femmes*?"

"Alas, I don't know whether my dance will ever reach a conclusion. It's a thousand gold écus that the contagion will steal from me, if I don't continue the mystery on Easter Tuesday. I beg you to stay until then, Giborne, my poppet."

"Macabre, my gallant seigneur, I would render you flatnosed and perplexed by leaving your lair and your ugly face, so I'll continue to be patient in this harsh slavery, provided that you give me enough to eat."

"Why don't you devour the dead, eternal glutton? Aren't you fat and swollen enough? Truly, in a time of famine you'd ruin the Pope himself with your silversmith's gob. Resolve to fast."

"I fast far too much, without being Christian! Simply remember the profits I'm worth, the services that I render you, the beautiful accoutrements I got from the Lombards, in return for a capital crime!"

"Yes, yes, wife—it isn't the first child you've stolen from a mother's bosom, and our honest Bohemian relatives do no different wherever they go. It's time to take all this to the Boîte-aux-Lombards."

"I've got a raging hunger, and my supper has gone all the way down to my heels; aren't there still a few bits of sausage and chaff bread? You put away the remains of a meal too quickly, and liberate them too late, Oh, if only I ate as well as a dog! If I could only sniff the fumes of the rotisseries of the Châtelet or the Rue aux Oies! My empty stomach no longer remembers having eaten, and is demanding a collation; my teeth are avid to bite."

"Bite a few stumps of your flesh for want of meat, my darling she-wolf; you can postpone your appetite until tomorrow without grass growing in your jaws. Go collect my dues, which I go to work."

"When will these fatigues and perils come to an end? Macabre, my poor seigneur, do you not see death mocking your hoard? The dead will avenge themselves on you by reserving the plague or the Provost's justice for you."

"Don't cast me such an evil lot, Wife, or I'll make you dance without the rebec. No, I don't have the time or the strength to disinter fifty corpses every night, which are as bare as their mother's loins."

"Undoubtedly the contagion is making such copious ravages that the daughters of the Hôpital Sainte-Catherine are saving their linen to bandage and bed the living; believe me, my lad, stop making such great efforts in this hard labor."

"Assuredly, my pet, I won't disturb the sleep of these hospital vagabonds who are only dressed in ulcers, but I won't leave a better windfall to the worms: the late Sire de la Vodrière was buried this morning..."

"It's possible that he's wearing rings and jewels in his tomb, after the fashion of gentlefolk; I invite you to strip him—but after that good haul, I advise you—I beg you—to decamp with your savings, which are stuffed in some corner."

"I have no savings but my acting and my dance, all my profits being in the hands of friend Croquoison, who is my banker, although he denies it. May I die a cruel death if I don't return in the end to the place where I was born!"

"In the company of our Bohemians, roosting on the ground and beneath the sky, telling fortunes, dancing sarabands and living at society's expense! I'll no longer suffer the bitter hunger that I endue in this jail."

"That hunger importunes me, my darling, and I put it at the service of whoever wants to feed it. Have you thought that, with famine coming, bread will be sold for its weight in gold, and that I won't make a sou or a stitch from the plague?"

"So we need to leave, without waiting for all those evils to combine, and take away the booty of our thirteen years; we'll go to the German lands, Macabre, among our ancient relatives, beneath our tribal tents."

"Wife, wife, there's no urgency, and there'll still be time next month—so go and traffic with the Lombards, and extract our profits, while I go make the dead dance. Destiny will return us to Bohemia one day!"

Giborne, who felt a furious hunger baying in her guts, looked round for any fragments of supper that might have escaped her voracity and Macabre's parsimony, but she only collected a few crumbs from the stone table, whose original usage was recalled by a Gothic inscription. She grumbled, while clicking her jaws, and, having loaded the enormous package of horribly fetid linen on to her shoulder, she sullenly followed the Bohemian, who walked ahead of her, holding up the lamp. She did not listen to the recommendations to commercial prudence that her husband addressed to her, with a litany of God-protects for the honest Seigneur Croquoison.

She went out of the *petit guifs* cautiously and slipped under the charnel-houses to the Porte de la Ferronnerie, which she opened quietly and did not close behind her, with the intention of returning soon by the same route. She traversed the Rue Saint-Denis at a run, where no lights were shining and no sound could be heard, and knocked three times on the shutters of the Boîte-aux-Lombards, repeating the password *Maschuah*, which signifies Messiah.

There was a silence of hesitation inside, and then Giborne was introduced, with her baggage. Culdoë, Nathan and Croquoison were already assembled, the first plunged in the meditation of a Jewish grimoire, the other two conjecturing in whispers as to the probability of the still-secret vow.

"Prophet Elijah said me!" said Culdoë, hammering his forehead with his fist. "Where shall I find a woman who'll second he sacrifice at this hour? For the mystery can't be accomplished without a feminine intermediary, and the Lord, for want of that, won't find my vow agreeable. It's written that the daughter of Eve represents the sin that reigns over the world, and the expiation invoked from on high. Some old woman is necessary by way of a scapegoat."

"Yes, indeed, my daughter," said Croquoison, relieving Giborne of her burden, "our cemetery is fertile, the harvest abundant! It would certainly be impertinent to allow so many yards of good cloth rot in the ground with neither use nor profit. The dead are not unemployed, and I admire the way that Macabre, working alone, undoes every night the work of every day. Is his rebec not a fairy that works harder than twenty human gravediggers?"

"That poor old man," the Bohemian woman replied, "is broken by age and toil; he'll soon be quitting the trade and the city; that's why he's counting to you to return to him the treasures put in your safe-keeping, Messire."

"What's this talk of treasures?" Holopherne replied, mechanically, surprised as well as tempted by the word. "Yes, daughter, I do suspect my friend Macabre of possessing a considerable hoard, but I haven't seen the shadow of it."

"Ha! I doubted that the deposit had been committed to you, Messire, and suspected that the villain Macabre was fobbing me off with that pretence. It's possible that he's buried his money; may it please fate that he extracts it from the sepulcher and resuscitates it!"

"Friend," said Nathan to Croquoison, after having examined, felt and sniffed the linen, "these drapes aren't worth six écus, because of the plague, and from now on I wouldn't touch them with a fingertip for a ton of gold, by Moses!"

"Come on, Messire," Giborne retorted. "Give me ten francs, or Macabre will think I've stolen his profits. As for the future, I renounce this perilous merchandise, and don't want to catch the plague for so little."

"Yes, indeed, Jeremiah," said Croquoison, holding his nose and taking a step back. "She's right—the plague's lurking in these winding-sheets, which it would be as well to douse in vinegar, for fear of deadly exhalations. Master Culdoë has got us stuck in a stupid business; all the linen of the dead is of mediocre interest by comparison with life, not to mention health, so Macabre can sell these rags and their contagion elsewhere."

"You're overreacting," Nathan said. "Once these pickings are washed and purified, I'll gladly make them into shirts, handkerchiefs and napkins, since Culdoë's vow will protect us against the malady."

"Give me what I need to eat, please," cried Giborne, her tongue hanging out like that of a dog extenuated by heat. "I have Saint Anthony's Fire in my stomach and my teeth are rabid."

"It's a good angel that sent you to us," said Balthazar, who had been agreeably astonished by the shrill sound of Giborne's voice in the midst of his Hebrew reading. "Come with me, woman, so that I can talk to you in private."

He got up from his chair and led her to the room on the first floor, where the plaints of the child were audible at intervals, coming from the top of the house. He sat Giborne down at a table, on which he silently set out bread, salt and roast lamb. The Bohemian woman did not wait for a invitation to do honor to that improvised repast; she paraded her avid eyes and hands over everything she could grab, and allowed the morsels indiscriminately, cramming them into her capacious mouth with a whistling aspiration similar to the sound of a pump in motion.

"My daughter," Culdoë aid to her, with a pensive gravity, "I've heard it said that you're an Egyptian, hence knowing neither God nor law; that's why I implore you to serve me in my religion, and to play the role that I shall teach you."

"Gladly," said Giborne, her mouth and hands full. "I remember having rendered the same office to the Christians during the procession in expiation of the plague in the year 1434, when I went naked and disheveled, following the Holy Sacrament."

"It's not a matter of such villainies, but of a vow I made to the God of Israel for the joy of the rediscovery of my son and the glory of the Jewish nation; you shall have rich recompense for holding the bowels into which the blood will poor..."

"The blood of an ox or a lamb, for you use no others in Jewry, being scornful of the flesh of swine? By the waning of the moon, it pleases me to celebrate Easter with you, and to seat myself at your table with a gallant appetite."

"No, my daughter; in accordance with the fashion of true servants of Moses, we must, on this night of the passion of Jesus, the false prophets of the Gentiles, martyr a little child as an excellent offering to heaven."

"Indeed, Messire," replied Giborne, unmoved. "The sorcerers and divineresses of Bohemia are accustomed to similar spells, and with the blood of a newborn one can cure all sorts of evils, including dysentery."

"I'm aware of its inestimable effects, principally in the ancient custom of circumcision, but I intend to offer it to heaven, as an exceedingly propitious holocaust, which will attract divine benefits to our lives and fortunes."

"The infant that I delivered to you yesterday as the price of the accoutrements for the dance was required for that objective? I'll help you as best I can, and ask no other recompense than a daily ration of meat and bread."

Master Culdoë, in whom religious fanaticism silenced hereditary avarice, did not limit himself to promising Giborne the ration of provender she was claiming in anticipation of the famine, but also handed her a sum of six gold crowns, worth twelve livres, which she was careful to separate from the price of the linen, and gave her technical instructions regarding the nature of the services that he required of her.

Giborne listened meekly, without permitting idle reflections to interrupt the copious feast by means of which she was taking precautions against present and future hunger.

Culdoë warned her to leave their two accomplices in ignorance of the project that completed setting out, and decided to go to the cemetery alone to begin with, where Giborne would join him as midnight chimed, along with Nathan and Croquoison.

Macabre did not wait for his wife's return to commence the night's hard labor; he deployed an extraordinary vigor in reopening the grave of the Sire de la Vodrière, who had been buried separately and rather deeply, by reason of his nobility; a pole, surmounted by a placard, indicated the place that the funerary monument was to occupy.

The night was as glacial as the day had been hot and suffocating; the large and reddish moon rose slowly into the dark azure of the sky, and, like a sepulchral lamp, illuminated the cemetery with a vaporous clarity that seemed to rise from the earth.[22] Macabre worked with ardor, thinking about the jewels, rings and amulets that the dead of quality often carried into their last refuge; he murmured a monotonous song in the barbarous Bohemian idiom, and furnished an exclamation of his cracked voice to every thrust of the spade with which he beat time.

He leapt into the hole to remove the freshly-shifted earth, and the coffin groaned beneath his weight; he had soon hoisted it out of the grave by means of a stout rope, and used pincers to wrench away the lid, the nails of which were scratching the cheeks of the deceased enveloped in the wrappings of death.

The pain of that slight wound, and the cold of the night, shook off the lethargy of the Sire de la Vodrière, who suddenly began to live again; he did not wake up as yet, but his congealed blood warmed up and caused this arteries to throb; his heart, in which he life as concentrated, vibrated at unequal intervals; a warm moisture circulated through all his limbs, and an indecisive respiration was exhaled between his

---

[22] Unlike the actual moon, the literary moon is a narrative device and convenience; although the actual moon could not contrive to be shining at midnight the day after eclipsing the sun in the early afternoon, the literary moon has no difficulty at all.

clenched teeth. He had no organic faculty; he was still lying inert, afflicted by atony.

Macabre leaned over the open coffin and felt breath on his cheek; he thought that the breeze was warming up as skimming the ground; weakening the sounds of his strident voice, he set about lifting the dead man out of his narrow bed, and laying him down, quite stiff, on the bare ground, in order more easily to strip away the winding-cloth, whose quality he had verified with the attention of a connoisseur.

He undid the first knots of the strips wound around the legs, and unfolded the sheet wound several times around the body, but his hand, placed on the cadaver's breast, shivered on finding an interior heat there. He stepped backwards, and fell into the ditch, with that earth, mingled with bones, that rained down on top of him.

Fear penetrated his mind, previously inaccessible to the superstitions of the people and the terrors of the tomb; he imagined that the spirits of the dead that he had troubled in their repose were coming to attack him and bury him alive; he uttered stifled plaints, writhed convulsively, making his bony carcass creak, as if to deliver himself from an invisible constraint.

He succeeded in getting up, and, more reassured, launched himself out of the sepulcher in which he had feared being buried. An incorrigible habit had immediately taken him back to the dead man, who turned large bright and staring eyes toward him.

Horror took possession of Macabre, who gazed without seeing. He almost fell backwards into the grave again, dragging the corpse of the Sire de la Vodrière with him, along with the winding-sheet, which he ripped with the convulsive clutch of his fingers.

He screeched like a barn-owl and fled precipitately, looking back to make sure that the dead man was not following him, and mistaking for phantoms the crosses with which he collided and the high tombs reflecting the moonlight. He did not draw breath until he reached the threshold of the tower and crawled into the shadow of his cellar.

"By the soul of the sun!" he said, extending his arms to ward off the frightful illusion that was obsessing him. "It's a presage of death, the dead returning from the sepulcher! I'll surely never see again the Bohemian land where I was born!"

The Sire de la Vodrière, gradually recalled to life by contact with the damp earth and the ventilations of the air, stirred gently, without changing his location or his posture; he loosened the bonds of the shroud, stretched out the arms that had been folded over his breast, separated his bruised legs, which had been stuck together and raised his head. Then, weakly, he let it fall back against the edge of the coffin. He propped himself up on his elbow, however, and that natural position determined the flow of his blood; the perception of objects returned, still feeble and confused, before memory; he could not take account of the circumstances that had brought him to this place and in that condition.

He remembered having been asleep for a long time, but he did not recognize the cemetery. When he stood up, however, his limbs covered with cold sweat and subject to strange frissons, he was frightened by the darkness and silence that reigned everywhere. He looked around for his wife and son; he brought together the trailing ends of the shroud to protect him from the cold that was congealing the marrow in his bones, and wandered sadly among the tombs.

The thought of his wife became more lucid and more dolorous; he ran under the charnel-houses, beating the walls with his blue fists, trying to get out of that funereal enclosure.

The Porte de la Ferronnerie, still open, let him out into the street, a pale, haggard, disheveled specter shivering in his winding-sheet.

172

XIII. The Dead Alive and the Living Dead

The Hôtel de la Trimouille, was black and silent, except that in the facade on the Rue des Bourdonnais, a ground floor room was projecting a few rays of light outside, through the cracks in the shutters, and the occasional sound of voices. That was Guillemette and the leper, whose had been celebrating the funeral feast since morning.

A massive table watered with wine and hippocras, supported twenty bottles, the majority of which were empty and all were uncorked. A half-eaten ham, torn-up joints of meat, sausages with neither heads nor tails, half-consumed pâtés, breadcrumbs, spilled salt, broken glassware and plates: such was the accusing evidence of an uninterrupted orgy, ongoing after numerous interruptions for love and chat. The debris of a bench attested to the fervor of the combat, like a horse slain beneath a warrior. Those magnificent libations, in honor of Venus, Bacchus and the deceased, had not yet closed the eyes and mouths of the indomitable couple, possessed by a generous emulation; they were seated side by side, eating from the same bowl, and drinking from the same cup.

Guillemette, her elbows on the tablecloth, her skirt tucked up above the knee, her hair undone and hanging down, her robe negligently agape, all her garments dirty, torn and in disarray, was considering her leper with a rubicund expression of happiness, and irritating him playfully with frequent digs in the ribs. The latter, grave and impassive, no less dirty and even more indecently abandoned in his dress, only paused in his swigging in order to listen to the sighs of Aeolus imprisoned in his belly and to scratch the irritated swelling of his legs. He had bravely sustained the reputation of white lepers, proven by authentic examples.

"Damn!" cried Guillemette, swallowing a fistful of tripe. "It seems to me that you're rejuvenated in age and body, my dear dumpling; you weren't so green, hard and warm in the old days, back in 1415 of ugly memory."

"It seems to me, similarly," said Malaquet, without taking his glass away from his lips, "that you believe in fun and frolics, as in your youth. Has Malaquet a more ardent thirst than little Crespeau?"

"Be careful, my dear friend, of pronouncing the wretched name of Crespeau, which announces woes to come in recalling those of the past. Let's drown Crespeau in this jar of fortunate pickled herring that is open before us."

"All right, my good lady of the bottling-plant. I have no remorse for the deeds and actions of the said Crespeau, a joyous and gallant companion in love and drinking. Brrr! Do you remember our youth fondly?"

"Yes, very—you were the handsomest and most vigorous of tricksters, as I was the most amorous of twenty-year old madwomen. Do you also remember your sacrilege and your condemnation to be hanged?"

"Brr, I'll remember it all the way to the other life, and I'll drink to the health of the judge who condemned me and the executioner who would have made me dance on the gibbet. Brrr! May the great devil render them as much and more."

"Damnation! I fear being damned with you, who have persevered in your sin—for during twenty-three years of pilgrimage in the provinces of France and Germany, you haven't done penance in masses sung and candles lit. Nevertheless, you've earned pardons by your voyage to Rome, and if you'd pushed on as far as the Holy Land, the profanation of the vessels of Saint-Josse would have been redeemed. Kiss me, you impious Saracen!"

"O marvelous windfall! I'll tell you a tale, my fine leperess: as soon as the Jew Schoeffer was led through the streets with blows of the whip, I went to mock him and invited him to patience and humility, crying at his cries and grimacing at his grimaces; afterwards, I accompanied with my rattle the pillage of his house by Madame Isabeau's lackeys and pages;

the Rue des Précheurs was sacked as if by the English or cut-throats..."

"Oh, precious work, corrupter of all wealth! By the fact of denunciation to the law, half of the goods confiscated from the poor Jew belonged to you by custom, and so the lackeys ruined your profits."

"Brrr! Enjoyment is worth as much as wealth, and I would want to be a hair's-breadth wiser as the price of recovering my ears. I'm well revenged on that money-lender, who poured scorn on my estate without paying an obol. Brrr! The pillory was a harsh armful, and I wash my throat when I think that the wife and children of that villain Schoeffer perished in that riot. For myself, I got no booty but the holy vessels of the church of Saint-Josse, which the irreverent Jew was holding in pawn, and the said gold vessels, which I put in the kitchen, out of hatred of the curé of Saint-Josse, served me as a pisspot after drinking. Brrr! I'll wager they didn't become lepers, those honest vessels!"

"Blasphemer! Divine thunder will choke you in the form of a tankard or a ham. Faith! It's gambling everything against nothing, and the outcome of those profanations was your judgment, your flight, the loss of your ears and all the rest!"

"Brrr! During that long exile, I didn't once repent of the sacrilege, which caused me no grief or heartache, and I'd treat the vessels of Notre-Dame likewise for the honor of the juice of the vine. Brrr! I'm changing into a barrel."

"I'll wager my share of paradise that you'll die hard in punishment and go to the leprosarium of Hell. Envious wretch, why couldn't the price of that treason enliven our amours and license our marriage instead?"

"Bah! The invention pleased me, and I wanted to do it. Dry up, in the Devil's name—we'll have enough to go on the spree, Guillemette, for the Jew Schoeffer has come back expressly to pay the expenses of the party."

"Schoeffer who was Christianly whipped and banished? Does he still have houses, property, rents, pledges, merchandise and a pile of cash?"

"As much and more than ever. I recognized him by his attitude, six days ago, when he was passing through the cemetery. I shouted to him to give me alms, which he did, out of dread. Brrr! Schoeffer is now Culdoë.

"Balthazar Culdoë, master of the Boîte-aux-Lombards? We're well off, my dear Malaquet; let's try to sell the bearskin a little more dearly this time—and I'll be the one to denounce the abominable Jew."

"Assuredly, I've no wish to stir up trouble; the pickings will be very pleasant, my wife-to-be; nevertheless, I intend to share the confiscation with my dear son Benjamin, whom I love more than anyone for his honesty and kindness."

Guillemette consented, while jibbing sat the abandonment of a part of her dowry, and promised herself secretly not to admit Benjamin to the division of the spoils. Malaquet's confidence had been followed by expansions of tenderness and accolades, which the fiancée disputed with the bottled; she accompanied her indefatigable swilling with regrets and condolences regarding the de la Vodrière family; the leper provided a chorus by praising the deceased's cellar and kitchen.

They encouraged one another mutually to continue the demolition of the dishes and bottles; neither perceived that their reason was not longer afloat on the floods of sugared and spiced wine. Malaquet tried to dance to the sound of his rattle, and slid under the table, which he tipped over as he fell, with the remains of the supper. Guillemette attempted to lift him up and fell heavily on top of him, the table, the bottles and the food.

The hideous lovers, illuminated by a wax candle that was burning in an iron candlestick, clutched at one another like spiders, interlacing like serpents, wallowing in a sticky mess strewn with shards; filthy with wine and sauce, infected with grease and the most odious spillage of their intemperance, they were choking on amour, drunkenness and slumber, licking the floor coated with a gastronomic slime, chewing fragments of pottery, biting, scratching and pinching one another; they were howling, laughing and clucking; one might have thought that they were some two-headed monster, bristling with hands and feet.

Someone knocked loudly on the door to the street.

"Saintly Lover!" murmured Guillemette, huddling against the leper. "Here comes Satanas, who's heard your blasphemies, and will give you bitter remembrance of the vessels of Saint-Josse!"

"Brrr!" said Malaquet, standing up anxiously. "It's the men of the watch, come to find out who's making this undue racket. We mustn't open up to the spoilsports, who'll take us to the cells in the Châtelet."

"Quinsy take them by the throat! The villains will want us to shut up. Thank God! Might it be Madame Jehanne returning home? Did the good lady not perish in the Maundy Thursday crush?"

"Guillemette, take care not to let the night-birds in, and welcome them with a face of wood. Brrr! That racket's going to wake up the quarter, not to mention the dead in the cemetery. If they find me here I'll be fined and thrown out of the city."

"And I'd be declared a leper and quarantined in the hospital. Get out, my friend, without waiting for anyone to catch us. It might be the reverend father in God Thibault, wanting to know whether my poor lady has come back."

"Brrr! If I'm seen leaving the house they'll take me for a thief, and I have no ears to leave in pawn at the pillory. Help me to flee anyway, for the neighbors will be going to their windows and that knocker's ready to break."

"May the good God save my soul! Vile and filthy sacrilege, do you hear that pitiful voice? It's the shade of the late Monseigneur who's reprimanding us for having drunk his wine! Heretic, he'll remind you of the vessels of Saint-Josse in the pit of Hell!"

Guillemette, whose terror was stronger than drunkenness, succeeded in finding her equilibrium on her tottering legs, while Malaquet, who was more preoccupied by the fear of prison than the fear of the dead, made a crutch our of a leg

177

of the shattered table. Forgetting his rattle, his barrel, his cap and some of his garments, he trailed at his mistress's heels as far as the side door to the Rue Tirechape, by which he left, and ran away, hugging the walls in order to support himself as well as to hide in the shadows, while the door to the Rue des Bourdonnais resounded to blows repeated with increasing violence, mingled with cries of fury.

Guillemette invoked the saints and signed herself, advancing and recoiling in her oblique march, listening and shivering. The harsh and cavernous voice that was calling her by name, bore a singular resemblance to that of the late Sire de la Vodrière.

"Bedeviled Guillemette!" said the voice, dying away into confused sounds. "It's me who's come back! Do you want me to die for real this time, of anger, thirst and cold? Oh, the malicious servant! Where, then, is my wife Jehanne?"

"In the name of the divine redeemer who forces demons to flee!" said Guillemette, falling to her knees in the vestibule. "Back, tempter! I'm a repentant sinner, and I count on burning eight one-livre candles for having eaten the flesh and dunk the wine, in spite of the Holy Friday fast! Depart, Messire Satanas, and I'll show you where to find a Jew to torment before he's put to the torture! Oh, don't imitate the voice of the defunct Monseigneur like that!"

"Don't you recognize me, vile witch? Have I caught a cold since yesterday? Isn't Madame Jehanne at home? I swear to God that I'll damn you to all the devils if you leave me to freeze outside my own house!"

That nocturnal racket had spread fear throughout the surrounding area, and the bourgeois, imagining that a gang of thieves was at grips with the men of the watch, were taking refuge in the depths of their beds with their heads under their pillows. The boldest or most curious came to stick their heads against the window-panes and plunged fearful gazes into the dark street, where a white form was moving in front of the Hôtel de la Trimouille. The death of the Sire de la Vodrière gave a formidable character to that apparition, which was playing the role of a soul in torment.

Guillemette persuaded herself that her resistance in keeping the door closed was augmenting the chances of her doom, and that it was necessary to obey the orders of a supernatural being. Her anxiety increased at every bound of the knocker, and every word from the revenant.

Her hands, which had gripped the bolts convulsively, drew them mechanically and turned the key in the lock. At the same time she experienced a redoublement of terror, and wanted to repair her imprudence, but she clung in vain to the wall trying to push back the door that she had opened; her fingernails dug into the stone, and her back received the imprint of the projecting ornaments of the sculpted wood. The door hesitated momentarily, and then, impelled by a superior force, hurled Guillemette to the floor, where she lay extended, shutting her eyes and beating the pavement with her forehead.

She had perceived the bloody and irritated face of her master, who, vaguely outlined in the folds of his floating veil, with his arm upraised, had the appearance of the exterminating angel.

"Miserable doorkeeper!" he cried, in a piercing tone. "Why delay so long in introducing me? Is it because Madame is in bed with some thief? Is it necessary that the gallant makes his escape? Beware of my meeting him!"

"The good God have mercy on me!" muttered Guillemette, who felt the phantom's icy fingers digging into her flesh. "You know full well that my dear lady hasn't come back. Give me time to confess my iniquities."

"Go fetch my sword, so that I can make an opening in your treacherous soul! What! Jehanne has gone? Jehanne has polluted my good name? It's you, dealer in amours, who have conducted this scandal and facilitated the adultery! Damnation!"

"Messire Defunct, I'll be damned like a billhook if you drag me down to Gehenna, for I've eaten flesh and broken the

179

fast on this holy day. Hear, if you will, the litany of my sins against you! Hear me!"

"Speak, cowardly whore—have you not tipped your lady and mistress into the precipice of impurity? On your life, on your salvation, confess your black misdeeds! It's thanks to you that my criminal spouse has broken the sacred sacraments of marriage!"

"Alas, alas, late Monseigneur, I'm unworthy, infamous, imprudent and more than I can say; I have greatly offended your cellar and also your kitchen; the ham reserved for Easter has entered into the dance, and also your best wine."

"It's not a matter of wine or ham, false refiner; I don't care about the cellar or the kitchen; I'll send you to Satan, your master, but first, declare your actions with regard to my wife, and how I was cuckolded."

"Assuredly, most venerable deceased, I shall not deny it in order to have my soul saved, if not my body. I accuse myself before you of my disloyalty in obeying Madame, for whom I served her amours with Benjamin..."

"Benjamin! By the precious blood of Christ! Who is Benjamin? I demand that you discover him to my vengeance; this Benjamin, whoever he is, I intend to fight with any weapons! Oh, I hunger to devour his heart!"

"It was a sin on my part to contrive their meetings and conversation; may the good Lord absolve me for the candles I bought with that ill-gained money! My most excellent lady honored him with great love, and he received hr allegiance at the steam-baths..."

"Am I dead or alive? Is this dream or reality? You're lying, Guillemette, you're mocking in talking in that fashion. The thing is impossible. Oh, you great whore, you sly pander, you can dispatch your last paternosters. It was at the steam-baths, you say?"

"Forgive me, late Messire, Caillebotte alone invented the scheme, and concocted the beverage on the very day when you came, with your sword drawn; I was mortally afraid, and I swore not to aid their dishonest amours any longer. Benjamin hasn't come back here since then."

"Why did I not render my soul to God rather than here this dire mystery? Jehanne has coiffed the conjugal head with horns! No it's an insolent lie. So, who is Benjamin? In what place can he be found? Is he a gentleman?"

"Do you not know all these things in the other world, my good late seigneur? The said Benjamin is the son of friend Croquoison, master of the gravediggers at the Cimetière des Saints-Innocents—he's the one who buried you this morning."

"Living God! This surpasses all mockery! Has this despicable rival attacked my person? Is it true that I was put in the ground? I've lost all remembrance of it. The calumny is far too outrageous. Where's Jehanne? Hurry up and fetch her."

"Don't order me to do what is beyond human power, my charitable late seigneur; you can't be unaware that Madame disappeared in the crush at the *danse macabre*, and has doubtless perished like so many poor people, whom God will pardon!"

"Jehanne is not in the house? Are you trying to get rid of me? Lord God, spare me this anguish! Jehanne, my good wife, my sweet spouse! The crowd stifled her in spite of my efforts! She's dead and entombed!"

"I haven't omitted anything in my confession, most compassionate defunct, so go away, and only tell me how many masses and memorial services are necessary to complete your purgatory. I promise you forceful prayers, if Madame and her child are not resuscitated to acquit my debt in your memory. By my fig! I forgot my greatest remorse: it was negligence and not perverse intention, when your little son was seized and carried off by the Bohemian woman."

"Rescue me with a lightning-bolt, sovereign Savior! What! My dear son is similarly implicated in my evil fate? That tender infant has not survived his mother? How is it that I have issued from the sepulcher to which those two deceased are recalling me? Jehanne dead or stolen, the child stolen or dead! My nobility and my fortune to whomsoever can restore them to me! I'll absolve the infidelity of the one and love her as before! Unlucky spouse and desolate father! Adieu to everything!"

The Sire de la Vodrière, whose mental weakness had succumbed to the reiterated shock of so many dolors, did not pronounce another word, and went to sit down in the courtyard on a stone pedestal, where he remained, cold and motionless, unseeing and unthinking, deprived of sentiment, already as if dead. His fixed and dull eyes were unable to find a tear; his hands were stiff, trying to tear his heart from his bloody breast; the whiteness of the moon surrounded him with a fearful prestige, although the crow of the cock, at midnight, did not make him disappear after the fashion of specters.

Guillemette, who had buried her master herself, and who had seen him descend into the grave, was too ignorant and too superstitious to attribute his return to a natural cause, to a extraordinary hazard; she recognized the voice and the features of the Sire de la Vodrière, but she convinced herself that she had nothing but a shade before her eyes, and was astonished that prayers were impotent to chase it away.

Eventually, she familiarized herself with the object of her terror to the point of considering him from afar; finally, she went back into the ground-floor room, where the light had soon reassured herm once she had subjected the inside door to a solid barricade.

She continued listening, and the effect of the wine, suspended by that of fear, reacted spontaneously again on all her senses at once; she curled up in a corner in order to sleep.

Malaquet, whose anxiety had not passed the threshold of the house, regretted the sleep that he had commenced, and searched for a dung-heap in order to make a soft pillow of it. He embraced the boundary-markers and muttered an unintelligible monologue; the only memory he retained related to the police ordinances that forbade lepers to sleep in the city on pain of exile and a fine.

He struggled with a heavy and blind drunkenness; he walked in a zigzag, in surges and stumbles. The noise that he could still hear in the Rue des Bourdonnais invited him to go away, and having beaten the walls of the Rues de la Chausseterie and de la Ferronnerie, he found himself opposite the open gate of the cemetery, into which he entered, staggering.

The impression of the cool air that had woken him up momentarily was no longer shaking the Bacchic torpor with which his mind was impregnated; he was losing the remainder of his strength with every step; the ground was lurching under him, the charnel-houses were spinning, the houses could no longer maintain the equilibrium that he lacked. He collided with an object that he encountered in his path; it was the Sire de la Vodrière's empty coffin.

May I be a leper to the tip of my nose," he said, falling down on the edge of the grave, "if it isn't a wolf-trap! Brrr! I'll have a charnel-house and a leprosarium built with my friend Schoeffer Culdoë's deniers. To drink in the vessels of Saint-Josse! Brrr! Who's cut off my ears? They'll grow back in their own time, like the buds of the vine. Benjamin, he holds lepers in high esteem and cherishes them! Culdoë, he does wrong in scorning and molesting them! Brr! I could drink the Seine if it were made of wine! Guillemette, come here that I might kiss you! O soft couchette! Brrr! I was one of a band of cut-throats, and never cut anything but purses. At daybreak tomorrow, the Lombard will be seized by the law, and I'll sound the rattle at his execution. Brrr!"

For want of saliva and breath, the leper left increasingly long intervals between each phrase as the influence of the orgy became more imperious; he had been asleep for some time while still dreaming aloud.

Midnight had not chimed when Balthazar Culdoë emerged from the Boîte-aux-Lombards alone, carrying a burden under which his old age bent: a cross of blackened wood, a covered basket, from which veiled plaints escaped, a thick book and a sealed box. He walked warily, interrogating the surroundings, with were profoundly calm, with a piercing eye.

He was surprised, on arriving at the Porte de la Ferronnerie, to find it wide open. He waited, listening attentively, before venturing into the cemetery, which was entirely illuminated by the moon; hearing no alarming sound, however, he hastened to go in, closing the gate quietly behind him.

He went straight to the tomb of Saint Richard, a monument of coarse stone three feet high facing the church, under which the infant martyr, crucified by the Jews at Pontoise, in a street that retains their name, had originally been buried. He deposited what he had brought on the slab of the tomb and began by setting up the cross against one of the sides of the monument—which, since the establishment of the church, no longer contained the relics of St. Richard.

He was interrupted in his precipitate work by a human groan coming from a short distance away, repeated several times. He thought about running away, and recommended his soul to the god of the Jews. The distinct pronunciation of his name filled him with horror, though, and he almost repented of his vow, which was inverting the laws of nature by giving speech to the dead. The breeze was brushing his contracted features like the breath of an invisible spirit.

Confidence returned with the silence in the air. Then he perceived, in the moonlight, a man or a cadaver lying next to a coffin and a grave. He shivered, wondering whether he ought to move closer, but the thought that the man might get to his feet stopped him. Tales of corpses miraculously expelled from holy ground because of their state of damnation were so widespread that he adopted that supposition to be begin with, but after a thousand detours and hesitations, he moved close enough to distinguish the supposed dead man and recognized the sleeping Malaquet.

A somber joy lit up in his gaze, and caused his entire body to thrill.

God of Israel, he thought, delighted by the contemplation of his enemy in his power, *it's you who are delivering him to me! He's worth a hundred extraordinary torments. Because of him I was whipped and banished; because of him I lost my wife, my children and my possessions. I take Heaven as my witness that I had done him no harm, It's possible that he'll betray me tomorrow and ruin me for a second time. Should I grant him mercy? Should I prevent him from ruining me again? It's only the blood of a Christian.*

"Brrr!" said Malaquet, ruminating his plans and his hopes in a dream. "That Israelite dog doesn't work on the Sabbath. His name is Schoeffer and he was banished in perpetuity. Brrr! Benjamin, my beadle, here's your share of the booty."

Master Culdoë, possessed by a horrible inspiration, smiled bitterly at those words, which revealed the leper's perfidy. He unsheathed a cutlass that he had in his belt and directed its point toward Malaquet's breast—but he suddenly changed his mind, on noticing the grave and the bier.

He smiled more frightfully, examining the sleeper's crimson and blissful face. Then he seized him by the feet and drew him into the coffin, the lid of which he subsequently replaced on top of the unfortunate drunkard. His heart leapt with vindictive satisfaction with every blow of the hammer.

When the coffin was nailed shut, he tipped it into the grave, which he filled with earth, indifferent to the muffled sounds of a voice that was repeating his name. Malaquet had not ceased his slumber and his happy dreams.

"Will you wake up now?" said Culdoë, joyfully trampling down the filled-in grave. "Crespeau, envious and hard-drinking leper, go tell the judges of the parliament that it's Schoeffer the Jews who has buried you alive!"

XIV. The Crime of Pingres

Having satisfied his vengeance as well as his assuring personal safety by means of an atrocious crime, Balthazar Culdoë knelt down on the grave that enclosed a living being, and thanked the God of Israel for having given him victory over his enemies.

After giving thanks, he continued the preparations for the sacrifice that he believed to be agreeable to his God. The cross having been solidly erected, he took from the basket a little child, entirely naked, his mouth gagged by a handkerchief to muffle his cries. He attached that innocent victim to the wood of the cross, suspending him there by the arms, tied with strong cords that bruised the flesh and bent the bones. The child, exhausted by hunger and pain, struggled weakly and let his head fall forwards; he implored his mother from the depths of his soul.

Culdoë covered him with a red veil and deposited the instruments of torture on the tomb: a circumcision knife, glass bowls, pincers, long fish-bones and long needles known as *pingres*, a word derived from the Latin *spina*, which etymologists would have explained be recalling that parliament had condemned to death, for the crime of *pingres* or *épingles*, several Jews who had crucified Christian children on the night of Good Friday, an act of religious fanaticism quite frequent in the Middle Ages, especially in Germany.[23]

---

[23] This tongue-in-cheek explanation excuses a scabrous item of wordplay. The French noun or adjective *pingre* now means "miser" or "miserly," so the phrase cited here and employed as the chapter title translates into modern French as "the misers' crime." *Épingle* means "pin." The account of the crucifixion of St. Richard of Pontoise on Good Friday 1163 apparently originates from annals compiled by a canon at Cambrai named Lambert of Waterloo, although it is also mentioned by two

Culdoë had scarcely terminated these sanguinary preparations than Jeremiah Nathan and Giborne were introduced into the cemetery by the master of the place, Holopherne Croquoison, who would rather have been asleep in his dwelling. Midnight was chiming in the churches, and the convents were waking up to the bell for matins. The three newcomers approached the tomb of Saint Richard, where only Giborne was neither surprised nor moved by the spectacle, which she had expected to find.

Nathan put his hands over his eyes in order not to see, for that scarlet drapery seemed to be moving like a bloody specter, and was rendering vague sounds. Croquoison made the sign of the cross in his initial alarm and reached for his rosary. Culdoë, his gaze inflamed and his hair unkempt, ordered him solemnly to stay, and constrained him to do so by force.

Indifferent and mute, Giborne had already picked up two vessels, which she held out, like a woman habituated to that cruel office. The child writhed more desperately, and his lamentations became more distinct.

Culdoë began to speak in a prophetic accent; the spirit of the abyss possessed him. "Know the mystery, sons of Abraham and brothers in Moses! When the false messiah, Jesus, was judged in Jerusalem by our priests, the Jewish people willed that the blood of that impostor should fall back on our posterity. In consequence, the Lord, to test us, has permitted us to be banished, persecuted, hated, pillages and put to death..."

"Yes indeed," said Croquoison, not reassured by this commencement. "It seems to me that a similar fate is destined for us if we're discovered in this sacred place, practicing diabolical magic."

---

other near-contemporary chroniclers; the scurrilous story appears to have spread rapidly, and encouraged further allegations of the same kind, some referring retrospectively to earlier supposed events.

"Patience," said Nathan, who saw nothing suspect in Culdoë's exordium. "Let us discover what our vow might bring; it is possible that the Great Work demands such singular dispositions."

"My friends," Culdoë continued, becoming gradually more animated, "the veritable Messiah is imminent, and his coming will put a stop to the iniquitous treatment of the Jewish nation by the Christians. While awaiting that happy time predicted by the prophets, it is good to acquire the Lord's grace for oneself and one's family. So, in accordance with the ancient Hebraic custom, I have vowed the blood of a Christian child to celebrate the Passover, and I have summoned you because of your faith in our glorious religion, you who have sworn my vow above the book of the Torah."

"Come on, my Master," exclaimed Croquoison, trying to get away, "you can't be serious. Crucify a child! Do you want to be boiled or burned? I have no such desire."

"Hold on, friend," replied Nathan, with a grimace of disappointment. "It was a matter of a hidden treasure, it seems to me, if not of gold, to be opened up; will good Christian blood fill our money-bags?"

"You will remain here until the accomplishment of your vow," Culdoë retorted, in a tone of irresistible authority. "Otherwise, I'll denounce you as my accomplices if I'm held to account by the law. Is it not better, friends, to play your part in the enterprise? Beneath this tomb a child was once interred that the Jews of Pontoise had bled in this fashion in their paschal ceremonies; the altar will thus be more pleasing to our God."

"Truly," said Nathan, rallying to the example of his associate, who seemed to be in ecstasy, "the blood of a Christian immolated as a sacrifice is appropriate to various usages, according to the opinion of the rabbis; it cures dysentery in men and women, scars the wound of circumcision, increases amity between those who mingle it with their food, and serves as a marvelous leaven for the bread of the Passover, as well as a thousand graces on high."

"By the sacrifice of Abraham," said Culdoë, arming himself with the cutlass, "the blood that will flow in memory of the passion of the false king of the Jews will produce the inestimable benefit of causing the sovereign Creator and the angels to rejoice."

"But the enterprise is extremely imprudent," Croquoison interjected, looking around and listening to see whether anyone might be coming to arrest them. "If anyone sees us from the nearby houses, we'll be punished by iron and fire soon afterwards."

"Friend, have complete confidence in the spirit that possesses me," said Culdoë, distributing the *pingres*; this rite is often carried out in subterranean places, but out of scorn for the Christians I have chosen this tomb, of which no stone will remain on top of another at the coming of the Messiah. I only command you not to waste any of the blood, to imitate the punctures that I shall make, and to second my prayers. Giborne, collected the celestial manna. Death to Christ!"

Culdoë, who was directing that refined murder, slowly drove the *pingres* into the legs of the infant, whom the pain cause to writhe in frightful convulsions, and the Bohemian woman received in the vessels the blood that spurted from the wounds.

Nathan was immediately fanaticized by the sight of the blood to which Jews then attached a miraculous virtue, and he plunged several *pingres* into the victim's arms, who uttered inarticulate plaints. Only Croquoison, who did not have any hateful ferocity toward the Christians, with whom he lived voluntarily, turned his eyes away in silence, unable to dissimulate the horror that the torture caused him.

Giborne carried out her task with an inflexible exactitude. The child's body, pierced by the fish-bones and pins driven into his flesh, was drained of his blood and his life while Culdoë murmured a monotonous chant, which Nathan accompanied with fervor.

At the moment when Culdoë cut the infant's sexual parts with his cutlass, however, the later, by virtue of a supreme

189

effort of anguish, detached the handkerchief that was gagging his mouth, and called for his mother with terrible howls, that were s far beyond his age as the torture was above his strength.

At these vociferations, which the calm of the night rendered more resounding, Giborne upset one of the vessels of blood, and ran away toward the Tour de Notre-Dame-du-Bois to seek shelter there.

"By the shade of Samuel!" cried Culdoë, tearing at his hair. "The mystery is not proceeding in accordance with the ancient rites! That impertinent witch has fled at the propitious moment—and without returning the money, the villainess!"

"By Notre-Dame!" Croquoison interjected, beside himself. "Are you going to let the treacherous infant scream like that, so that he can wake up the quarter? By the tribe of Levi, is it to please God that we'll be tortured?"

"Omnipotent Lord, who caused the race of Abraham and Jacob to triumph," Culdoë went on, steeping his lips in the warm blood, "accept from my hands this dear offering, for which you have returned my son Benjamin to me!"

Master Croquoison did not share the religious exaltation of the two Lombards, who were prostrated face downwards; transported with rage and terror, he did not wait for those frightful screams to be extinguished with the life of the victim. He fully understood the danger of his situation, and cursed the trap into which he had fallen by virtue of a excess of trust. His character, naturally mild and good, hardened at the idea of the punishment that he was imprudently risking, but he took possession of the bloody cutlass, and, closing his eyes, all his limbs stiff with horror, he plunged it into the infant's heart.

The child uttered a feeble sigh, let his head fell loll forwards, and cried no more.

Meanwhile, Jehanne de la Vodrière was lying in the Loge-aux-Fossoyeurs, sick with a delirious fever.

Benjamin, not finding her there on his return from the inhumation that he had completed reluctantly on learning the name of the deceased, had immediately gone up into the char-nel-houses, where he had found his lover lying on a bed of bones, and transported her, unconscious and badly bruised by her fall, into the hideous cellar that had been witness to their happiness.

He warmed her up with his kisses, and set her down, still unconscious, on the couch that was still warm from their love-making. He covered her with caresses and tears; he thought that she was dead, but joy returned to him at the same time as sentiment to her; he was on his knees beside her bed when she woke up, uttering a shrill screech in memory of her recent misfortune; then she wept abundantly, without making any response to Benjamin's futile consolations.

Once, she pushed away the gravedigger's hands in dis-gust; the ardent fever that had set her head ablaze had almost robbed her of her reason. She demanded to see her husband and her son; she hid herself in her lover's arms to avoid a na-ked sword that she saw gleaming over her bosom; she mut-tered prayers for the dying and the dead; she wanted to get up and go back to her house; she re-envisioned the scene in the steam-baths and became terrified by a past peril that could not be renewed henceforth; she made her confession through sobs of repentance; she imagined hearing the holy words of Père Thibault; she passed from despair to hope, and from tears to smiles; she cradled her infant in her arms, presented her teat to him, and gazed at him fondly, the poor thing!

Benjamin dared not summon a physician or a barber, who might rob him of the enjoyment of his possession by an indiscretion, and perhaps expose him to judiciary pursuit for the crime of rape. He took advantage of a momentary lapse, which rendered Jehanne torpid, to run to Master Moutard, the grocer-apothecary, and buy various juleps that he sold for us-age against the plague.

Those innocent preparations procured the invalid a tran-quil and reparative slumber, during which Benjamin, leaning on the edge of the bed, did not quit her with his eyes or his thoughts. When she awoke, however, the redoubled fever was accompanied with vertigo and raving madness, with intervals of lucid melancholy.

"My excellent friend," she said to Benjamin, in one of those physical abatements in which mentality acquire the upper hand, "I do not regret having loved you, and of loving you so much, but why disguise your estate, which I now know?"

"Good and indulgent lady," he replied, kissing her feet in order that she would not perceive his blush, "if you had rejected and scorned me, I would have found remedy for my shame in the river. From now on, I swear to you, I shall not labor in that base profession."

"I shall arrange that, my dear Benjamin, and my gross riches will serve for your usage. No, henceforth, you'll no longer dig graves. Oh, wretch, was it not you who interred that worthy gentleman, my noble lord and husband?"

"Alas, dear Jehanne, set aside that fatal remembrance. It was not me who dug the grave; I merely buried him. Dispel these images of mourning. See our love, so cheerful, so prosperous, so young and so alive! I would not take a Duc's crown in place of your great amity, for you love me with a fine force, as I love you, and will do for so long as my heart has the breath of life. Jehanne, I am more fortunate than the king in his court of barons, since you consent to love my poverty!"

"Messire!" cried Madame de la Vodrière, gripped once more by the delirium of the fever. "Don't kill me, I beg you! Resheathe your menacing sword, and have pity on me. Benjamin, my beloved darling, hasten to depart before my husband sees you, for that jealous villain will not grant you any mercy... Give your plaintive mother a smile, my lovely child... See how nicely he's growing! Who is that dead man they're putting in the ground? Who is that gravedigger?"

Madame de la Vodrière had spent all day in that agitation of body and mind, which nothing could contrive to calm; her husband, her son and her lover were the three objects that represented themselves incessantly, together or by turns, to her wild eyes. The nervous excitation became so violent that she would have smashed her skull against the wall if Benjamin had not retained her in his arms.

The latter, no less pale and distressed, forgot to take any nourishment and maintained an immobile vigil beside his mistress, who often failed to recognize him any longer. The illness became visibly worse as night fell; the crises became more frequent and more prolonged. The fever resolved itself in cold sweats and unbearable hot flushes; it required enormous efforts to keep her in the bed, which groaned at her suppressed bounds.

Benjamin struck his forehead, bit his fists, invoked both the God of the Jews and the God of the Christians, wept, and sobbed, while these distressing symptoms finally reached an unexpected conclusion in a complete torpor, which lasted until the advanced hour when the lamentable cried of the crucified child rose up in the cemetery.

Benjamin, sunk in dolorous contemplation, had paid no heed to the various noises of footsteps and voices that had succeeded one another in the cemetery, but he pricked up his ears at those disquieting screams, to which he would have liked to put a stop at any price, before Jehanne's sleep was interrupted by them—but what he feared occurred almost immediately, while he was blocking the ventilation-shaft with a plank in order to intercept the outbursts from outside.

Jehanne launched herself out of the sheets, damp with sweat, careless of her nudity, her black hair flowing over her white shoulders, her pupils dilated, her hands clasped, her neck stretched, and her body trembling. She listened, hoping that she as dreaming.

"By Heaven, is it my child who is crying in that fashion?" she said, half-suffocated by fright. What is this place? This isn't the Hôtel de la Trimouille! God protect him from all encumbrance, that's the voice of my dear son!"

"Madame, I beg you to be silent," said Benjamin, trying to put her back to bed. Jehanne, there are sorcerers and magicians celebrating their Sabbat in the cemetery, and they'll molest us for spying on them. I don't have the power that's necessary against their spells; I have no weapon against their sticks. My darling, those strange cries derive from their diabolical mysteries!"

"No, assuredly not! Listen! Listen! My poor child is calling for help! I'll go; I want to go! Oh, Messire, someone has hurt him, I imagine. It was his voice that wailed so cruelly. Oh my God! What has happened that he has almost died?"

"I beg you not to make your illness worse, beloved Jehanne! Remain under your coverlet to seat out the fever; don't torment yourself because of those magical cries, which are frequent in this cemetery, where necromancers hold councils."

"You shall not stop me going to see, Messire, for I need to know who is crying thus. I'm half-dead of anguish. Don't delay me anymore, Benjamin; I would feel too poignant a remorse if my child came to any harm for want of help. Let's go!"

"Jehanne, ill as you are, the damp night air will do you grave harm. Stay in bed while I research the origin of those loud cries, which have excited you unnecessarily. I'll return right away to tell you what I find."

Jehanne, whom that sudden impression of fear and anxiety had animated with a false energy, fell back on her couch, weaker than when she had emerged from it, her face colored, her lips tremulous and her eyes bulging. That temporary return of strength was followed by a total exhaustion, of which Benjamin hastened to take advantage in order to stratify the desire that she had expressed so obstinately. He wrapped her up so as to recall the warmth that had immediately left her in the cold temperature; he urged her to calm a frivolous presentiment that he was about to belie; he encouraged her with hisses, and promised her not to be absent any longer than the time necessary to visit the cemetery.

Having armed himself at hazard with a gravedigger's pickaxe, Benjamin slipped silently out of the lodge, and, having distinguished in the moonlight a group of men around Saint Richard's tomb, he marched straight toward them, brandishing his pick. He had so firmly persuaded himself in advance that he would have to deal with sorcerers and their familiar demons that his courage increased on only encountering men.

The latter, absorbed in their criminal occupation, did not perceive the approach of the young man, who, before recognizing them, had the leisure to verify the nature of the gathering. He saw the child suspended from the cross, the vessels of blood, the *pingres* and the bloody cutlass.

He was petrified by horror.

"Infamous murderers!" he cried, his pickaxe raised. "What abomination have you conspired and perpetrated? Are you zingaris, Turks, mages or sorcerers? Expect exemplary punishment, the gibbet or the pyre, cowardly child-killers!"

"Indeed, friends, we ought to be afraid," said Croquoison, who was now battle-hardened, having taken part in the crime. "This tiresome individual is none other than Benjamin, my son—which is to say, yours, Culdoë. It's necessary to associate him with our vow."

"What! Damnation!" said Benjamin, struck with astonishment and indignation. "Is it you, Father, who has just shed this pure blood in a detestable spell? Am I the son of a murderer, then? No, you're not my father..."

"That is the oracle of nature," Culdoë interjected, throwing himself into Benjamin's arms, who pushed him away fervently. "My son, my dear and beloved son, whom I once lost, I am the one who is your only and veritable father!"

"You, my father!" cried Benjamin, with a scornful incredulity that soon gave way to an involuntary respect. "If I'm necessarily your son—God grant that it is not so!—in what place and at what time are you giving me that name?"

"Yes, and you'll pay me the promised ransom, which I have surely earned," Croquoison put in. He was reassured by an affirmative gesture from Culdoë. "Benjamin, I'm not your father, but rather this man, Balthazar Culdoë, a rich Jew, master of the Boîte-aux-Lombards."

"Alas! I disown my life," said Benjamin, sadly. "I would have preferred to be the issue of a paltry and honest laborer. Have you no shame and repentance for this misdeed, worthy of the fire? Who is that child? Is it you who have martyred him?"

"I have glorified myself thereby," replied Culdoë. "Do you observe the Jewish religion? I have offered the Lord this sacrifice in rejoicing at having found you again. Dip your fingertips in this blood in order to share in the offering."

"No, never, by the Arch-Saint! I will not commit such an execrable pact. I suggest that you flee to the most distant land—make haste, Monseigneur, for you will be burned. Oh, what harm you have done to that poor child!"

"Rather ask that we become Christians," Culdoë interjected, bitterly. "Benjamin, my son, the Christians on whom I am avenging myself by the sacrifice of one of their children, persecute, pillage, torture, imprisoned and kill the lineage of Abraham, from which you descend. These Christians, whom I hate as much as they hate me, have beaten me with sticks and banished me from the kingdom; have murdered my wife, your mother, and my children, your brothers; have ruined my former commerce, and will probable resume the same iniquitous vengeance tomorrow. Look at your scarred side, your broken arm, and the traces of blows on your head. Interrogate Croquoison, who picked you up, charitably, on the brink of death. Come on, Benjamin, do not forgive the Christians, who do not forgive us: return war for war, wound for wound. Come to sit by my fire, and prepare the Passover bread..."

Culdoë drew Benjamin away, who, stunned by this unexpected recognition, trembled at the thought of returning to Jehanne's presence, and submitted reluctantly to paternal authority, allowing himself to be taken to the Boîte-aux-Lombards, while Nathan and Croquoison carried the vessels full of blood and the instruments of the sacrifice, without attempting to hide the body of the victim, which they abandoned on the cross.

As they were preparing to close the cemetery gate again, Macabre's rebec vibrated in the air, tormenting it with discordant sounds that expanded thereafter in a funereal melody, at first slow and monotonous, and then varied, rapid and powerful.

"Indeed, friend," said Croquoison, making the sign of the cross out of habit, and fleeing, "that accursed music is the presage of cruel death! Beware!"

XV. The Two Households

Macabre, who, in his initial terror, had hidden in the depths of his cellar, which no noise from outside reached, soon forgot the revenant in favor of his treasure, which he regretted having left alone. He went rapidly up the stairway, forgetting that the entrance to the tower was open, and only felt himself revive in palpating his cherished gold pieces, which he never wearied of stirring voluptuously.

Lying curled up on the damp stones of the platform, he surrendered himself to his bizarre passion, which rejoiced in the susurrus of metal money; he rolled, he writhed, he swooned, and all the while his quivering hands, dipped in the gold, intoxicated his senses with spasmodic pleasure.

After a few hours of delight, which had exhausted his strength and irritated his nerves, he took down his rebec and animated it with the harmonious tickling of the bow; he played a touching and sublime funereal canticle, a kind of solemn and gracious swan song, which descended from the heavens to return there.

Macabre, shivering with a prescient emotion, bathed the enchanted strings of the instrument with tears, which, in his fascinated eyes, returned life to the dead and changed the order of nature.

"When shall I return to the land of Bohemia?" he said, assessing the stars of the night. "Shall I ever have sufficient wealth? Plague and famine are coming, inciting me to flee them. Alas, is it written that I shall not see my companions again, and the cherished land of my birth? Shall I ever rest, save in the tomb? I cannot transport my rich hoard to the abode of the dead. Sing, rebec, sing my departure—tomorrow! But what will become of the dance that I began…?"

The Bohemian, incessantly pursued by a sinister presentiment that turned his thoughts toward Bohemia, set down his rebec and gazed at the cemetery as a laborer gazes at his sown field.

Then he remembered the cadaver that he had seen move and return to life. He accused his mind of vertigo and his eyes of illusion, but he persevered in his belief, against which the proofs of thirteen years rose up in vain; the marvelous offered itself to him for the first time in the death that he had thus far observed in an entirely material form.

He vaguely distinguished a pale object surmounting the tomb of Saint Richard, and a half-naked phantom walking slowly beneath the charnel-houses of the Ferronnerie. He imagined that he recognized the Sire de la Vodrière, and, in order to escape that apparition, which he attributed to the prestige of his music, he hastened to go back down to his underground lair, where his terrors vanished.

Giborne, who was unworried by his absence, renewed every night, had not waited for him to lie down in the coffin, where she was fast asleep, her slumber weighed down by the copious supper she had on her conscience. She was snoring like a grunting pig, sharpening her appetite for the day to come.

Macabre, whose otherworldly reverie was troubled by that snoring, returned immediately to worldly thoughts. He wanted to know the pecuniary result of his wife's commission, and shook her rudely, whereupon she returned to semi-consciousness.

At first she only replied by sonorous yawns and hideous contortions. Impatiently, Macabre poked and prodded that mass of inert and pendulous flesh.

"Wife!" he shouted, in his hoarse voice. "Are the Lombards men of probity and honest commerce? Have you exchanged the dead's linen at Master Croquoison's counter? I'll wager that those Jews have shown themselves Jews thrice over in respect of me? Isn't it so?"

"My gentle seigneur," murmured Giborne, "does it not seem to you that I have acquitted that employment honorably?

I have not dissipated a single drop of blood; perforate the armpits, groin and soles of the feet."

"Are you coming back from a witches' sabbat and feast?" Macabre interjected, demanding a financial response. "Have you swilled wine like a leather bottle? Death of my life! Tell me the result of the bargain, and give me the price of my linen. You can sleep afterwards."

"Is that you, my husband? I feel the blazing amour that solicits me to stick to you; come, my amiable musician, dance the gay confusion! Am I not dainty and pretty? By the Moon! Is there any more sovereign remedy for the plague and hunger than rubbing one's lard?"

"Damn the slut!" replied Macabre, avoiding her caresses. "She's been eating and drinking like a monk! Back, mad cow, avid she-wolf, vile frog! Hurry up and give me the money that you haven't squandered on your wretched drunkenness."

"By the rope that will hang you, cemetery-ragpicker," Giborne retorted, outraged to be so poorly rewarded for her affection. "Carrion crow, robber of tombs, charnel-house musician! Go away—where are your skeletal twins? Take these six francs, and make sure they don't fly away, vile usurer of sepulchers, ugly henchman of death!"

"Six francs!" objected Macabre, who took them in an indecisive hand. "Is that really all? Six francs! The sum is utterly inadequate—these Lombards are more Jewish than the English. Six francs! That's pitiful!"

"Go forth yourself and get as much, Messire Graverobber. Your rebec would have a hard time getting more. There's no more demand for your rags in this time of plague, and you'll catch the disease from your corpses, if you haven't already."

"This is an impertinent traffic, Giborne. I thought Monseigneur Croquoison was full of generosity. Six francs! That's not the value of my work; there were a hundred and twenty winding-sheets, two hundred shrouds and many other pieces of fine cloth."

"Why didn't you keep a few yards in order to bury yourself? Tell the big chief, damn it. Why don't you go to the counter yourself, monster of nature? They'd have given another franc to see your carcass and your dead man's mug."

"On your body," said Macabre, dully, interrogating her with a piercing gaze, "is it true that my linen produced nothing other than these six gold francs? Have you not drunk part of the sum? You'll restore the rest yourself, thief!"

"A truce on these false suspicions, my friend," Giborne retorted, laughing. "Certainly, I've had the fantasy of transmuting these resonant francs into wine, but the worthy Culdoë met the needs of my thirst; I've supped enough for a week."

"May death protect you, vile drunkard!" muttered Macabre, searching Giborne's clothing. "I'll throw her out, fustigate her, curse her, that infidel depository! By my Bohemian fatherland! She's kept half the income! Six crowns!"

"Leprosy take you by the legs!" cried Giborne, who perceived her husband's design too late to obviate it. "That's my money—six crowns that Messire Culdoë put in my hand. Give me back my money!"

"I've recovered mine, which you've bitten into by culpable enterprise. I suspected as much! Ah, treacherous Giborne, you've stolen the best of the booty! I order you to tell me where you've hidden your stolen goods. How much have you pillaged in thirteen years?"

"Evil good-for-nothing! I reproach myself for having served your profits and interest too well, but I swear by the divinity of the sun that this money belongs to me, and that I earned it by assisting in the sacrifice of a child by moonlight—so give me my six crowns."

"No, Wife, no one tells me such lies; the linen was worth at least twelve gold pieces, and my calculation is perfect on that score. In future, I'll prevent this pilfering. Stop insulting me, Giborne—try to take my life rather than my écus!"

"You're the one who's the thief. I won't be robbed without putting up a fight! My six crowns! You've usurped my legitimate property! I'll gouge your eyes, bite your cheek and suck your blood, if there's any in your veins."

Inflamed by the drink as much as by anger, Giborne hurled herself at Macabre to take back the coins, which he hid in his bosom; she hurt him so much with her fingernails and teeth that he made use of his strength to get the better of his furious adversary; he strangled her and almost choked her with his skeletal arms, but she dragged him down with her weight as she fell to the ground, where they rolled in the darkness, the lamp having gone out in the course of the horrible struggle, in which the woman could be heard choking and the man creaking in all his bones.

Eventually, Giborne, bruised by the sharp limbs that dug into her plump flesh, begged for mercy with oppressed groans, and groped her way back to the bed in silence.

"Macabre," she said, in a low voice, pronouncing an irrevocable oath in the manner of her homeland, "all intelligence between us is finished henceforth; I've suffered too much from your injustice and tyranny; I'll have my revenge before long—yes, I'll be revenged for thirteen years of blows, molestations, misery and famine. O genteel lover of Death, I'll send you to see your lady!"

The Sire de la Vodrière had remained seated in the courtyard of his deserted house, where his pale immobility was not frightening anyone but himself. The wind chilled his naked body without causing him to go in search of clothing or shelter; life had retired entirely to his heart, and his sightless eyes were as devoid of tears as his mouth was of words. An atrocious interior torture was tearing at him relentlessly. His thoughts were spinning in an infernal circle in the wake of his wife and son, whom he saw dead and bloody, while he heard mocking laughter and jeers directed at his conjugal misfortune. That chaos seethed in his mind, through which passed, as before a mirror, memories of joy and mourning. Nothing showed externally in his death-mask face.

At three o'clock in the morning, however, the old man stood up straight and stiff, exhaled a profound sigh and left the house, tucking up the pleats of the shroud. He did not look around, but marched gravely toward his goal at an assured pace.

He arrived, without any detour, at the Porte de la Ferronnerie, and went back into the cemetery with the intention of lying down in his grave again, but that place, where he had been separated from Jehanne, evoked gentler emotions in him, and his eyelids moistened. He walked under the charnel-houses, striking his forehead and breast, folding his arms and joining his hands.

Jehanne, retained shivering in her bed by an insurmountable weakness, had vaguely heard an argument in strange voices, which Benjamin's had dominated momentarily, but the voices has drawn away, along with footsteps, and the silence that soon followed in the vicinity was only troubled by the murmurs of the wind, which brought with them the funeral accents of Macabre's rebec. Subjugated by that supernatural harmony, which had a plaintive echo in her soul, Jehanne listened with an inexpressible tenderness; all the fibers of her sensibility were brought into play and vibrated with those prophetic chords; she shed tears without effort and without constraint: tears of bitter dolor, meek resignation and inconsolable habitude; she wept thus for as long as Macabre's supreme song was exhaled.

She had lost the memory of her cruel situation, including the memory of Benjamin, who did not come back. When the airborne sounds ceased to intoxicate her with a forgetful melancholy, she felt the anxiety and despair more vividly of an abandonment that she dared not interpret, judging it calamitous in any supposition. Benjamin had abandoned her; Benjamin had fallen into the hands of a murderer; the shade of the Sire de la Vodrière had risen from the tomb against Benjamin. But what about those infantile screams, still resounding in the maternal heart, those cries of atrocious suffering, so strange at that hour and in that place? She experienced a sensation of cold in her extremities, a squeezing sensation in her heart; her eyes had become haggard and her teeth were chattering.

Nevertheless, she found the courage to get out of bed and get dressed; she dragged herself out of the Loge-aux-Fossoyeurs and advanced, tottering, all the way to the tomb of Saint Richard.

She uttered a loud scream and, about to fall, embraced the cross from which her child was suspended, horribly mutilated and disfigured.

She had recognized him.

"Woe is me! Woe to our child! Woe to you!" cried a voice that seemed to her to rise out of the ground. "Jehanne, culpable and ingrate spouse! It's you who have murdered my son! It's you who have cast me into the sepulcher! The Lord God punishes the wicked! Try to expiate your sins down here, Jehanne, or come to sleep with me in my nuptial grave! Woe to you! Woe! Woe!"

Jehanne was stupefied by this menacing imprecation, and waited for the earth to open up to devour her miserable existence. It was a frightful, inextricable nightmare that enveloped her.

Without tears and without groans, she contemplated the dear victim and the barbaric mutilations, the skin traversed by pins and the bits of the pincers, and the shed blood already dried on the stone.

She thought she was dying.

Suddenly, an icy hand gripped her arm; she turned her head and proffered a second scream on perceiving the Sire de la Vodrière, paler than his shroud, his eyes staring and his features distorted by infernal laughter.

They fell down together, linked by that last embrace, at the feet of their crucified son.

She had fainted; he was dead.

XVI. The Charnel-Houses

The following day, the traces of the crime of *pingres* that had been committed during the night were found, and the semi-naked bodies of the wife and the husband, over which suspicions floated, ever vulnerable to appearances. Popular opinion had soon invented a story, however, in which the marvelous supported plausibility to provide a diversion from the terrors of the plague. It was said and believed that, Madame de la Vodrière having sacrificed her son at a witches' sabbat, her husband had surged forth from the tomb to frighten her in her rascality.

Master Croquoison, anxious and overwhelmed by remorse, hastened to have the Sire de la Vodrière—who had broken the ban of death, and whom the witnesses were talking about taking to the Montfaucon gibbet as a sorcerer—buried for a second time, more profoundly.

Jehanne, who was still possessed of a passive life that could scarcely be distinguished by the movement of her lips, was taken back to her house, where Père Thibault did not spare her any aid of medicine or religion.

Benjamin was imprisoned in a room in the Boîte-aux-Lombards, behind the padlocks, bolts and iron bars that Culdoë had opposed to impetuous imprudence.

The latter Jew, penetrated by the duties that he extended from his execrable murder, was kneading flour with the sacrificial blood in order to celebrate the Passover.

The Bishop of Paris, Jacques Duchâtelier, whose avarice and dissolute morals cause sufficient rumor in his time for historians to attach scandal to them, went to the cemetery decorated by his pontifical ornaments and accompanied by his clergy; the crime of *pingres*, which was always attributed to Jews, was formally observed, and the profanation of the cemetery recognized. In consequence, the Bishop ordered that the

205

dead should no longer be buried there until penance had been done for the crime and the place had been purified.

That prohibition, which the same Bishop had imposed on the cemetery once before, on the occasion of a quarrel that had taken place in the church of the Saints-Innocents in 1437, was an infallible means of levying an obligatory tax on the devotion of the parishioners. Perhaps, however, the Provost of the city, Ambroise de Loré, who was in charge of public health, was hurriedly seizing the pretext in order in move inhumations away from the center of the capital for the duration of the plague, whose epidemic was becoming more intense and widespread with every day that passed.

Adam de Cambrai, the first president of the parliament, assumed responsibility for the investigation of the crime, the authors of which were not in custody.

The people, indignant at the atrocious murder, to which they attributed the ravages of the malady and the symptoms of famine, assembled in a crowd around the cemetery, the gates of which had been closed at the moment when Macabre was about to pay dearly for his permanent sojourn with the dead.

That effervescence of thought did not dissipate with the multitude, which was nourishing dark projects of vengeance against the Jews. The Provost sent his sergeants to invite the good inhabitants of Paris to disperse, for fear of contagion, and they all retired making energetic threats, calling for death and pillage, which more than one Lombard understood in the depths of his shop. The respect and love that the Provost had been able to inspire, however, prevented grave excesses and bloody reprisals that day.

Croquoison detested his sin even more, on thinking that the fallow cemetery would not produce anything but grass.

On Easter Monday, Guillemette, not yet fully recovered from the night of Good Friday, and tormented by the disappearance of the leper, came back in the evening from a pilgrimage to the churches of Saint-Julien-des-Ménétriers, Saint-Marie-l'Égyptienne and Saint-Laurent. She had dispatched many paternosters, burned many candles, kissed many relics, distributed abundant alms and invoked numerous saints, but her conscience was not tranquil, and the absolution of a confessor, whom she had compensated generously, added further weight to her remorse, for, in combining the reminiscences that her drunkenness had not entirely effaced, she convinced herself that the Sire de la Vodrière had appeared to her as a sign of impending punishment, and that the soul of her defunct master would pursue her until she had expiated her mortal sins: the adultery she had favored and the flesh that she had eaten on a holy day of fast. The latter sin could have sent her to the pyre for heresy. She wished ardently for Malaquet's return, in order to denounce Culdoë and doom him by accusing him of Judaism under his former name of Schoeffer; that denunciation seemed to her to be agreeable to Heaven as well as her own interests, since she would obtain her share of the confiscation of the wretch's wealth; she rejoiced in that action as a good deed.

At hazard, she went in to the cemetery, where the plague had diminished the number of idlers who had come to watch the exhumation and transport of corpses whose scrupulous families were having them transferred to other cemeteries, or into churches, since the excommunicatory prohibition imposed on Saints-Innocents. As she passed under the charnel-houses she bumped into a fat woman, whom she recognized by her costume rather than her face.

Giborne, who had also recognized her, without appearing to, lowered her red hood and attempted to escape into the shadow of the vault—but Guillemette was no less quick to follow her, and to stop her by grabbing her skirt.

"By all the saints whose relics I've every worshiped!" she exclaimed, with a gross chuckle of satisfaction. "It's my holy guardian angel who has sent me this encounter! Yes, well, here you are discovered, false Bohemian, child-stealer!"

"What are you saying, with your crazy and malevolent tongue?" retorted the Bohemian woman, whose green tint was covered by a crimson blush. "Do you want to try to weigh my fist? Let me go about my business, or I'll mash you in no time, bitch!"

"Damn you, fortune-teller—we have an account to settle frankly. If you want to play with nails and teeth, I can hold my own in that language, but I'll call on someone to take you to prison, my darling."

"Why to prison, good lady?" retorted Giborne, changing her tone and her expression. "I prefer the tavern, if you please. By the way, I've seen you somewhere before, I don't know where or when. Wasn't it the convent of Sainte-Catherine, O joyous whore?"

"No, wife of a zingaro; it was the other day in the Rue des Bourdonnais, at the door of the Hôtel de la Trimouille; if you remember, I gave you wine, bread and ham, at the price of which you stole Monseigneur's child."

"Oh, the dishonest calumny! May I be an impious and bad Christian if I laid a hand on that child! To be sure, the wine was good, the pork better; destiny surely owes you recompense, venerable lady."

"By my faith, malign sorceress, I'll procure you a fire of faggots and sulfur. That poor child was most cruelly killed on the night of Our Lord's passion. It was you who carried out that damnable sacrifice!"

"No, my dear, charitable lady! Don't raise your voice, in case someone hears you! I'm completely innocent of the murder and the sacrilege. Don't say that, I beg you—they'll put me to the question. I'm not responsible for the sin."

"Who hurt the son of the late Messire de la Vodrière? Who besides you, sabbat whore? I intend that the criminal should be delivered to the law for the vindication of this profanation. Name the murderers!"

"I'll do that, in order to please you, my clement hostess, on condition that you forgive the people in question. In addition, I advise you not to say anything about how the mystery was revealed to you: permit me to retire thereafter."

"God be praised! The malefactor will be punished for the repose of Messire's soul. Tell your story, Egyptian frog, and don't leave anything out. I'd gain indulgences by taking you to be hanged, but don't worry about the delay."

"You're a friend of virtue, my good lady, and I'll lodge you in my prayers; record your oath, and don't bring harm to someone who is helping you to do good. The child was put on the cross by Culdoë, master of the Boîte-aux-Lombards..."

"Culdoë!" Guillemette interrupted, almost embracing Giborne for the glad news. "Culdoë! Is that true and certain? It was Culdoë, the Jew, formerly Schoeffer? I'll have no lack of pardons, nor of écus, thank god!"

Giborne, trembling for fear that the revelation might not be sufficient to save her, and that her testimony might become the cause of her ruin, disappeared behind the pillars, while Guillemette, tearful with joy, no longer had any but one obsessive idea: repeating the names of Culdoë and Schoeffer. She was rejuvenated by ease, and tormented her soft plumpness with petulant demonstrations. She could not have asked any more of the Bohemian woman, who slipped out of the cemetery in order to avoid the gratitude of the chambermaid, which might have compromised her as much as the most direct accusations.

Guillemette took the walls as confidants of her vengeance and her interest; she thought she would be able to redeem her sins, appease the soul of the Sire de la Vodrière, and serve the hatred of Crespeau, the founder of her fortune; she would have liked to have already informed the parliament, the Provost and the Bishop of Paris.

A rougher and noisier crowd had assembled around the gravediggers who were exhuming the dead. The latter were found to be badly accommodated in their biers, stripped of their winding-sheets; people were voicing their astonishment at that particularity, which was being attributed either to a miracle or a sacrilege—for the fresh bodies, consumed or desiccated, all offered traces of violence, and the nails of the coffin-lids had been extracted.

The people looking on crossed themselves.

"I suspect that the deceased were not in a state of grace," said a monk, who was carrying a heavy sack back to the monastery. "They are baying now in Hell or Purgatory, for not having given alms to God's mendicants."

"It's black magic," relied the apothecary-grocer Moutard. "It's the Bohemian Macabre who causes these griefs and pollutes the holy ground; his abominable dance has engendered the plague, for which I've already sold him twenty bushels of rhubarb."

"In the time of the late king Charles V," retorted the old cabbage-chopper Courlebois, "The Provost of the city maintained everyone's rights, and the dead weren't robbed any more than the living. Perpetual damnation to anyone who violates the sanctity of tombs!"

"It's possible that the Jews have disturbed the fate of the dead Christians by enchantment," objected a sly gravedigger, "and I invite you to consult Master Croquoison on that score, who has the care of Saints-Innocents and two hundred écus in annual income."

"By Saint Babolin! Master Croquoison is an honest seigneur," said someone among the spectators who were exchanging various opinions.

"It's the envious who are saddened and annoyed by the good fortune of others."

"I've heard it said that in recent times, the dead coming from the Hôpital Sainte-Catherine don't have the wherewithal to hide their shame."

"Damn! Is it the poor who are taken from the ground for fear of excommunication?"

"The worms might have eaten the drapes."

"No—linen doesn't rot before the flesh."

"Indeed! Saracens wouldn't commit such odious crimes!"

"I'm going to be buried in holy ground, by the holy cross!"

"Friend, don't hasten to open my grave in this holy place; the people here are badly dressed!"

The gravediggers, in search of the body of a grocer from the Rue aux Fers, had just discovered a sealed coffin, which they lifted out with difficulty because of its unaccustomed weight; it exhaled a bitter odor of sour wine; the cover stained with violet infiltrations was removed, and everyone fled, except for one lone man in a fur-trimmed overcoat, who did not budge, any more than the dead man, when the inhabitant of the coffin was brought to light, clad in a good robe of gray sackcloth, all his limbs contracted, his eyes bulging from his head, his mouth twisted, swimming in a noxious liquid mixture of food and wine, which he had expelled as he expired.

The gravediggers had not been the last to run away, thinking that they might see an apparition loom up before their eyes, but the fully-dressed corpse did not emerge alive from the coffin, in which his atrocious agony had prolonged several centuries in two hours of life.

Curiosity gradually brought the idlers back, whose circle thickened around the bier. The distorted features of the unfortunate man were examined avidly, along with the fingernails sunk into his lacerated breast, his ripped tongue, the bitten and disjointed planks stained with blood. They understood the desperate struggle that he had been obliged to deliver in his narrow prison, in which he had rolled and writhed like a reptile, until he had perished, stifled and drowned in the hideous remains of his last supper.

The interrogation was conducted by eye, silently, and the gravediggers, leaning on their spades, dared not touch the soiled cadaver, which seemed ready to revive in the warm inspirations of the air. A mute horror reigned all around.

"Holahey!" cried someone, in abrupt intonations. "It's the white leper of the charnel-houses—the one named Malaquet. He's probably buried himself in order not to end up on the rubbish-tip."

"How is it that he's forgotten his rattle and his barrel?"

"That leper stinks like carrion—he'd make vinegar smell good."

"A worthy and brave dungeon. What demon has laid him upside down in that cask?"

"Our genteel Malaquet was wickedly put to death?"

"My God! He's suffered extraordinary distress, poor fellow!"

"Summon the clerk of the Châtelet, to make a report of the adventure."

"By the Holy Grail! It's devilment and sorcery! Look, the wretch was alive in the tomb!"

"The Jews who martyred the infant have committed the crime."

"I suspect that it was divine punishment," said a grave-digger, with an air of conviction, "for this is the bier of the late Sire de la Vodrière, who was initially buried in the same place. Who can tell whether God or the Devil would have buried the living man in the dead man's place."

"Well, my masters," said the old man in the fur-trimmed overcoat and conical bonnet, "don't mourn for that drunken scoundrel who has left his ears in the pillory: it's the fake leper Crespeau, who was condemned to be hanged for heresy and sacrilege in the year 1415, if you remember; the body of the said Crespeau belongs to the law of Paris, and I beg you to attach it to a gibbet with a placard manifesting his sins and his vile death by miracle."

"Belly of a bitch!" said someone, surprised. "Crespeau became Malaquet!"

"Crespeau, who drank, ate and pissed in the vessels of Saint-Josse!"

"He escaped the gallows!"

"Really! Who said so?"

"Seigneur Culdoë, master of the Boîte-aux-Lombards."

"Culdoë!" interjected Guillemette, with a cry like a hyena. Having drawn near distractedly, attracted by the noise, she had recognized her faithful leper, and was weeping, annihilated by the horrible scene. "Not Culdoë, honest folk, but Schoeffer the Jew!"

Culdoë stepped backwards at that name, articulated in a clear and curt voice, which came from the middle of the group. Paling and blushing at the same time, he sought his accuser with one eye, while the other sought a retreat in case it was necessary to flee.

This beginning, which promised an interesting episode, enlarged the tightly-knit circle of the audience, among whom whispers and laughter were circulating. The cadaver, Culdoë and Guillemette found themselves surrounded in by a living wall, as if to provide a dueling-field for the settlement of their quarrel.

Guillemette, excited by the grief occasioned by the inanimate object at her feet, moved to confront the immobile Culdoë, whom she menaced by gaze, by gesture and by speech. He saw that he was trapped, and resigned himself to it.

"It's you, circumcised miscreant," she said, circling around him, "it's you, Israelite dog, vermin of Abraham, canker of Moses, it's you, in truth, who defeated my friend Malaquet by treason! It's you, Master Schoeffer!"

"Woman, I don't know what's inducing you to abuse me," said Culdoë, affecting a forbearance that was on the brink of turning to rage. "Have I perchance done you some wrong that can be repaired by gold or silver? I'm Culdoë, master of the Boîte-aux-Lombards."

"Yes, by Malaquet's soul! It's Culdoë I want to ruin, body and wealth; now, Culdoë is the same Jew Schoeffer who was whipped and banished perpetually twenty-three years ago; your riches will acquit the bringer of the denunciation."

"By the sacred memory of my forefathers, Woman, that's a filthy lie, and I shall prove that you're lying before Messire the Provost. I'm a Lombard of the Papal States, and as good a Christian as anyone in the world."

"Oh, my poor Crespeau, do you hear these temeritous blasphemies! You, a Christian, Culdoë! You, a Christian, Schoeffer! Who has put that honorable leper in the ground, who was of such good humor! Who crucified the child on Good Friday!"

"Seamstress of slander," the Lombard interjected, clenching his teeth and his fists, "cease outraging my venerable old age; cease calling upon me the chastisement that the Lord has in store for you. I swear to everyone that I do not traffic in usury, but in alms."

"For the price of blood! Schoeffer-Culdoë, I denounce you publicly as a Judaizing Jew, and as the author of the crime of *pingres*, which has brought about the desolation of the bosom of the church. Stop him from getting away, the child-killer!"

"You'll die before me, by the holy patriarch Abraham!" howled Culdoë, exasperated by the cries of the dead that were assailing him. "Yes, I'm the unfortunate Schoeffer, once so wickedly tormented, who has his revenge today!"

Culdoë and Guillemette grabbed one another bodily with a reciprocal fury, pulling at one another, insulting one another and disputing the advantage of the struggle.

The crowd applauded and laughed uproariously.

Culdoë knocked Guillemette down, who had raked his face with her fingernails and bit his throat; he dragged her by the hair and threw her almost dead on to a flat tombstone; she coughed and agitated convulsively, to the ferocious acclamations of the assembly. He lifted up an enormous stone, with a tremendous effort, suspended it over his vanquished enemy and let it drop from his full height.

Guillemette's head burst like a nutshell, and the gray matter gushed out.

The murderer would have been torn to pieces on the spot by the indignant multitude, if the city archers had not come running with their iron truncheons. Culdoë, disengaged from a host of adversaries, who were urging one another not to spare him, black with bruises and crushed by blows, was taken to the Châtelet, where there was no shortage of witnesses against him, although he persisted in denying his crime and his accomplices.

A search that was made that same evening at the Hôtel des Lombards procured irrefutable evidence: the vases of blood, the bread mixed with blood, the bloody cutlass and *pingres*. Jeremiah Nathan, Benjamin and Holopherne Croquoison, arrested together, went to the cells to wait a sentence that could be foreseen before the punishment had been determined by the caprice of the tribunal; the tortures would then be diversified for the entertainment of the people.

Giborne learned about this circumstance from the rumor that was its immediate aftermath, and although Guillemette no longer had a voice with which to accuse her of the theft of the child, she shivered at being at the mercy of Culdoë, who might perhaps have named her already. She hesitated as to whether she ought to spend the night in Paris and returned very perplexed to the Tour de Notre-Dame-du-Bois. She had avoided speaking to Macabre since their nocturnal altercation, the stigmata of which reminded her of her oath of vengeance.

She pretended not to notice the Bohemian crouching pensively on his tumulary seat; she lay down in her coffin and tried to go to sleep, but she imagined that she could hear the archers coming who had orders to take her into custody; that terror drowned out the baying of her famished stomach.

She was beginning to get drowsy when Macabre, who no longer stated awake in order to rob the dead, quietly stood up, leaned over her to see whether she was asleep, and then left the cellar without closing the door, the rusty scrape of which might have woken Giborne up.

The latter listened to her husband draw away, creaking, and climb the steps. Then the clicking sound of gold succeeded that of bones. She got up spontaneously and stopped, panting, at the foot of the staircase, which transmitted to her ears, like an organ-pipe, the vibrations of the metal stirred in scales, fifths and octaves by musician's hands.

The Bohemian woman's heart leapt in her breast, impatient to be launched toward the harmonious instrument whose existence so close to her she had not suspected.

The aurisonic melody became more arrhythmic, more confused and more inspired; a strident respiration and osseous creaking were audibly mingling with the cadenced resonance of the gold. Then the triple sound diminished by degrees, and faded away entirely.

The silence encouraged Giborne to seek out the cause of that strange music, and, having groped her way up the seventy steps of the staircase, mute beneath her measured paces, she arrived at the entrance to the platform, where Macabre's recumbent body barred the way.

The Bohemian, his arms plunged into his open treasure, his eyes blank, his limbs taut, was inebriated by an itch of delicious avarice and singular melomania. His wife smiled at both the spectacle and a black thought; her gaze embraced the precious hiding-place in which so much gold as shining.

"Darling gold, amorous gold, beatific gold, hesitant, sonorous and resonant," the musician murmured, about to recover the consciousness paralyzed by sensuality. "Alas, shall I never see the land of Bohemia gain, where I was born? Oh, my cherished homeland!"

"No, by the earth our mother!" exclaimed Giborne, exploding with joy. "Remain dead in the cemetery that you love to much while alive! Macabre has played death enough, and the hour has come to enter the dance, evil miser!"

As she pronounced these insults, which struck Macabre's ears like a thunderclap, still dazed as he was by joy, she lifted him up by the feet, placed him on the parapet and shoved him off, with a grating laugh by way of an adieu.

The skeleton fell, stifled by the rapid trajectory of the fall, and rendered a hollow noise like a rotten tree-trunk. It could be seen from the top of the tower, stiffly lying on its back, yellow and grimacing in the moonlight.

Giborne had no sooner committed that murder than she felt remorse and sensed danger, but the gleam and the sound of the gold, which she stirred with as much pleasure as Macabre, dazzled and intoxicated her; she lost irreparable time enjoying her new property, feeling it and gazing at it before having made it safe; for her, the present was the future.

When she compared the weight of the treasure with the difficulty of a prompt flight, she experienced the dread of being forced to sacrifice a part of that embarrassing fortune.

The idea occurred to her of having recourse to the interested good offices of friend Croquoison, who would procure a safer refuge for her person and her écus. She went down from the tower and stepped insouciantly over her husband's body, which seemed to be defending the issue from the *guifs*. She ran to the house of the master of the gravediggers and found it guarded by archers of the watch, who stopped her to have a drink with them.

She was wily enough to escape before daybreak, when the wine had delivered her from that dangerous company, which was snoring in the street, and went back to the cemetery. She returned, palpitating, to her treasure, which she had earned by thirteen years of harsh privations.

There was not enough of the night remaining to get out of Paris carrying more than twenty thousand gold pieces, which the Cut-throats, the English, and even the French would have regarded as a good prize in an epoch so poor in coin. She conceived the plan of hiding it in the garrets of the charnel-houses until she was able to effect her retreat without any accident.

She immediately set about the translocation of the treasure, which she deposited under the auspices of a pile of skulls that caused hr heavy step to oscillate.

It was necessary to go back and forth between the tower and the charnel-houses several times, but the fragments of winding-sheet that she employed for the displacement of the coins were not reliable depositories, and a number of coins of various sorts always filtered through the interstices of the worn cloth. Red in the face and utterly out of breath, Giborne was in haste to put an end to these difficult journeys, which dawn was about to render impossible, and did not perceive the spilled coins that she sowed in her tracks.

Finally, exhausted by fatigue and need, she curled up behind a rampart of bones and went to sleep on the gold, which did not appease the intestinal furies of her devouring hunger.

The gravediggers who were the first to arrive at the Cimetière des Saints-Innocents were alarmed on finding Macabre lying dead at the foot of the Tour de Notre-Dame-du-Bois; they recoiled at first, then became bolder, and, familiarizing themselves with the dead man that they had feared so much while he was alive, they undressed him and propped him up against the wall, where idlers came to examine and touch him.

The adventure was interpreted with marvelous commentaries, and even the less credulous were persuaded by the sight of that once-animated skeleton that the demon had chosen the accursed form in question in order better to preside over the calamities that he had caused to weigh upon the city in the last thirteen years. Hence, no one had the audacity to insult the cadaver, which one might have thought desiccated by a long sojourn in sandy ground. A few signed themselves as they considered it, and others proclaimed a miracle.

In the meantime, the actor's residence was visited. People descended into the hideous cellar and climbed up to the platform; the inspection of those places corroborated the popular opinion that attributed a supernatural power to Macabre. The interior of the tower did, indeed, resemble a sorcerer's lair.

The gravediggers noted, in support of the diabolical nature of the player, that his wife had disappeared.

The general curiosity was stimulated by the joyful cries of a vagabond who picked up a gold coin on the threshold of the *guifs*, and, as everyone began searching for a similar windfall, the most avid or the most clear-sighted fell upon the numerous coins spilled along Giborne's route. They were sought out, they were collected, and they were disputed as if they were gifts from Heaven; and they led a pack of bloodhounds along their trail, who penetrated into the garrets.

One gravedigger, having discovered the Bohemian woman lying curled up in a corner, launched a trenchant blow at her, which she received on the temple; her sleep became eternal after a slight sigh and a sensible contraction of the facial muscles; she did not even open her eyes.

The gravedigger's malice was spontaneously imitated, and if Giborne has still had a breath of life, she would have exhaled it under the hail of projectiles unleashed upon her, along with the laughter and the coarse insults of the crowd. She was stoned with skulls, tibias and a rain of bones that buried her entirely beneath a mass of human debris.

Afterwards, weary of that barbaric sport, the gravediggers, students and vagabonds pulled out the bloody and mutilated corpse, which they attempted to reanimate, but that belated humanitarian impulse had the unexpected result of revealing the treasure, which was pillaged by a hundred hands avid for prey, in spite of the equivocal origin of the considerable sum.

The charnel-houses trembled under the weight of a frightful battle in which everyone was fighting on his own account; they swarmed and howled; there was an inextricable pell-mell of arms, legs, heads, bodies and bones.

An hour later, the floor was stained with blood and paved with pulverized skeletons; twenty victims, strangled or disemboweled, formed a cortege for the Bohemian woman, whose tormentors had torn her apart with their teeth, their fingernails and their knives, in order to see whether she might not have a second treasure in her entrails.

Thus was dispersed, in a matter of minutes, the gilded soul of Macabre.

In a large, carpeted and paneled room in the Hôtel de la Trimouille, Jehanne de la Vodrière, who had been prey to a continuous delirium for a fortnight, devoid of reason, had descended from weakness into a melancholy torpor. She was no longer writhing in convulsions; she no longer exhausted herself in inarticulate cries; two weeks of implacable, ardent, unparalleled despair had surpassed the strength of a frail female body.

Père Thibault had not wiped away his tears during that fortnight, which had been fourteen years for his paternal heart. The assistance of religion had been no more effective than that of medicine; he had waited beside his daughter's dolorous bed while that fever of the soul had run its course; he had not taken an instant's rest in those long hours, which he abridged in prayer; he forgot nourishment, sleep and other bodily needs in order to drown himself in anxiety and alarm.

Finally, God, whom he invoked incessantly, had become manifest in a benevolent crisis, and Jehanne, pale, thin and debilitated, had smiled softly at the old man, who wept with joy on seeing her calm on the bed that had witnessed so much suffering.

Suddenly, there was the sound of people passing along the Rue des Bourdonnais, and the trumpets of the Provost's criers alerted ears to open. The cry was proclaimed by a resounding voice:

"Hear this, good gentry, bourgeois and manual workers of the town, city and university of Paris; Messire the Provost makes it known to you that today, because of the contagion, you have to restrict yourselves and remain in your dwellings during the execution at Les Halles of the four Jews condemned by the warrant of the high chamber of parliament, presided over by the Messire the noble Simon Charles, for the crime of *pingres* villainously perpetrated on the Holy Friday of the Passion in the Cimetière des Saints-Innocents, whom God absolve in regard of the punishment."

Jehanne, with eyes, nostrils and eyes agape, listened with stupid attention; she raised her head from her pillow and held her breath. Père Thibault, made anxious by that attentive pose, could not prevent himself from taking a palpitating interest in the cry.

The crier, who has paused to swallow a glass of red wine that someone had had the kindness to offer him, continued in a firmer and more resonant tone:

"It appears from the interrogations, testimonies, questioning and judgment, that the so-called Culdoë, once convicted of Judaism, whipped through the streets and banished in perpetuity under the name of Schoeffer, returned to this good and Christian city, notwithstanding the express prohibition, and lived there as master of the counter of the Boîte-aux-Lombards, situated in the Rue Saint-Denis. The said Culdoë, by damnable invention, wanted to immolate to his god, in accordance with the customs of his pernicious religion, a baptized child, whom he bought from a Bohemian woman, it is said, presently defunct; which child, belonging to Messire Louis de la Vodrière, chevalier, was taken by night to the said cemetery, put on a cross above the tomb of Saint Richard, once crucified in the same manner, and pierced with a thousand wounds, such that he rendered his soul to the celestial Creator. Culdoë was assisted, aided and counseled in this abominable practice by Jeremiah Nathan, his associate, Benjamin, his own son, and Master Croquoison, warden of the cemetery and the gravediggers. Thus, by the good pleasure of the Messieurs, on this day of the fifteenth of April in the year of grace 1438, at three o'clock in the afternoon, the said four Jews will be placed in the Pilori des Halles, to be reprimanded and executed there in the following fashion: Culdoë, Nathan and Benjamin boiled in oil, and Croquoison, also guilty of having robbed the dead committed to his care, flayed alive, by the office of Jean Tiphaine, legal tormentor. Finally, the bodies of the individuals in question having been reduced to ashes and scattered in the wind, their movable and immovable property are and will remain consecrated to the domain of Monseigneur le Roi, with the charge of having portrayed on the frontispiece of the house of the said Croquoison the figure of a stripped patient, in eternal memory of his wickedness toward the poor deceased, whom God has put in his holy paradise. By that, the profanation of the cemetery will be expiated. Amen."

Jehanne had listened to that cry without manifesting the emotions that were colliding in his mind and reviving her memories; she was still listening with the same insistence when the crier had gone away, dragging his procession of dumbfounded idlers elsewhere. Then she fell back upon her bed, which she moistened with silent tears, and wanted to die.

The good Père Thibault, who did not suspect the real cause of that affliction, recommenced his Christian and paternal allocutions; he tried in vain to turn away from a subject to which Jehanne incessantly returned, and ended up relating the details of the trial with respect to the murder of the child. He imagined that the vengeance of the law would be a balm for a mother's broken heart, but he hid from her the detail that suspicion, having hung over her, had almost caused her to appear before the law herself. Fortunately, Benjamin had entirely exonerated her in confessions that respected her reputation as a wife.

Jehanne felt joy reborn within her on learning of that generosity on the part of her lover; she hung on the recitation, which she only interrupted in the curious interests of her passion; she wanted to hear talk of Benjamin.

"Oh, describe again, my venerable Father, and keep on describing the noble countenance of that Benjamin, who is, however, merely the son of a Jew, a gravedigger and a player of farces. He declared how he kept me prisoner in the lodge in the cemetery?"

"Assuredly, and without their being any need to prove the question; he claimed that he wanted, by means of that abduction, to prevent a search for the child and to steal your jewels; in fact, the gold cross from your rosary, engraved with your name, was found in his clothing."

"Oh, the heroic young fellow! No prince or baron could emulate that magnanimity, which will be remunerated on earth sooner than in Heaven. In addition, you say, he recoiled from having to steep his hands in the child's blood."

"By Saint-Jacques, he was obstinate in maintaining that verity, and the anguish of the torture was unable to extract an admission of his consent to the crime. Nevertheless, it appears that your were locked, during that day and night, inside the Loge-aux-Fossoyeurs, until, having broken your bonds, you encountered the late Sire de la Vodrière, issued from his grave by miracle or black magic..."

"Messire, refrain from reminding me of that horrific mystery, at the idea of which understanding abandons me. Is it possible and veritable that you recognized Benjamin for having baptized him in the parish of Saints-Innocents?

"God's will be done! When I was deacon in that church, the son was baptized of Master Croquoison, gravedigger, who had been suspected of Judaism and showed his good will toward the Catholic religion by that act. Today, however, the false Croquoison is a convinced Jew, and the son he had returned to his friend Culdoë as Jewish as any in the Jewry. Thus, parliament thought that it would be profitable to show no mercy, in order to maintain the people."

"Parliament has judged badly, Monseigneur, and Benjamin seems to me to be innocent of everything. This news, which I know in time, has almost returned me to health, and I shall, if you please, sleep for a brief interval, while you go to offer a prayer to my advantage."

Père Thibault, who was reassured by these sensible words and the apparent calm of the invalid, thanked Heaven for that sudden cure, and immediately went to Saint-Jacques-de-la-Boucherie to burn candles and say a celebration mass, while the bells rang incessantly for the dead.

Jehanne, although on the brink of fainting with exhaustion, was no sooner alone and free that she got up and dressed

223

without making a sound. Twenty times over she thought that she would never accomplish her design, but love and fever inspired her strength; she dragged herself out of the room in spite of the vertigo and weakness that gripped her at every step. She succeeded in getting out of the house without being seen, by the door to the Rue Tirechape.

It was three o'clock in the afternoon.

The plague had made such frightful progress in Paris in a fortnight that it threatened to render the city a desert, after having depopulated it four years earlier. The admirable devotion of the Provost Ambroise de Loré and the presidents Adam de Cambrai and Simon Charles could only temper the evil, the intensity of which was augmented by the rainy season and the famine. They also watched over the material conservation of the city, the outskirts of which the English and bands of Cutthroats were coming to harass. Thanks to them and the bourgeoisie they called to their aid, discouragement did not take hold of numerous laborers, who were nourished by digging graves and working on the fortifications.

The interior of Paris presented a deplorable spectacle: in the streets, solitary and obstructed by ordure, refuse longer being collected, no one was abroad but starving packs of stray dogs, invalids being transported to the hospitals and corpses being transported to the plague-victims' cemetery, blessed outside the city walls.

The Hôtel-Dieu only offered tortures instead of the relief that the poor had been accustomed to find there for so many centuries; the mortality had become so devouring in that refuge of charity that the master, the brothers and the sisters had fled for their personal safety. Fifteen hundred unfortunates, with no bread, medicines or remedies, lay in confusion in the vast rooms, bunched on rotten straw; they were attacking one another, tearing one another apart and eating one another. In all the hospitals there was a total lack of linen, provisions, hands and medicaments.

The squares and crossroads, the areas around churches and the forbidden Cimetière des Saints-Innocents served as hospices for thousands of moribund individuals buried among the cadavers in a noxious and moldy dung-heap, raising their arms toward the heavens, mouths full of foam, visages swollen with pustules, skin taut and carbonized, writhing in convulsions, stiffening at the approach of death, motionless, haggard and mute or joining shrill voices in a lugubrious concert of knells, prayers and plaints, which were exhaled night and day from that vast nucleus of suffering and pain.

All human sentiment had disappeared, to give way to the most pitiless egotism; family and friends only existed in name; the fear of contagion broke all bonds; people murdered one another for a morsel of bread.

However, in spite of the public calamities in which everyone shared, and in spite of the Provost's ordinances, a considerable crowd had gathered in Les Halles for the execution of the four Jews, which was calculated to distract and amuse the people. The Pilori des Halles, the most celebrated of all those that existed in Parisian law, probably derived its name from *puits Lori*, which encompassed its primary enclosure, enclosing a courtyard, stables and an outhouse in which to keep the bodies of the executed felons that were exposed at Montfaucon.

In 1438, the pillory, which was reconstructed in the sixteenth century after having been burned by the populace, who killed the executioner during the exercise of his functions, was the Provost's principal ladder; it was there that great felons, except for forgers, had the privilege of being hanged, boiled or decapitated. There is reason to believe that the octagonal tower pierced by high arched windows, supported by cylindrical pillars ornamented with dentellate fleurons and surmounted by a stone spire with a weather-vane, was anterior to the fire of 1515, which only consumed the wooden frame and outbuildings. The pillory still served as a constraint in the Revolutionary epoch.

That octagonal tower, from which the patient was shown to the people during his confession and final interrogation, had, at the height of its open windows, a large oft-repaired scaffold known as the *gibet des Halles.* That permanent scaffold, which the carpenters of the woodcuttters' guild had to maintain in a good state, did not tremble on its bolted and iron-barred joists. A headsman's block in heart of oak, channels to receive the blood and a gibbet were the usual attributes of noble works. This time, however, in view of the evils of the day, which rendered the choice of popular diversions more exacting, a stake and an enormous cauldron of oil had been added to the habitual equipment of the master juridical tormentor, who had been working since daybreak with his robust assistants, clad in their black and scarlet livery.

While the gentry of the parliament and the archers clustered in the rooms of the neighboring markets, which had been washed with vinegar to chase away the odor of fish, the four condemned men were waiting, securely bound, in the prison of the Pilori until the time came for them to be summoned above. They were able to hear the bellows animating the flames in the furnace, the oil boiling and the dull murmur of the crowd, imitating the cauldron. They had already rejected, by silence or insults, the Christian exhortations that Brother Richard attempted to make them accept, and the Franciscan had left them momentarily to prepare themselves for a holy conversion.

"By the Divine Cross," said Croquoison, who had not forgiven Culdoë their common misfortune, "did you hear that holy man, that hard and diabolical heart? Yes, of course I'd accept his religion if it would save my life."

"By the abyss in which Dathan, Korah and Abiram were swallowed,"[24] said Culdoë, indignantly. "Philistine, Bethsamite, Gentile, do you want to hold the sacred law of Moses up to derision? If I weren't in chains, I'd prevent that."

---

[24] In *Numbers* chapter 16.

"Alas, friend," replied Nathan, shaking his head, "we're doomed, body and possessions; that monk has no power to grant us absolution from the sentence, and to hire a cowardly abandonment of the faith of our fathers, he'd give us a confessor."

"Benjamin, my beloved son," said Culdoë to his son, who made no reply, "our unjust death might perhaps advance the coming of the Messiah, so I summon you to maintain a firm and steady courage, as a loyal Jew should."

Benjamin, plunged in an impassive reverie, refused to share his father's fanatical sentiments, and regretted nothing in life but his amours.

Croquoison, was tearing at his beard and hair, martyrizing himself with his fists and fingernails, still cursing Culdoë's fatal vow, while the latter only interrupted his advice to his son in order to draw nearer to the Lord, in ecstasy.

Jeremiah Nathan wept for himself and his treasures.

The crowd was less dense and more peaceful than on an ordinary day of execution and market; it was only emitting a buzz of impatience and curiosity, through which sighed, at intervals, the lamentations of the plague-ridden, from the direction of the Cimetière des Saints-Innocents, and whining voices begging for alms. Even so, the hangars of the markets were covered with spectators sitting on the tiles, the repair of which cost some two hundred Parisian sols after every important execution. The women and children were distinguished by the petulance of their gestures and clamors. Death-knells never ceased chiming in all the bell-towers.

There was a resounding cry of joy when, on the stroke of three o'clock, Jean Tiphaine led his four subjects into the lantern of the pillory, but that habitual joy was merely an impulse, soon compressed by the particular sorrow of each individual, and a monotonous murmur circulated in the crowded amphitheater of the markets, devoid of jokes and laughter, with no projectiles or insults hurled at the patients.

From one minute to the next, among that contagious aggregation, someone was seen to fall, to writhe, to vomit corrupt blood and to expire in hideous agony.

"My brothers in Jesus Christ," declaimed Brother Richard, who had reappeared, with new arguments extracted from a pint of spiced wine, "I call upon you to renounce Satan, his pomps and his works; although the flaying and boiling is about to commence, it is not necessary for you to continue your torture in Gehenna; so, come into the bosom of the Catholic Church, and bequeath a few chaplaincies to the good Franciscan brothers."

"By the holy name of God," said Croquoison, kissing the Franciscan's robe, "deliver me from this dangerous pass, and I will abjure the doctrine of the rabbis, and will even don monkish garb and dedicate all my possessions to founding a convent."

"That is an honorable thought for which Saint Francis will reward you," said Brother Richard, "but, your possessions having been confiscated by law, it is only licit for you to extract a gift therefrom for the ransom of your soul and pious works. A hundred thousand chariots of the devils, the worldly vanities of corporeal corruption! I can, by the virtue of my prayers, save your soul from death and damnation; I can comfort you with hope that this hour..."

"Go away, quicker than you came, vile Christian!" shouted Culdoë, making him retreat to the edge of the scaffold with a glare. "Get away now, for fear of being unable to do so later! We are not infidels and renegades forsaken by the Lord."

That thunderous sally from Culdoë did not conciliate the pity of the audience, and fragments of tile whistled past his head. He was not intimidated, and blessed his companions in torture while Holopherne Croquoison was tied to the stake, his entire naked body shivering, still bruised by the stigmata of the questioning.

Jean Tiphaine took personal responsibility for the flaying, and his valets had only to throw the other three condemned men into the cauldron.

Croquoison uttered shrill screams merely on seeing the knives glittering in the sunlight in the hand of the executioner, who was sharpening them.

Nathan was already dead of fright.

Benjamin, pale and fatigued by his tears, looked toward the Rue des Bourdonnais, unworried by the boiling oil; his intrepid countenance, his handsome and noble face, and the pleasing appearance of his entire person, gained the interest of the assembly, especially the women, always kindly disposed to an agreeable exterior.

"By the congress of La Manche!" said one of the fishmongers among them, "that Jew has a comely neck, and his peers aren't so numerous that one can waste the seed in this fashion."

"Truly, if I weren't married, I'd demand to espouse him for a day, in accordance with custom."

"By Saint Herring, my good ladies, that pretty lad would rather die than have such an ugly wife!"

"Hola! I'll consent to his choice—let him name the most worthy!"

"Truce, Messire executioner!" cried a voice, the only one capable of moving the young man, indifferent to his fate. "I have come, in accordance with the ancient custom of the *gibet des Halles*, to save from death, and also to espouse, Benjamin!"

That timid and tremulous voice attracted all gazes to a woman whose pallor was scarcely colored by shame, standing on the steps of the high stone cross that rose up beside the pillory. The woman in question was supporting herself on the stem of the cross, and seemed as troubled by her strange step as weak with malady.

Benjamin, who was the first to perceive her, opened his arms to her, and would have launched himself toward her had he been permitted to do so.

Culdoë frowned, and considered his son, who, transported by joy and gratitude, saluted Jehanne with a smile; there was a spontaneous sentiment within the crowd in favor of the woman who was sacrificing herself thus for the interesting young man.

"I venerate the ancient privileges of Les Halles," said Jean Tiphaine, advancing to the edge of the scaffold, "but it is necessary for the woman who offers herself thus in marriage to declare her name and qualities in the due form; in addition, a Jew must convert to the Roman Catholic faith to merit its mercy.

"I am Jehanne Coutanceaux," she said, without hesitation, "widow of the nobleman Louis de la Vodrière, and I declare publicly that it is my desire to take for a husband the said Benjamin, who is not a Jew, having been baptized in the church of Les Saints-Innocents, as the investigation revealed. I demand that he should have the right of my supplication, and that we should be taken before a priest immediately, in order that he might bless us."

That frank and generous declaration completed the favorable disposition of the people, who were very glad that a noble lady should have recourse to old popular customs; the spouses were applauded, and no one remarked on the fact that Jehanne was clad in mourning.

Benjamin had blushed and was fighting a residual scruple relative to his religion.

Culdoë was in a crisis of fury, which did not overflow s yet in words; he was waiting for the resolution of his son.

Nathan remained insensible to everything, and Croquoison was looking around urgently, seeking a charitable soul with his eyes.

Brother Richard urged Benjamin to a striking abjuration.

"Indeed, Mesdames," said Croquoison, "will you abandon me in this pitiful circumstance? I have never been married and am only fifty years of age' look, I am both sturdy and mature; I am employed as the master of gravediggers at the Cimetière des Saints-Innocents; I have income enough to by the crown of a comtesse for whoever might want one. Hurry up, my good ladies! Who will have the wealth of young Croquoison? Yes, indeed, what a fine husband I will make!"

A unanimous burst of laughter greeted that tender invitation, but not even the poorest and most toothless presented herself to steal the flayers' work; the unfortunate fellow's nudity served as a convincing text for those enemies of marriage; Croquoison did not gain by such a meticulous examination, and it would have required a blind woman to be content with his feeble conjugal value.

"My dear and honored father," said Benjamin, on whom the clerk called to record his grace, "if only that excellent lady who is saving me from certain death could give you similar support!"

"Does that mean that you are renouncing your God?" interjected Culdoë, in a thunderous voice, as he was being dragged toward the cauldron. "I adjure the fire of Sodom and Gomorrah to consume you before the eyes of these worshipers of the golden calf! What! You would deny the God of your ancestors, Benjamin? You would receive the accursed name of Christian? Oh, wretch! Better not to have found you than to have found you alive and perjured! Better to know that you were dead with your mother and your brothers! No! Say that you are and will remain a Jew; say it, my dear son, at the expense of this terrestrial life! Yes, surely, the offspring of my race will not defect from the paternal religion! By the holy tabernacle, Benjamin, confess your faith and come to die!"

With these words he broke the cords that bound him and seized Benjamin by the arm, who was being led away, sad and joyful at the same time. By virtue of that abrupt movement, he tore away the bandages in which the young man's hand, mutilated by the iron spikes of the torture, were bound; blood began to flow from the wounds again, and Culdoë let go at that sight, which excited the indignation of the people. It was thought that the father had wounded his son, who was taken down into the room beneath the pillory; the cries of death that resounded against the Jews stimulated the executioner not to delay the execution any longer.

"Circumcised miscreant," said Brother Richard to Culdoë, whom Benjamin's apostasy had exasperated to the utmost degree of rage, "there're is still time; rally to the example of your son and detest the false gods, idols and demons that you have adored; look at the cauldron, the image of the punishments of Hell, and prevent the eternal fire from harnessing you to the hundred thousand chariots of the devils. Give me and honest legacy to the profit of the Order, and I will absolve you of your vile sins!"

"By the spirit of the Lord who guides me," shouted Culdoë, no longer in possession of himself, "Christian drooler, gentile, tempter, I'll pay you the account of your sermons. Go first to see whether the fire of Gehenna roasts and scalds! Go replace the relapsed, whom I curse, abominate and condemn! Become a Jew in your turn!"

Brother Richard, who had high hopes of reconquering his popularity by means of a pompous conversion, had not quit Culdoë, whom he was pursuing with Latin arguments and French insults to deafen his ears; he was radiant with his triumph in the presence of that wide-eye crowd, ever-accessible to pious stagecraft. He was marching beside his martyr, whom he supported with an obliging arm, while weighing him down with the weight of a heavy crucifix, which he placed on his shoulder, as Jesus Christ had borne his cross. While he was climbing the steps leading to the edge of the bronze cauldron however, moving backwards in front of Culdoë, the latter bent down, blaspheming, and, lifting him up by his feet, hurled him into the boiling oil, which splashed mightily and rained down at a distance.

The horrible scream that emerged from the cauldron was repeated by a unanimous echo of terror and execration, accompanied by a hail of stones and laughter, inextinguishable when the red and inanimate corpse of the Franciscan was fished out by the hair.

Culdoë laughed too at his accomplishment.

Suddenly, there was a diversion in the nature of the cries and the laughter, which were soon modified into acclamations when the sergeants led Jehanne and Benjamin in procession to the Grand Châtelet, through the middle of a double hedge that opened up of its own accord in the crowd, walking together and gazing at one another with an expression melancholy with joy.

The couple traversed Les Halles, followed by a curious multitude, by the maledictions of Culdoë and the howls of Croquoison, flayed alive.

XVIII. The Marriage

The church of Saint-Jacques-de-la-Boucherie was besieged by a crowd of people who were jostling to get in, without fear of the proximity of the plague-victims piled up in the cloister, half-dead and dragging themselves to fetid gutters to slake an insatiable thirst. Some were devouring the hay that the curé had given them for bedding; others were gnawing bones that had already been gnawed; some were listening to the indistinct murmur of the church, where prayers were being offered for a miraculous salvation; others were getting up to discover the cause of the crowd that had come to witness the marriage of the condemned man.

Benjamin arrived from the Châtelet via the Rue du Crucifix; he was pensive and oppressed; the glimmers of joy passing over his face were charged with clouds and funereal presentiments. By his side, Jehanne, excited by fever and her devotion, which cost her less than those around her thought, smiled, pale and suffering. Père Thibault led them silently, his arms folded over his breast, his head in his cowl. The acclamations redoubled.

"Do you remember the women's Steam-Baths, handsome lad, gracious pet?" said a cracked voice. "Truly, I thought of saving you from Master Jean Tiphaine's accolade, and I'm sorry that this lady spoke before me. I had a fancy for a young and gallant husband, rather than love a white leper like my sister Guillemette!"

Benjamin turned around more rapidly than if he had been bitten by a snake. He recognized Caillebotte, and withdrew his bloody hand, which she had clasped in hers, moist with purulent sores.

Caillebotte, whose horribly ulcerated face attested to incurable ravages, clung on to Benjamin's clothes and fell down on the steps of the Pierre-au-Lait.

The young man experienced a frightful constriction of the heart on stepping over that still-warm cadaver; he considered the hand that Caillebotte had touched and raised to her lips. Jehanne made him forget his anxiety by inviting him quietly to kneel down.

The two spouses were in front of the altar!

The marriage ceremony continued in a bleak silence, while Benjamin tottered and covered his eyes with his cold hand; his face changed; he felt his veins burning, his breast and face ablaze and his feet icy; the words expired in his mouth, the thoughts in his brain. He resisted momentarily.

"Jehanne, widow of the late Sire Louis de la Vodrière," said Père Thibault, with tears in his eyes, "Jehanne, my dear daughter, will you accept for your husband and seigneur Benjamin here present?"

"Yes, I accept him and receive him as such," replied Jehanne, uniting her hand with that of her spouse. "Henceforth, I am and will be his humble and faithful servant."

"Benjamin, son of Culdoë the Jew," the priest went on, severely, "who is now a baptized Christian, do you take for your spouse and servant Jehanne here present?"

"Yes!" Benjamin replied, his voice weakening after that explosive word. "I am and will be her faithful spouse down here and on high. Adieu, Jehanne! Our espousal will be completed in Heaven!"

Those final words were only heard by Jehanne, who, seeing him faint, had thrown herself into his arms in order to embrace him alive.

They fell together at the foot of the altar, and the people who filled the church, frightened by that fatal marriage, fled and dispersed tumultuously.

Benjamin had died of the plague.

That same evening, at the hour of curfew, Père Thibault, who had taken Jehanne, resigned to devote the remainder of her days to the service of God and the sick, to the Hôpital Sainte-Catherine, was returning from his painful mission, absorbed in his despair and his prayers, when he was attacked in the Rue des Bourdonnais by a pack of hungry wolves that had swum across the river and were spreading out in the city.

The following day, the shreds of his monk's robe were found, with his sandals, his rosary and misshapen bones, on the bloodstained cobblestones. The Chambre des Comptes published by trumpet an ordinance that promised twenty Parisian sols for every wolf taken dead or alive.

For as long as the contagion lasted from which fifty thousand people perished, Jehanne de la Vodrière demonstrated an admirable zeal in the care that she lavished on the plague-ridden. God did not want as yet to take a life employed in such a Christian manner, but she had been subjected to so many dolorous proofs in losing., one after another, her son, her husband, her lover and her father that she refused to reenter a world that offered her nothing but irreparable voids; she resolved to complete her work by a public penitence, and after having essayed a retreat of two years in an attic in the hospital, she pronounced vows of perpetual reclusion, distributed her wealth to religious communities, hospices and churches, and on 11 October 1442 entered a cell that she had built in the Cimetière des Saints-Innocents, adjacent to the wall of the church, from which a barred window permitted her to hear the offices.

There was a celebration for her installation in the cell, whose doorway was walled up on her, and the sermon pronounced for the occasion from the Préchoir compared the recluse to the Gospel parable of the light under the bushel.

Jehanne died the following year, in the imbecility of devotion, but was not canonized after her death because a sister of Saint-Catherine named Alix la Bourgotte, having become a recluse in her imitation, inherited her cell and her odor of sanctity, and even attracted the respect of Louis XI, who dedicated a bronze monument to her in a chapel in the church of the Saints-Innocents.

Macabre's skeleton, which the superstition of the vulgar had surrounding with a cult of sorts during the plague, was conserved in a cupboard in the charnel-houses of the Rue Saint-Denis. It was regarded as a talisman and as an emblem of the power of death, without its origin being remembered. It was only displayed on All Saints' Day to pious visitors of the dead, and that custom became so established by tradition that when Macabre was accidentally broken he was replaced with an ivory statue representing a human skeleton three feet high, whose right arm was draped with a shroud and left bore a deployed scroll with the rhymed inscription of the *danse macabre*.

That masterpiece of sculpture, which has been mistakenly attributed to Germain Pilon, is the sole precious debris that now remains of the Cimetière des Saints-Innocents.

SF & FANTASY

Henri Allorge. *The Great Cataclysm*
Guy d'Armen. *Doc Ardan: The City of Gold and Lepers*
G.-J. Arnaud. *The Ice Company*
Charles Asselineau. *The Double Life*
Cyprien Bérard. *The Vampire Lord Ruthwen*
Aloysius Bertrand. *Gaspard de la Nuit*
Richard Bessière. *The Gardens of the Apocalypse*
Albert Bleunard. *Ever Smaller*
Félix Bodin. *The Novel of the Future*
Louis Boussenard. *Monsieur Synthesis*
Alphonse Brown. *City of Glass; The Conquest of the Air*
Emile Calvet. *In a Thousand Years*
André Caroff. *The Terror of Madame Atomos; Miss Atomos; The Return of Madame Atomos; The Mistake of Madame Atomos; The Monsters of Madame Atomos; The Revenge of Madame Atomos; The Resurrection of Madame Atomos*
Félicien Champsaur. *The Human Arrow; Ouha, King of the Apes; Pharaoh's Wife*
Didier de Chousy. *Ignis*
Michel Corday. *The Eternal Flame*
Captain Danrit. *Undersea Odyssey*
C. I. Defontenay. *Star (Psi Cassiopeia)*
Charles Derennes. *The People of the Pole*
Georges Dodds (anthologist). *The Missing Link*
Harry Dickson. *The Heir of Dracula*
Jules Dornay. *Lord Ruthven Begins*
Alfred Driou. *The Adventures of a Parisian Aeronaut*
Sâr Dubnotal *vs. Jack the Ripper*
Alexandre Dumas. *The Return of Lord Ruthven*
Renée Dunan. *Baal*
J.-C. Dunyach. *The Night Orchid; The Thieves of Silence*
Henri Duvernois. *The Man Who Found Himself*
Achille Eyraud. *Voyage to Venus*
Henri Falk. *The Age of Lead*
Paul Féval. *Anne of the Isles; Knightshade; Revenants; Vampire City; The Vampire Countess; The Wandering Jew's Daughter*
Paul Féval, *fils. Felifax, the Tiger-Man*
Charles de Fieux. *Lamékis*

Arnould Galopin. *Doctor Omega*; *Doctor Omega and the Shadowmen* (anthology)
Judith Gautier. *Isoline and the Serpent-Flower*
Léon Gozlan. *The Vampire of the Val-de-Grâce*
G.L. Gick. *Harry Dickson and the Werewolf of Rutherford Grange*
Edmond Haraucourt. *Illusions of Immortality*
Nathalie Henneberg. *The Green Gods*
V. Hugo, P. Foucher & P. Meurice. *The Hunchback of Notre-Dame*
Romain d'Huissier. *Hexagon: Dark Matter*
Michel Jeury. *Chronolysis*
Gustave Kahn. *The Tale of Gold and Silence*
Gérard Klein. *The Mote in Time's Eye*
Fernand Kolney. *Love in 5000 Years*
Paul Lacroix. *Danse Macabre*
Louis-Guillaume de La Follie. *The Unpretentious Philosopher*
Jean de La Hire. *Enter the Nyctalope; The Nyctalope on Mars; The Nyctalope vs. Lucifer; The Nyctalope Steps In; Night of the Nyctalope*
Etienne-Léon de Lamothe-Langon. *The Virgin Vampire*
André Laurie. *Spiridon*
Gabriel de Lautrec. *The Vengeance of the Oval Portrait*
Alain le Drimeur. *The Future City*
Georges Le Faure & Henri de Graffigny. *The Extraordinary Adventures of a Russian Scientist Across the Solar System* (2 vols.)
Gustave Le Rouge. *The Vampires of Mars; The Dominion of the World* (w/Gustave Guitton) (4 vols.)
Jules Lermina. *Mysteryville; Panic in Paris; To-Ho and the Gold Destroyers; The Secret of Zippelius*
André Lichtenberger. *The Centaurs; The Children of the Crab*
Jean-Marc & Randy Lofficier. *Edgar Allan Poe on Mars; The Katrina Protocol; Pacifica; Robonocchio; Tales of the Shadowmen 1-9*
Xavier Mauméjean. *The League of Heroes*
Joseph Méry. *The Tower of Destiny*
Hippolyte Mettais. *The Year 5865*
Louise Michel. *The Human Microbes; The New World*
Tony Moilin. *Paris in the Year 2000*
José Moselli. *Illa's End*
John-Antoine Nau. *Enemy Force*
Marie Nizet. *Captain Vampire*
C. Nodier, A. Beraud & Toussaint-Merle. *Frankenstein*
Henri de Parville. *An Inhabitant of the Planet Mars*
Gaston de Pawlowski. *Journey to the Land of the 4th Dimension*

Georges Pellerin. *The World in 2000 Years*
Ernest Pérochon. *The Frenetic People*
Pierre Pelot. *The Child Who Walked on the Sky*
J. Polidori, C. Nodier, E. Scribe. *Lord Ruthven the Vampire*
P.-A. Ponson du Terrail. *The Vampire and the Devil's Son; The Immortal Woman*
Henri de Régnier. *A Surfeit of Mirrors*
Maurice Renard. *The Blue Peril; Doctor Lerne; The Doctored Man; A Man Among the Microbes; The Master of Light*
Jean Richepin. *The Wing; The Crazy Corner*
Albert Robida. *The Adventures of Saturnin Farandoul; The Clock of the Centuries; Chalet in the Sky; The Electric Life*
J.-H. Rosny Aîné. *Helgvor of the Blue River; The Givreuse Enigma; The Mysterious Force; The Navigators of Space; Vamireh; The World of the Variants; The Young Vampire*
Marcel Rouff. *Journey to the Inverted World*
Han Ryner. *The Superhumans*
Brian Stableford. *The New Faust at the Tragicomique;The Empire of the Necromancers (The Shadow of Frankenstein; Frankenstein and the Vampire Countess; Frankenstein in London); Sherlock Holmes & The Vampires of Eternity; The Stones of Camelot; The Wayward Muse.* (anthologist) *The Germans on Venus; News from the Moon; The Supreme Progress; The World Above the World; Nemoville; Investigations of the Future*
Jacques Spitz. *The Eye of Purgatory*
Kurt Steiner. *Ortog*
Eugène Thébault. *Radio-Terror*
C.-F. Tiphaigne de La Roche. *Amilec*
Théo Varlet. *The Golden Rock. The Xenobiotic Invasion; The Castaways of Eros; Timeslip Troopers* (w/André Blandin); *The Martian Epic* (w/Octave Joncquel)
Paul Vibert. *The Mysterious Fluid*
Villiers de l'Isle-Adam. *The Scaffold; The Vampire Soul*
Philippe Ward. *Artahe*
Philippe Ward & Sylvie Miller. *The Song of Montségur*

MYSTERIES & THRILLERS

M. Allain & P. Souvestre. *The Daughter of Fantômas*
A. Anicet-Bourgeois, Lucien Dabril. *Rocambole*

A. Bernède. *Belphegor*; *Judex* (w/Louis Feuillade); *The Return of Judex* (w/Louis Feuillade); *The Shadow of Judex*

A. Bisson & G. Livet. *Nick Carter vs. Fantômas*

V. Darlay & H. de Gorsse. *Arsène Lupin vs. Sherlock Holmes: The Stage Play*

Séamas Duffy. *Sherlock Holmes in Paris*

Paul Féval. *Gentlemen of the Night; John Devil; The Black Coats ('Salem Street; The Invisible Weapon; The Parisian Jungle; The Companions of the Treasure; Heart of Steel; The Cadet Gang; The Sword-Swallower)*

Emile Gaboriau. *Monsieur Lecoq*

Goron & Emile Gautier. *Spawn of the Penitentiary*

Rick Lai. *Shadows of the Opera: Retribution in Blood*

Steve Leadley. *Sherlock Holmes: The Circle of Blood*

Maurice Leblanc. *Arsène Lupin vs. Countess Cagliostro; Arsène Lupin vs. Sherlock Holmes (The Blonde Phantom; The Hollow Needle); The Many Faces of Arsène Lupin*

Gaston Leroux. *Chéri-Bibi; The Phantom of the Opera; Rouletabille & the Mystery of the Yellow Room; Rouletabille at Krupp's*

Richard Marsh. *The Complete Adventures of Judith Lee*

William Patrick Maynard. *The Terror of Fu Manchu; The Destiny of Fu Manchu*

Frank J. Morlock. *Sherlock Holmes: The Grand Horizontals; Sherlock Holmes vs Jack the Ripper*

Antonin Reschal. *The Adventures of Miss Boston*

P. de Wattyne & Y. Walter. *Sherlock Holmes vs. Fantômas*

David White. *Fantômas in America*

Pierre Yrondy. *The Adventures of Thérèse Arnaud*

SCREENPLAYS

Mike Baron. *The Iron Triangle*

Emma Bull & Will Shetterly. *Nightspeeder; War for the Oaks*

Gerry Conway & Roy Thomas. *Doc Dynamo*

Steve Englehart. *Majorca*

James Hudnall. *The Devastator*

Jean-Marc & Randy Lofficier. *Royal Flush*

J.-M. & R. Lofficier & Marc Agapit. *Despair*

J.-M. & R. Lofficier & Joël Houssin. *City*

Andrew Paquette. *Peripheral Vision*

Robert L. Robinson, Jr. *Judex*

R. Thomas, J. Hendler & L. Sprague de Camp. *Rivers of Time*

NON-FICTION

Stephen R. Bissette. *Blur 1-5. Green Mountain Cinema 1; Teen Angels*
Win Scott Eckert. *Crossovers* (2 vols.)
Jean-Marc & Randy Lofficier. *Shadowmen* (2 vols.)
Randy Lofficier. *Over Here*

ART BOOKS

Jean-Pierre Normand. *Science Fiction Illustrations*
Raven Okeefe. *Raven's L'il Critters; Rave's Faves*
Randy Lofficier & Raven Okeefe. *If Your Possum Go Daylight...*
Daniele Serra. *Illusions*

HEXAGON COMICS

Franco Frescura & Luciano Bernasconi. *Wampus*
Franco Frescura & Giorgio Trevisan. *CLASH*
L. Bernasconi, J.-M. Lofficier & Juan Roncagliolo Berger. *Phenix*
Claude Legrand, J.-M. Lofficier & L. Bernasconi. *Kabur*
Franco Oneta. *Zembla*
L. Buffolente, Lofficier & J.-J. Dzialowski. *Strangers: Homicron*
Danilo Grossi. *Strangers: Jaydee*
Claude Legrand & Luciano Bernasconi. *Strangers: Starlock*